DESTROYING ANGEL

A Rose McQuinn Mystery

Alanna Knight

CHIVERS

British Library Cataloguing in Publication Data available

This Large Print edition published by BBC Audiobooks Ltd, Bath, 2008.
Published by arrangement with Allison & Busby Ltd.

U.K. Hardcover ISBN 978 1 405 64430 3
U.K. Softcover ISBN 978 1 405 64431 0

Printed and bound in Great Britain by
Antony Rowe Ltd., Chippenham, Wiltshire

*To Alex Gray and Lin Anderson,
my dear friends and favourite
Femmes Fatales, with love.*

CHAPTER ONE

I thought that danger belonged to the past and that happiness would last forever.

But I was wrong. Soon I was to lose the two most dear to me. Once again I had not heeded the harsh truth that happiness is to be counted in brief moments, too often in hours only, although fate occasionally grants a few extra days. That is all we can hope for.

That early autumn of 1897 was blissful for me due to a long and eagerly awaited visit from Pappa and Imogen Crowe, who had cause to celebrate. Orphaned, when she was sixteen she had been brought over to London by her Fenian uncle who had secretly planned to assassinate Queen Victoria. They were both arrested. Now past forty, her wrongful conviction as an Irish terrorist had been acknowledged by the British Government as a miscarriage of justice.

Recent celebrations had included a visit to my home in Solomon's Tower where we enjoyed a succession of divine days and—for Edinburgh—divine weather. For me, every day was another awakening to joy. My fiancé Jack Macmerry, Pappa's son-in-law elect, joined in the family celebration and so did Thane. Normally so elusive with strangers, my shy deerhound looked in cautiously, wagged his tail and permitted the newcomers to pat his head.

A merciful Fate, with a taste for irony, provided no inkling, no intuitive flash in that time of magic how close I was to losing those I held dearest.

On the day Pappa and Imogen left to continue their travels to the Highlands I was aware that Jack was unusually thoughtful, a preoccupation I put down readily enough to the stress of working as a detective inspector with the Edinburgh City Police. I smiled indulgently, recalling how I had enjoyed watching Jack with Pappa, ex-Chief Inspector Faro, as they compared notes. How I had warmed to the intimacy of those moments, which had almost persuaded me that I was doing the right thing in marrying Jack.

But I did not marry him.

When at last I recovered from the almost fatal events of the disastrous Golden Jubilee visit to his parents' home in Peebles where we were to have been married, doubts again crept in at the prospect of legalising our life together, which we had enjoyed for three years without the benefit of a marriage ceremony.

The main reason for my reluctance to tie this particular knot was a growing certainty that with it must end my career as a Lady Investigator, Discretion Guaranteed. There had been hints and more than hints, stern reminders, that Jack—a clever young detective

with ambitions to become a chief inspector—
could not be expected to tolerate a female
sleuth as wife. Especially one who dabbled in
domestic crimes which anxious clients
considered for their own varied, and not
always respectable, reasons unworthy of police
investigation.

'Most unsuitable.'

Jack had long made it plain that such a role
would place in jeopardy any hopes he had of
elevation to the higher ranks of the City
Police. And it did not take long for me to
realise that, much as he protested his love for
me, I had a rival. His ambition was even
stronger.

The choice was mine and it had to be made.
Did I love him enough to sacrifice a promising
and flourishing career? The answer was simply
that I could never be just Mrs Macmerry
warming her husband's slippers by the fire. I
was a Faro, after all, and my father's daughter.
Solving crimes, for good or ill, was my
inheritance.

But even as I rehearsed and discarded
suitable words I was in for a disagreeable
surprise when Jack, following me indoors after
we had waved goodbye to Pappa and Imogen,
solemnly declared that we had urgent and
important matters to discuss.

Once again I presumed that this was to
discuss a date for our wedding and, armed with
a plausible excuse to merit yet another delay, it

never occurred to me that Jack might be having second thoughts himself. In fact, I could hardly believe what I was hearing as he stumbled through the words.

I was being told by Jack, my faithful devoted Jack, that he had met someone else. A young woman in Glasgow.

He spoke rapidly, just a little above a whisper. Obviously very embarrassed and deeply upset by this confession, I almost pitied him as he stammered that he thought he was in love with this young lady, but needed time to think it through. Would I be agreeable to a short separation, 'a little breathing-space' until he had made up his mind and was certain this was not just a fleeting infatuation.

Suddenly I was aware of my own reactions. Shaking, my heart beating wildly, I had never been so shocked. It was unbelievable. I blinked rapidly. Surely this was a dreadful nightmare, one from which I would awaken any moment with Jack's arm about me. But I didn't wake up. This was not the stuff that dreams are made of. This was real life. Truth, rejection, harsh and bitter.

Quite correctly in the circumstances, he did not stay at Solomon's Tower that night and I lay sleepless beside his empty pillow with the certainty that the love I had taken for granted was about to be snatched from me.

The irony was that all the while I had been craftily considering a convincing escape clause, so too had Jack, but with a much stronger reason.

I was honest enough not to pretend that my heart was broken. That had happened once already when my husband, Danny McQuinn, vanished in Arizona three years ago. I had to accept that he was almost certainly dead and I would never open the door of Solomon's Tower, as I had so often in dreams, to find him smiling, waiting to take me in his arms.

I had rebuilt my life without him and, although Jack's rejection was a grievous blow, I had suffered worse in my life: the loss of a beloved husband and an infant son. I had survived.

I was not completely lost. I still had my career, Solomon's Tower and Thane.

Or so I thought . . .

*   *   *

Yes, I still had Thane and any day now my beloved stepbrother, Dr Vincent Beaumarcher Laurie, junior physician to Her Majesty's Household, would visit Solomon's Tower, as he did whenever the Royal train was stationary for a few hours in Waverley Station on the journey to or from Balmoral Castle.

Without Jack I would devote myself to my thriving career. Jack might well scorn domestic cases, but I was relieved. True, there was a certain sameness about absconding wives or husbands, thieving servants, lost wills and frauds—all too predictable to merit more than a brief note in my logbook, where only murders justified a detailed case history.

But I certainly had no wish for murders. There I was treading—often innocently unaware—on dangerous ground. I shuddered to remember that on two of my previous investigations but for the timely intervention of Jack and Thane I would have become the killer's next victim. I had them to thank for my deliverance.

*   *   *

When Vince arrived two days later, I told him that Jack and I were to separate for a while and there would be no wedding in the immediate future. I hoped to sound casual. For Jack's sake and perhaps as a sop to my wounded pride, I preferred to take the line that this was a shared decision, especially as Vince liked Jack and should we get together again, might thereafter regard him in a poorer light.

His reaction was unexpectedly non-committal. He merely shook his head, called Jack a fine fellow and hoped that I might not regret agreeing to such a proposal. I was relieved that he did not make as much fuss as I had feared. Indeed, he seemed more preoccupied than usual on this brief visit, and I had encountered the signs of frequent throat-clearing, suppressed sighs and uneasy glances often enough through the years to recognise that he was the bearer of unpleasant news.

It couldn't be anything involving Olivia and the children; he had already told me at first greeting that they were in splendid health, thank you, and sent their love. Nor could this concern Pappa and Imogen, whose visit he had just missed. Her Majesty, then; could it be something to do with his court appointment? Had he fallen foul of some protocol or misdiagnosed some Royal condition?

Yes, with reassurances at the ready, I decided that would be the reason. But then he asked suddenly:

'Where is Thane? I expected to see him.'

'He was here just before you arrived,' I said. 'You know what he is like—'

Vince nodded, clearing his throat again, and glancing unhappily towards the window. Then, leaning forward, he took my hands. 'It is really Thane I want to talk to you about. I know you have always been doubtful about his origins.' A deep breath and his grip on my hands tightened. 'Rose, I have to tell you. I have found his owner.'

My heart lurched. Suddenly I felt sick with apprehension. 'After all these years,' I gasped. 'It's impossible—I don't believe it.'

'Three years, Rose. Stranger things have happened. And I'm afraid what I have to tell

7

you is true. Hubert Staines—you have heard of him? No? An artist, a great photographer. Family groups are all the rage just now and we met at Balmoral when he was commissioned by Her Majesty to take a series with her grandchildren and great-grandchildren.

'Hubert lives in Northumberland at Alnwick and, as there is a railway station—a convenient diversion for the Royal train on visits to Alnwick Castle—he suggested that I call on him. A lovely manor house, the site of an ancient priory on the edge of the Duke of Northumberland's estate. We got along splendidly and he showed me his collection of magnificent photographs, quite outstanding. We had much in common, and he visited us in London recently to take photographs of Olivia and the children.'

Vince paused, bit his lip and sighed. 'Olivia has your painting of Thane in the dining room, in pride of place above the mantelpiece—'

I felt momentarily flattered as, pausing, Vince sighed. 'I could see he was much taken by it. He kept going back for a closer look. Then he turned to me and said, "Quite extraordinary, Vince old man, but would you believe that I have—or had—a deerhound exactly like him?"

'I explained that you were the artist. He asked where you lived and when I told him Edinburgh and of the mysterious circumstances in which you had found

Thane—or rather in which Thane had found you—he questioned me closely and asked when all this happened. When I said three years ago, he looked startled. "What a strange coincidence. That is when we lost Roswal, or rather, I did. I was at Holyrood on a commission for HM, Roswal was with me and we were walking on Arthur's Seat. There was a heavy grey mist and it was chilly too, but he had to have exercise. Usually so serene and biddable, that day he was agitated, restless. I thought the weather had upset him, but suddenly he took off, bolted like an arrow from a bow. Always obedient at home, he had never been known not to respond to a command. Not this time, alas. I whistled and called and waited, and then I searched and searched, but all in vain."

'Poor Hubert,' said Vince. 'He shook his head and looked so sad. "I have never seen him or his likeness again until—" And pausing, he pointed to the painting of Thane and said solemnly, "until this very day. I had to leave Edinburgh and there was nothing I could do, except break the news to my poor little stepdaughter. A frail, lonely child; an invalid. She was heartbroken. Roswal had always been hers from puppyhood. She is now gravely ill with consumption."'

Pausing, remembering, Vince sighed. 'Poor Hubert,' he repeated, 'he looked at me with his eyes full of tears, and whispered, "Her

9

weeks, perhaps even days, are numbered, and all she asks and still prays for every night is that she will see Roswal again—before—before—" '

Vince left the sentence unfinished and a silence fell between us. I said nothing. I was too stunned. There was nothing in this world I could think of except—selfish and heartless as it must sound on paper—that this could not be happening to me.

Thane was mine.

I dreaded what was now expected of me and knew that I would resist it—that I would do anything, anything to keep Thane. As for Roswal, I remembered that was the name of the deerhound Sir Walter Scott had written so lovingly into his novel, *The Talisman*. Roswal had been the cause of considerable friction between his owner the Scottish crusader Sir Kenneth and his Royal commander, King Richard.

'What I am going to ask you, Rose, may not be easy for you,' Vince began hesitantly.

'I can guess,' I said bitterly. 'You want me to hand him over to this Hubert Staines, that's it, is it not?' I cried. 'Well, I cannot do it. What's more, I will not! Thane is mine. Oh, Vince, please, forget this conversation. Forget you ever told me. I beg of you, don't ask me to do this,' I sobbed—I who so rarely shed a tear.

Vince again grasped my hands. 'Hear me out, Rose, there's a good girl. I told Hubert you had become devoted to Thane and he to you. How he had saved your life—Hubert already knew about Stepfather, he had heard of Chief Inspector Faro, of course, from the Royal family, and when I had told him about your activities as a lady detective, he understood how vital Thane had been to protect you—'

I wriggled from his grasp, my hands over my face, moaning in protest as he went on. 'Rose, Hubert only asks that you take Thane to visit him in Northumberland so that Kate may see him once again in her last days on earth. Surely you cannot refuse this request,' he added sternly.

Ignoring that, I said bitterly. 'And when I take him away again?' I said bitterly. 'What then? How could I possibly do that—?'

Vince took my hands again. 'Look into your own heart, Rose. This is a dying girl's last wish. You will only be required to stay until—until that unhappy event then you and Thane will be at liberty to return home. There is no other obligation. Hubert has other dogs, but Roswal was Kate's. How can you refuse?' he repeated reproachfully.

I knew that I was trapped. It was so easy, too easy, to put myself in Kate's shoes. But first I had one of two questions.

'Have you met this little girl?'

'Kate? Alas, no. She was in a Newcastle hospital on my visit—being examined by a

11

consultant in respiratory diseases. Hubert said it was his last hope that some means might be found of prolonging her life, for cure there is none.'

'What about her mother?'

Vince shook his head. 'Sadly Hubert is a widower. Mary died last year, the result of an accident, I gather. He was too upset to talk about it. Mary had been married before and as there were no children to this second marriage, Hubert is absolutely devoted to Kate. It's a sorry, tragic business, Rose. He is heartbroken at the prospect of losing her so soon after his dear wife. He has taken many photographs of them both, the very essence of family life. I'm glad he will have those at least to comfort him.'

'What is she like?'

'Beautiful, but so frail. Her eyes were remarkable for a child, as if she had seen all the world's sorrows. My heart was touched too when I heard her sad history—'

I shook my head, turned away. I didn't want to hear any more heart-rending accounts of Hubert Staines' tragic life that would make a refusal impossible.

'There is one other consideration,' I said. 'One you obviously haven't considered. How on earth will Thane react to being removed from here and taken on a long journey down to Northumberland?'

Vince's mocking shrug clearly indicated his

reactions. 'He made the journey to Peebles with you and Jack by train and seemed to take no ill effect from what I have been told.'

'Yes, but this is different.'

'How different?'

'Because it concerns him, his past. I must know how he feels about meeting—meeting his former owners.'

'I don't see how you are to do that, Rose,' he said sternly. 'After all, he is only a dog.'

'He has feelings,' I said angrily. 'Just like the rest of us.'

Vince's despairing shrug again said clearly what he thought of that absurd idea.

'A pity he isn't around. The Royal train will be heading south just as soon as HM completes her visit to Holyrood. We could have arranged for a stop at Alnwick, and telegraphed Hubert to collect you there. A half hour's journey later you could be at his home,' he added encouragingly. 'How would that suit you?'

I thought of the carriage waiting to take Vince back to Waverley Railway Station and shook my head. 'I cannot possibly go back with you, even if Thane were here. I need time to prepare.'

We got through the next half hour somehow, and for the first time I wasn't sorry when Vince's visit ended, since my anguish at losing Thane made it difficult to resume our usual family conversations and my normal curiosity about Royal events was stunned into silence.

As the coachman outside signalled Vince's departure time, he stared out of the window towards Arthur's Seat.

'What on earth has happened to Thane? He usually rushes in to greet me. Most odd,' he added. A reproachful look suggested that I might be concealing him somewhere.

But the carriage had hardly disappeared from view when Thane appeared—from the direction of the kitchen. I realised he had been staying out of sight and I did not doubt he had heard every word of our conversation.

I told him that we were going to Alnwick.

I stroked his head. Did he remember Hubert Staines and little Kate? Of course, he couldn't reply. I would have to wait and see—and hope. Hope that he was not and never had been the missing deerhound, Roswal.

CHAPTER TWO

Two days later all was arranged. Hubert Staines had sent a telegraph, offering to meet me with his carriage at Alnwick Station. I declined. I wanted the independence my bicycle would allow and did not want to inflict on him the possible embarrassment of accommodating it too.

Realising the anxious outcome of Thane's future could only be prolonged by delay, we boarded the southbound train the next day. As there were several empty compartments, we were not sternly dismissed to spend the journey in the goods van, as had happened before, and we reached Alnwick with only a minor delay.

The train braked abruptly, throwing us from our seats, doors were flung open and a rush of porters dealt with a cow that had found its way onto the level crossing between a cluster of houses and the decayed workings of an unsightly colliery pithead.

Expecting a simple platform and tiny waiting room similar to others along the line, I was surprised when the train steamed into Alnwick's ornate station, its splendid architecture equalling Edinburgh's Waverley and in the same category, I learnt later, as Newcastle and York.

Built in 1870 to replace the original modest railway halt, its mission was to accommodate the new fashion of travelling by train—set by members of the Royal Family—and the aristocracy's constant flow to the Duke of Northumberland's handsome Castle which dominates the landscape.

As Thane and I left the train, I had to admit that our progress along the platform created quite a stir. I was aware of curious passengers staring out of compartment windows, unable to restrain their astonishment at the sight of a young woman wheeling a bicycle along the platform accompanied by a dog the size of a Shetland pony.

Perhaps the bicycle aroused the most comment, and as we walked to the station exit, with its elegant canopy and painted seats, I was already beginning to regret opting for sturdy independence by declining Mr Staines' handsome offer of a carriage to meet us. As well as wanting to save him the embarrassment of trying to load my bicycle into his carriage, I had rejected his offer because I had been told that Staines Manor was only two miles distant from Alnwick. 'You cannot miss it' (according to Vince) 'on the Great North Road to Newcastle.'

As the train steamed out of the station, I had a glimpse of an ancient wall, a medieval tower with an archway that led into the town. New places are my delight and I was well pleased at the prospect of exploring Alnwick and, considering that what awaited our arrival in Staines was melancholy indeed, I was glad of this opportunity for temporary respite. Was it remotely possible that instead of the tiny market town I had expected, there might even be a theatre, an assembly hall for concerts and like entertainment?

I regarded my bicycle fondly. It offered freedom of movement without having to call upon the Staines' carriage. A thoughtful contemplation of Bartholomew's map had revealed several tempting landmarks of historical and archaeological interest that I hoped to visit. As well as Alnwick Castle there were others of note—Warkworth, Bamburgh, Dunstanburgh, some of which were ruinous— and I was glad indeed that I had packed my sketchbook.

Such were my thoughts as we headed downhill. In fact I was so involved in the prospect of these fantasy adventures that I suddenly realised I was lost.

That promised signpost to Staines had failed to appear!

I was at a crossroads, but the only sign was to 'Gibbet Hill'. A name that might arouse feelings of melancholy and caution in the criminally minded, the sign pointed sharply back along the road we had travelled instead of directing us to Staines. Closer inspection revealed that the signpost was leaning at a rather unhappy angle as if it had been the victim of a carriage accident, or had suffered in a high wind or from a bout of malice from person or persons unknown.

Helplessly, I looked around and decided that Gibbet Hill had been well chosen for a criminal's last sight of a bleak and barren moorland world, devoid of hope and stretching to infinity.

All signs of the handsome castle or indeed of any visible habitation on the vast horizon had vanished. The cold, grey sky's sole occupants were a few large unidentifiable birds hovering in the manner that such creatures do when seeking their prey on Arthur's Seat, which seemed by comparison a friendly park.

Homesickness swept over me. Why, oh why, had I started on this venture? Already I feared the worst, for this was no gentle Border village guarded by the undulating Eildon Hills. As far as I could see this was a wild and savage land; the feeling of sudden death, of treachery and ancient violence still lurked in the gaunt and stricken landscape.

Here were boulders that under some lights might take on the look of moving phantoms, and heather moors whose bleached roots could, to one possessed of even a moderately lively imagination, reassemble into a chilling likeness of human bones.

We were lost under a rapidly darkening and unforgiving sky, where isolation and despair stretched forth from every mute crag. Every now and then I imagined I caught the echoes of a twilight world, long vanished, where prehistoric monsters roamed this desolate land.

The welfare of my bicycle necessitated cautious proceeding. A punctured wheel was the last thing I needed, and as what passed for a road turned into a boulder strewn path winding uphill I dismounted and prepared to walk, with an unperturbed Thane trotting alongside.

Some distance further on, and wondering what on earth to do next, in desperation I said: 'Where do we go from here? Come on, let's see some of that much-vaunted canine instinct.'

Thane regarded me reproachfully for a moment from under those magisterial brows and, using the pause to sniff delicately at a clump of bracken and attend to the needs of nature, he returned to my side, sat down and waited for me to tell him what to do next.

I looked around despairingly. Soon it would be too dark to travel in safety. Nothing lay in sight by way of shelter built by human hands beyond a sheep pen in the middle of a field. Open to the four winds, it would have to suffice until daylight.

I had no fears that anyone would steal my bicycle, so I climbed over the fence, which Thane took in one leap. As we neared the stone structure, I realised this was no sheep pen but something much more ancient. A fragment of the Roman wall built by Hadrian two thousand years ago to keep the Scots at bay. He had certainly succeeded, and I was a prime example.

Suddenly at my side, Thane growled low in his throat, and across the field I saw moving towards us in the gloaming the pale ghosts of cattle. Then I realised what I was seeing: the legendary Chillingham white cattle, a few miles off their terrain perhaps. The original cattle, they were well-established long before the Romans invaded, and their survival from prehistoric times was said to be due to the fact that no one had ever been able to domesticate them. From what I had read and heard from Pappa, who had had a narrow escape from being gored to death on one of his Border cases, they were highly dangerous to humans.

Such facts were hardly reassuring, since there was nothing between us but the length of a field, down which they were making a fairly rapid and steady progress.

Thane looked at me and then at the wall, as if to say, 'Take shelter.'

I needed no second bidding, but clambered over fully realising that the remains of an ancient wall would not offer much defence.

And what of Thane?

Thane had not moved. He stood his ground. The cattle drew nearer. Now only a few yards separated us from them. Although smaller than our domestic cattle, their horns were long and sharp. Above the beating of my own heart, I heard their angry snorts, pawing the ground, heads lowered . . .

Was this how it was to end?

First Thane, gored and killed—and then—and then—

Dear God, please . . .

I looked at Thane. The cattle looked at Thane. And then as one, they bowed their

20

heads and, turning slowly, retreated back the way they had come.

I found myself breathing again. It was over. The incident closed before that prayer had time to reach heaven, Thane jumped the wall, wagged his tail and lay down beside me, a sigh indicating: Don't worry, you're safe now.

And I realised this phenomenon was not something new and strange. It had happened before and I had observed Thane's effect on all four-legged things. Cows, sheep and horses ignored him completely, dogs and cats merely walked on past him.

As if he were invisible to them. Perhaps he was.

Now, although we were out of danger, the cattle gone, the present indication was that we would be spending the night in the fragmentary remains of what had once been a bathhouse abandoned by the Roman legion.

At least it wasn't raining and the wall with its sunken floor was reasonably sheltered. I had often slept under the stars in the Arizona desert during my pioneering days with Danny McQuinn. And it was cold there, too, when the temperature dropped considerably during the night. I did not expect much in the way of a comfortable lodging, but wrapped in my woollen cape I must have slept, for when I opened my eyes the sky was flooded with moonlight.

But where was Thane?

Panic seized me. I stood up, called him, and then realised that I had the bleak and barren landscape all to myself. I was completely alone.

Alone, that is, apart from a large bird of prey hovering close. Dangerously close, in fact. About six feet above my head.

The moonlight touched its wings and left no doubt of what it had in mind. I was marked down for supper.

'Shoo!' I screamed, waving my arms.

The bird continued to hover.

Seizing my cape, waving it wildly, I screamed again.

Suddenly, I saw a peep of light on the horizon and a bulls-eye lantern came swinging across the moorland. It was being carried in a hurry by a tall man with Thane dancing around him.

As they approached, in the moment before I recognised my rescuer, I realised that I was witnessing something extraordinary.

I had never imagined a deerhound dancing with joy. But that was exactly what Thane was doing.

'Mrs McQuinn!'

The lantern was anchored and the man came over the wall.

CHAPTER THREE

He was no stranger.

We had met once before under terrifying and sinister circumstances during my first months in Edinburgh. This was Chief Wolf Rider, a Sioux Indian from the Wild West Circus, now transformed into a semblance of an English gamekeeper by a garb that suggested an Aztec high priest in fancy dress costume.

Smiling, he helped me over the wall, looked down at Thane, and nodded solemnly. 'So the deerhound has stayed with you, protecting you from danger.'

I ignored that enigmatic introduction. 'His name is Thane.'

Three years ago no one believed he existed. Thane was then very good at keeping himself to himself and only deigning to appear to me.

A deerhound! On Arthur's Seat! A figment of my imagination, they said, all except Sergeant Jack Macmerry.

Now everything was happening at once. The bird of prey swooped down, I threw up my hand to protect my head and yelled out, but the peregrine falcon settled happily on Wolf Rider's gloved fist and shook out his feathers.

'Kokopele is quite tame. He helped me find you. Pleasant change to tracking down his prey,' he said.

That touched another memory. Kokopele was the mythical flute-bearer of the Navajo Indians.

I shuddered as Rider went on: 'It is your deerhound you have to thank for keeping the white cattle at bay,' and, looking over his shoulder, 'but we would be wise to get out of this field immediately.'

'Where are we?'

'On Staines' estate, but this part is the cattle's territory and they are notoriously suspicious of strangers—and quite unpredictable. Follow me.'

We made our way rapidly across the field to where my bicycle reclined gracefully against a fence. The sight of Chief Wolf Rider, without his Dakota Ghost Dancers from the Wild West Circus at Queen's Park, was completely out of context in these surroundings and awakened bitter memories of my return to Edinburgh.

Rider had come to Solomon's Tower to identify the body of one of his troupe. Riding on the hill, Wild Elk's horse had thrown him. Badly injured, he had crawled to the nearest habitation—my barn—and had died there.

Wolf Rider was a shaman and came to carry out certain Sioux rites before the young man could be buried. He told me that Wild Elk believed he was being stalked on the hill by a large dog, and he presumed that this animal had spooked his horse.

24

I looked at Wolf, walking ahead with Thane at his side. Meeting him again aroused painful memories that I shuddered to recall. I remembered his extraordinary and uncanny explanation that Wild Elk had killed an innocent white man who wore a Christian cross and, in accordance with Sioux beliefs, the dead man's spirit had entered an animal to seek revenge.

Danny wore a crucifix and Thane, a mysterious deerhound who lived on the hill, had chosen to befriend me. A coincidence, I told myself, refusing to be reconciled to such a terrifying idea, especially as I was clinging to the certainty that Danny still lived and that one day we would be blissfully reunited.

Now as I watched the man and the deerhound, there was none of Thane's usual shyness and caution with strangers. It was as if I was witnessing the reunion of old comrades, both possessors of that extra-sensory perception, well beyond my range, or indeed beyond the range of most humans.

I guessed I was observing a phenomenon. Rider and Thane inhabited a world bordering on the supernatural. A world of instinctive intuition of which I had only touched the fringes. It was as though their bond had been forged many lifetimes ago, many ages past.

Suddenly I was back in the present, surrounded by the menace of dark moorland, the feeling of danger in the air, despite the

25

softening effect of the moonlight. Shivering, aware of being cold and hungry and that I had not yet slept properly, a blessed apparition appeared fifty yards away.

A small estate cottage, known as a 'bothy' in Scotland.

Wolf pointed to the smoke rising from the chimney. 'This is where I live. There is food and a warm fire.'

His hand on Thane's shoulder, we covered the short distance rapidly. Opening the door he ushered me inside, set down the lantern and attended to the fire. Then, placing two bowls on the table, he said: 'Hot soup, this will soon warm you. And I have meat for Thane.'

The soup was delicious. It tasted of herbs and I decided I must have the recipe.

Watching with satisfaction as I tackled a second helping, he leant back in his chair and smiled. 'It has been a long time, Mrs McQuinn.'

'Indeed it has. And please call me Rose.'

'That will be my pleasure.' He grinned, briefly. 'There are moments in life, like my brief time in Edinburgh, that will always remain with me.'

I was surprised that he hadn't enquired what I was doing in the middle of nowhere. 'You didn't seem surprised to see me.'

'No. I was expecting you again—sometime. I knew we should meet again.' And before I could think of a suitable reply, he asked, 'What brings you to Staines?'

'A brief visit.' I wasn't prepared to give my reasons and added: 'What on earth are you doing in Northumberland? As I recall, you said in Edinburgh that you were going in search of your roots—your Scottish grandmother.'

'That is exactly what I did. And I found her—not in Scotland, but here in Staines.'

'Really!'

'She was the young wife of Hubert's grandfather, made wealthy by the coal on his land. A difficult man by all accounts, and as Miranda had a spirit of adventure, she became bored with rural life and went on a fashionable safari with rich friends to hunt buffalo in Arizona. However, they became the hunted instead. All were slain but the lovely Miranda, who was taken captive and kept alive by the chief. She had a child by him and never returned to Staines.'

'So you are distant cousins. What an extraordinary coincidence.'

And as I said the words, I recalled my practical father's scorn of coincidences.

'Always be suspicious of coincidences,' was his maxim.

For Pappa, everything had to have a purpose, and that was the philosophy in which I had been raised. There was another question looming:

'How did you meet Mr Staines?'

He shrugged. 'By chance, in London. The circus was closing and I was desperately in need of funds. What little I had would not last very long if I wished to return to Scotland. Then, at the end of the last show, Hubert Staines had been taking photographs and said he was impressed by the way I handled animals—I had taken over the lion taming act.'

With an apologetic grin, he added: 'Leo the Man-eater and I were great friends. He was very old and lacked teeth. We understood each other. He was a good actor and when asked to do so he could look impressively fierce, with his tail lashing furiously. He had a roar that shook the rafters and had small children screaming in terror when it looked as if he might leap out of the cage.'

And smiling at the memory, he shook his head. 'But he was more akin to a good dog than a king of the jungle.' Then, regarding my puzzled expression, he laughed. 'I can see you are wondering why a rich man like Mr Staines wanted a lion tamer. Is that not so?'

It was indeed, and he went on: 'His family had acquired a collection of animals and birds from their days as big-game hunters. Most of their trophies are now stuffed in menacing attitudes, on exhibition in the gun room. Staines followed the family tradition and learnt that art, said it was useful for a photographer. But he longed to do something that had never been done before.'

Pausing, he shook his head and gave me a quizzical smile.

'A man who likes a challenge. You will no doubt have recognised his connection with our remarkable grandmother. He wishes to capture a beast from the famous Chillingham white cattle, whose territory you have just invaded, and to breed a domestic strain. I understand that a wealthy white rancher in America has offered him a considerable amount of money and what he offered me was the last temptation.'

'To do what exactly?' I asked.

He shrugged. 'To work on his estate and to extract a new-born calf from the cattle to send to Texas.'

'Surely that will be very difficult—and from what you've told me of the cattle, very dangerous.'

Again that dismissive shrug. 'True, but I will receive enough money to return to Arizona—or to remain in Britain. I have grown rather fond of Scotland,' he added wistfully. 'It wasn't until I came to Staines that we found out we were related. Quite a coincidence.'

That word again, I thought.

'I will take you to meet him in the morning.'

'Why not now?' I asked.

'He had to go to Newcastle unexpectedly. A change in the weather, by which outdoor photography is dictated. He said he was expecting a visitor from Scotland, but did not

29

mention a name, only that this person was bringing back a dog that belonged to him—'

I bristled at that assumption as he went on. 'I think it would be best if you stayed here tonight. You are tired and need rest; I am sure it has all been a rather trying experience. Hubert is notoriously absent-minded, except where his passion for photography is concerned. Mrs Robson, the housekeeper, did not mention this morning that she was expecting a visitor. There will be nothing prepared for you.'

He smiled. 'You shall have my bed. I shall sleep in here—' And cutting short my protests, he said, 'Sleeping under a roof is a fairly new experience. I have spent most of my life in a teepee or under the sky. A bed of the kind provided with blankets and pillows of soft down is still a novelty.'

A slight pause then without the least embarrassment, he added: 'But you must be comfortable before you retire. There is a water closet at the side of the cottage—you may have noticed it.'

When I returned, perhaps aware of my doubtful acceptance of his hospitality—here I was spending the night in a cottage with a man I had met only once, but instinctively trusted— he bowed, opening the door to the bedroom.

'Take Thane with you, he will be company if you wake during the night,' he said, handing me my valise.

I had decided to send my small travelling trunk in advance, leaving my hands free. I need both for bicycling, but I had an excellent roomy saddle bag for my valise, very practical and by courtesy of Jack.

Jack, I thought, with a sudden shaft of pain. Is he lying in bed in Glasgow in the arms of his new love? Such imaginings are the circuit to despair. A full moon glowed in through a window that lacked curtains or shutters. Its light streamed across the room, exploring corners, like an eager watchful face.

I believed I would never sleep, though Thane settled down on the floor, unperturbed and soon snoring gently. At last I closed my eyes, and opened them again to find the moon had been replaced by bright sunlight.

It was morning, and Thane had gone. I opened the door, but there was no sign of him or of Wolf Rider. They had not been long absent, for there was a basin of warm water and a towel in readiness for my morning ablutions.

In the kitchen, breakfast had been prepared. There was a kettle on the hob, and I lifted the lid of a pan to find porridge. Rider had certainly adapted to some British habits, I thought, recalling the clean crisp sheets and pillowcase, provided by the Staines housekeeper no doubt, and easier than sleeping outdoors in our cold climate.

I had just poured a second cup of tea when

the door opened and Thane rushed in looking pleased, wagging his tail and dancing around his new friend. At least he was happy and I am ashamed to say that I felt suddenly quite envious and neglected.

Had the faithful Thane now transferred his devotion to Wolf Rider, deserting me as he had once before for Jack's father, in Eildon in June? Just months ago, when Jack's parents were preparing for a wedding that never happened, though my demise almost did.

I studied Thane. Perhaps he preferred male companionship.

Wolf greeted me with the conventional question—had I slept well?—and satisfied that I had done so, he said: 'Hubert is due back soon. I will take you over to the house. I called on Mrs Robson and she is preparing a room for you. As they don't have many visitors she was a little flustered, especially since, as I suspected, Hubert had completely forgotten to inform her of your arrival.'

I thought about Hubert's omission. If I had found my way to Staines Manor, I might well have been turned away, much to my consternation, not to mention my anger and humiliation.

'What of his stepdaughter?'

'Kate? She has a very good nurse in attendance, so Hubert can leave her although he prefers to be constantly at her side—' He stopped, sighed. 'Just now. She will be glad to see her lost deerhound again.'

'Do you think Thane is the missing Roswal?' I asked, unable to keep the anxiety out of my voice.

His expression was quite blank. He shrugged. 'An amazing coincidence—'

'Another one,' I said bluntly.

'Such things can happen. Life is like that.'

I said, 'I just wonder, if their deerhound was so devoted, why did he desert his master and run away at Holyrood?'

Wolf looked surprised at the question. 'Oh, I can understand that perfectly.' And giving me a penetrating glance he said, 'No one can own Thane, make no mistake about that. He obeys no laws but his own. He makes the choice; he will go to those who need him most. He chose you because you were the person he wished to be with. There is a possibility when he ran away from Hubert that he already knew of your existence.'

These strange words failed to comfort me for they fitted in all too neatly with the terrifying theory that I had forced myself to reject. That the spirit of my dead husband had entered this extraordinary deerhound whose mission in life had become to protect me. And Thane really was an extraordinary deerhound. As much as I had tried to dismiss it as an hallucination, I could not forget that I had seen this dog shot dead before my eyes a few months ago, but that he rose again, with no trace of wound or scar.

As if he read my thoughts, Wolf leant across the table and said solemnly, 'Enjoy Thane but remember you can only keep him with an open hand.' And making a tight fist he opened it again. 'Like love, if we attempt to close it, then it is lost for ever.'

And so we went to meet Hubert Staines.

CHAPTER FOUR

The manor house was old, one of hundreds scattered all over Northumberland and Durham, built in the late eighteenth century by wealthy land and coal owners. It was Georgian, but had none of the asceticism of Edinburgh architecture. This sprawling, rambling house, half timbered with a nod in the direction of something much older, was a mixture of Tudor and modernity, with a hint of Gothic in the twisting chimneys, and the pale ghost of a Border peel tower, which rested uneasily alongside mullioned latticed windows.

Wolf left me at the gate. As he walked away, there was a whimper of protest from Thane, which I sternly refused to indulge.

'You'll be seeing him again.'

Heading along the short drive to the front door, I nervously watched Thane for signs that he recognised his old home, afraid that he might joyously race towards it. But, reassuringly, he never left my side. Unused to accompanying me on visits to friends in Edinburgh, I was secretly relieved that he was displaying his natural caution towards new places, certainly showing neither interest nor curiosity about what we were doing here.

I suppressed a sigh of relief. Dogs have long memories and surely his first home would have had brought about a different reaction. As we reached the door, I felt almost happy, convinced that Thane and Roswal were not the same. Complacently, I felt that I could afford to be magnanimous in such tragic circumstances, and would go along with the dying girl's belief that this was indeed her lost deerhound.

And that, I was to discover, was my first mistake—of many!

I heard footsteps in the hall, and the man who opened the door eagerly stretched out his hand, but not to me—to Thane.

'Roswal, old boy,' he whispered. 'Welcome home again.'

A fine, deep, melodious voice, heavy with emotion. The upper-class voice of authority. A military man's voice. Orders given, requests that were commands to be carried out immediately.

A commanding figure indeed. Tall, well-muscled, strong. His head bent down showing thick, dark hair, lightly touched with white at the temples.

His expression was concealed from me and I watched Thane anxiously. Apart from twitching his ears, he made no move to leap forward and dance around Hubert Staines as I had witnessed just a few hours ago with Wolf Rider.

Suddenly Hubert became aware of my presence and held out one hand in polite greeting, the other still firmly patting Thane's head, who made no move apart from polite acceptance.

'Same old Roswal,' said Hubert, as he bowed over my hand.

'Mrs McQuinn, pleased to meet you. I do apologise. I am quite overwhelmed, as you can see. This is a moment I believed would never happen. As you can imagine I had given up all hope long ago.' And shaking his head sadly, he added, 'Even in my wildest dreams.'

I regarded him critically.

He didn't strike me as the kind of man who would be overwhelmed or troubled by wild dreams. He went on: 'And I have to thank you for coming all this way. I assure you, I am most grateful and you are most welcome—more than welcome.'

An odd similarity struck me at that moment. I have seen many a face in Princes Street that seemed to belong in a sixteenth-century portrait, but Hubert Staines' went back quite a bit further than that.

I took a deep breath. Here was Harry Hotspur to the life, a Northumbrian legendary hero, his rightful place the darker pages of Border history. His broken nose testified to ancient combat, and there were scars of war, too, now grown faint. All in all, he was meant for riding through Alnwick's tower, named after him, carrying a broadsword, not a photographer's camera. And on these ordinary nineteenth-century days, I wondered, did he ever feel the twinge of history?

I was to learn later that the first de Steyns who came over with William the Conqueror had been well established in Northumberland before the original Percys, Harry Hotspur's line, had died out for lack of male heirs.

Now, as he spoke, I was mesmerised by this reincarnation of a Border warrior, the high cheekbones tempered by a thick-lipped, sensuous mouth, a firm line that conceded nothing to curves, heavy-lidded, shrewd and watchful eyes, so dark their colour was indistinguishable, taking in all the world at a single glance.

Here was a man who had stepped straight from the pages of romantic fiction, a man that the vulnerable souls of gentle women would find irresistible.

Not so, Rose Faro McQuinn, I told myself firmly. I was not in danger. I had been a pioneer, had fought off Indians, and was of the suffragette mentality—a fighter for 'Votes for

Women'—I would not be swayed by handsome looks.

I was only half listening to his polite remarks and apologies, while receiving the impression of a no-nonsense man who would not tolerate fools gladly. And, as he turned his attention again to Thane, I believed he was used to having his own way but would also make sure of his facts, and would be unlikely to embark on a deception in order to procure a deerhound, especially as I fancied he could afford a whole kennel full.

Opening the front door wider, he bowed me into a panelled hall where the smell of aged wood mingled with wax polish. The walls were hung with trophies of the chase, killings the upper classes seem to relish, heads of deer and foxes eyeing them reproachfully in the glazed stare of their dying moments.

Thane remained at my side, trotting obediently across the hall to follow Hubert up the handsome oak staircase. I wondered what his thoughts were. Although I imagined that occasionally I could read his mind, on this occasion he remained enigmatically canine.

If only he could talk, tell me the truth of all this masquerade, I thought, as Hubert opened the door into a room similarly panelled. A massive bay window, with armorial bearings in the upper glass segments, overlooked a paved terrace some twelve feet below. A flight of stone steps led down the terrace to a formal garden, with smooth lawns that dissolved into a tree-lined estate, and a distant gleam of distant water.

Magnificent as the view was, without knowing why, I didn't like it. Feeling dizzy and slightly nauseated, I turned my attention to the huge stone fireplace supported by two unhappy looking medieval figures. Were they perhaps feeling more than a little threatened by the log fire burning briskly around the areas of their lower limbs while on either side well-worn leather armchairs spoke of comfortable evenings? An absence of the current passion for lavish ornamentation—not even a selection of his famed photographs or family portraits—hinted that although this was a man's room, it was not Hubert's favourite.

Nor would it be mine. I was to find out why later.

Invited to take a seat, I was gratified that Thane immediately moved to my side and sat down, ignoring the clicking fingers of his perhaps erstwhile owner, who shook his head a little regretfully, as though disconcerted by this lack of obedience.

Regarding me thoughtfully, he managed a somewhat rueful, 'Roswal always displayed an instinct to protect the weaker sex.'

I bristled as always at the reference to the weaker sex, but as Hubert came over and, bending down, put an arm around Thane's neck, there was something quite endearingly

39

boyish and vulnerable in his action. My attention was riveted on Thane, but there was no move on his part, no eagerness to lick that nearby cheek. His glance of despair signalled that he didn't care for this familiarity.

'Roswal is very well bred, you know, a gentleman among dogs—and bred by one of the finest of Scottish gentlemen. Your countryman, Mrs McQuinn, a great scholar and a fine novelist.'

Pausing, Hubert regarded me quizzically, his manner that of a school master posing a question to a truculent child.

'You must mean Sir Walter Scott,' I said.

'Who else!' he laughed.

Well done, Mr Clever Staines, that is your first mistake. Sir Walter could not have known Roswal. He died in 1832 and though Thane is remarkable in many ways, he cannot by canine standards be credited with sixty-five years.

But Hubert had the explanation ready. 'Of course you could not possibly know that Roswal was a descendant of Sir Walter Scott's favourite deerhound, Maida, whom he described as "a most perfect creature of heaven". It is she who sits at his side on his memorial in Edinburgh's Princes Street.'

Frowning, he bit his lip, and as if the thought had just occurred to him, he said, 'Indeed, that could be the answer.' Looking at me intently, he added eagerly: 'Don't you see—the reason why Roswal ran away from

40

me when we were out walking on Arthur's Seat? Perhaps some instinct told him that he was on his native heath—an attempt to return to the Abbotsford kennels.'

A very remarkable and highly improbable assumption, I thought, even if Roswal and Thane were one and the same. He went on: 'I remember the day perfectly; it was 15th May, three years ago. A day I shall never forget.' And giving me a sharp glance. 'When was it you first saw him?'

'About a week later,' I admitted reluctantly.

'So that's it! There now, that's settled!' he repeated triumphantly, leading the way upstairs and opening the door of a pleasant but informal guest room in the corridor alongside the family apartments, doubtless hastily prepared by Mrs Robson.

Setting down my valise, he said, 'Is that all your luggage?' I said that I had left a small trunk at Alnwick Station for collection.

'Rider will collect it.' He laughed. 'I must confess I am surprised. Ladies usually carry so much baggage. You are to be congratulated, Mrs McQuinn.' Turning to leave, he said, 'Tea in my study in, say, half an hour. Come, Roswal.'

A quick glance in my direction, and Thane followed him. At the door, Hubert turned, smiled: 'I'm delighted and relieved that we have solved the problem of Roswal's disappearance so easily. Quite fascinating!'

Left alone, his theory didn't fascinate me in the least. Nor did it account for the fact that although Roswal/Thane had been out roaming the hill for a week, his coat was clean and well-groomed, as if he had gone missing only hours before, as I had presumed when he appeared on Arthur's Seat.

At that thought, another more alarming possibility occurred to me. That Thane/Roswal had not been trying, as Staines suggested, to find his way back to Abbotsford, but had been tracking down his strange soul mate Wolf Rider, who was at that time with the Wild West Circus in Queen's Park.

I still firmly rejected Rider's belief that the spirit of a murdered man could enter the body of an animal to seek vengeance. If I really believed it to be true, and this story with all its coincidences, then I would have taken to my bicycle and headed for Alnwick Railway Station and the very next train back to Edinburgh.

And once safe home in Solomon's Tower, guarded by its ancient walls which had seen so much of Scotland's history, what then?

I could not bear to think about it. To continue living there alone, with Jack happy in the arms of his new love, and Thane happy to be back with his true owner.

CHAPTER FIVE

Hubert's study door was open. He sat behind a large, untidy desk littered with papers, some books and a scatter of society photographs of ladies wearing tiaras and diamonds—doubtless his wealthy clients. I learnt later that he had adapted the cellar into a darkroom for his photography.

Thane trotted over to greet me as Mrs Robson, plump and bustling, arrived with tea, scones and fruit cake. An odd choice for a mid-morning refreshment, I thought, but maybe this excellent fare was standard for visitors who, according to Wolf Rider, were rare.

It was certainly most welcome. I have a decided weakness for home baking and appreciate others' efforts in a field of domestic activity in which I am a non-starter. My ten years of marriage to Danny McQuinn were spent in the wilder outposts of Arizona, where food was eaten for survival rather than pleasure. Similarly, as my pantry in Solomon's Tower is spartan in the extreme, I am ashamed to confess that I become quite exhilarated, not to say downright greedy, at the prospect of anything vaguely appetising.

Mrs Robson poured the tea and set the plates silently, and curtseyed without making eye contact. When I praised this feast, she blushed and looked pleased in a shy way, while I could not fail to notice her rather challenging glance towards Sir Hubert. It suggested that compliments on culinary or any other domestic skills flowed seldom in her direction.

I ate alone. Hubert indulged in some more robust refreshment from an assortment of bottles on a side table, leaving me feeling somewhat embarrassed as I proceeded to demolish a couple of scones while yielding not to the temptation of assaulting the slices of cake.

Hubert, glass in hand, devoted little attention to Thane.

I was curious. He did not seem in any hurry to reunite the prodigal deerhound with his stepdaughter, and I decided he was waiting politely for me to dust off the last crumbs. In an effort to speed up the process, I asked, 'How is your little girl?'

He seemed taken aback by the question and, for a moment, quite confused. Surely he had not forgotten that she was my reason for being here. Recovering, he sighed. With a sad shake of his head, he said, 'She has disturbed nights but Collins reported that she slept well last night. Collins is her nurse and very reliable,' he added, tugging at the bell pull, at which the immediate appearance of a tall, thin woman of about forty, with tight pulled-back hair and a forbidding expression, suggested she had been either stationed outside the door or had slid down the banisters from the bedrooms upstairs.

'Ah, Collins, this is Mrs McQuinn.'

We shook hands and I learnt a lot from that first encounter. My powers of observation and deduction, inherited from Pappa, interpreted a brooding, naked glance in Hubert's direction, suggesting that my presence troubled her. They were not good actors and the atmosphere between them, despite the public show of formality, hinted that Collins was much more than a nurse and 'very reliable' in more intimate matters.

I was intrigued by the absence of a first name. What did he call her when they were alone with the bedroom door shut? Surely not Collins, the surname a formal address for upper-class servants.

Her anxious reception of me, which I suspected would be the fate of any young woman who crossed the threshold, hinted that whatever commitment she hoped for was not yet forthcoming.

What was the impediment?

Hubert was a widower. But as her shrewd appraisal summed me up as a possible rival, I could have put her mind at rest. Later, however, that would not be so easy as matters developed between her master and myself.

As I watched, she regained her role as nurse and was assuring Hubert in the polite tones of

45

a paid employee that Miss Kate was awake, had breakfasted, and was ready to see Roswal.

She looked towards me dismissively, but that was not to be. Hubert smiled and said, 'Mrs McQuinn must come along. Kate will wish to know all about Roswal's amazing adventures all this time away from us in Edinburgh. Is that not so, Collins?'

I got the impression that Collins was completely indifferent to such fascinating information and as Thane stood up she backed away from him hastily.

She was afraid of dogs, but Thane knew his place, always remembered his manners. Polite to strangers who he guessed might be intimidated by his size, he never bounded forward to leap and greet but waited patiently, allowing them to make the first move.

There was none but as we climbed the stairs he remained at my side, with the other two in the lead, and I was in for yet another surprise.

Having expected to see a frail, childlike creature, I was astonished to find that the girl sitting by the bay window was a beautiful, exquisite young woman with long, pale gold hair and enormous, deep blue eyes. Seventeen years old, she could have passed for twenty-five. Although fragile as Venetian glass, she certainly did not have the look of near-death from a long and terminal illness.

Anxiously I awaited Thane's reaction. He remained at my side, but when the girl put out her hand and said, 'Roswal', he glanced at me apologetically, a look of understanding passed between us and, tail wagging gently, he went over to her and sat at her side.

Again I was relieved, for there was no rapturous reunion here, nothing more than his usual acceptance of any stranger visiting me in Solomon's Tower.

Kate looked up from rather timorously patting his head and Hubert, hovering close by, said heartily, 'You remember Roswal, my dear?'

An odd question, since he had been brought to Staines on the grounds that she yearned for the deerhound as her dying wish.

Without looking up, she whispered, 'He is lovely. I remember that, but he is—so big.' Sighing, she frowned. 'He must have grown in the time he was away.'

'Three years is a long time in a dog's life,' was Hubert's soothing response.

Leaning forward, Kate kissed Thane's head and looked across at me. 'Thank you for taking such good care of him and bringing him back to us again.' And to Collins, who was standing by with nurse-like hands primly folded, she said, 'Will it be all right if he stays with me for a while?'

'During the day, yes, of course, Miss Kate.'

Thane raised his head in my direction, giving me a look of despair. 'He needs a lot of exercise,' I protested. 'He's not used to being

47

treated like a lapdog.'

Hubert came to our rescue, smiling at Kate. 'Since he has spent the last three years with Mrs McQuinn and is used to her daily routine, we must leave it so for the present, my dear.' Another reassuring smile. 'Especially as you are not well enough to go out of doors and take him for long walks—yet.'

Did he mean 'if ever'? I looked at him sharply, but his face remained inscrutable, and as Kate sighed and looked a little sulky at this decision, he added gently, 'We don't want him to run away from us again, do we, now?'

She shook her head and Collins said, 'It is time for your bath, Miss Kate.'

I blessed her for that as Thane took the opportunity of rushing back to my side.

'We will see you later, my dear.' Hubert kissed Kate's forehead and motioned us towards the door. As we descended the staircase, not a word of explanation was forthcoming.

In the hall he turned to me, saying, 'Lunch is at one o'clock. Feel free to use the library.' He indicated a door across the hall. 'Anything you need, just ask Mrs Robson.'

Dismissed with another of those penetrating looks, I went out into the fresh air and Thane, glad to be released, trotted ahead, eager to explore his new surroundings.

I had much to be thoughtful about. Most important, I was sure that Kate did not remember Roswal, although three years is a long time in a child's life. But then, at fourteen, grief for a beloved pet gone missing was worthy of comment; a bereavement not easily forgotten.

But what concerned me most was that she certainly did not resemble the child dying of consumption my stepbrother had led me to expect.

These two facts led to one logical question: What was the real reason Thane and I had been brought to Staines?

*   *   *

As the situation I had just left suggested that I might be in Staines longer than I had been led to believe, I decided that Thane and I should explore the grounds and get our bearings.

We were fortunate indeed. It was a truly beautiful morning, which bestowed a sprinkling of magic to hide the cracks and bruises of a somewhat neglected estate.

Following a narrow downhill path that led to a pond fed by a underground stream, and looking back, I discovered that Staines Manor stood in a commanding position above us, overlooking a tiny hamlet surrounding a green, complete with market cross and ancient church, while far to the right the rural landscape was scarred by a pithead.

Smoke from a railway train identified this as

the level crossing where we had encountered the stray cow on the approach to Alnwick.

On the outskirts of the village, there were skeletons of roofless houses and broken walls overgrown with grass, which suggested that Staines had known more prosperous days under earlier landlords, before coal had been discovered on the land.

Shading my eyes, from my vantage point I was sure that I could see a line of shining water mingling with the bright horizon, and the air carried the salt tang of the North Sea. Breathing deeply, I let the surroundings, silent and ancient, creep into my soul. The brooding stillness, the waiting expectancy of the hills where human sounds are quieted and the peace of ages creeps over sun-warmed earth and a scrambled quiltdown of distant fields.

There are moments when memory remains fixed and forever indelible. And often in a troubled, uncertain future, I was to return to this brief stillness, this tiny magic oasis with Thane at my side.

At last a shadow came over the earth, the sky filled with darkening clouds and I went in to a lunch set for four. Hubert and Collins (the nurse by designation ate at the family table) were joined by Wolf Rider, much to Thane's delight, whose exuberant welcome was regarded somewhat sourly by Hubert.

Mrs Robson leant over with her soup ladle and whispered sternly, 'Sir doesn't allow dogs into the dining room.' A fact I realised was rather obvious since Hubert's two Labradors remained outside having merely twitched their ears at Thane's appearance and thereafter ignored him.

'Will it be all right if he stays in the hall then?' It was hardly my place to apologise, since it was up to the master to give the order, especially as Thane was supposedly his dog. Having overheard, Hubert nodded and Thane trotted off with Mrs Robson, after a reproachful glance in my direction.

Hubert was aware that Wolf and I had met, and the conversation turned to Kate and her medication. I asked if the local doctor took care of her.

He sighed. 'Alas, no longer. We have now given up on doctors and conventional treatments. Kate had an excellent doctor at the hospital in Newcastle who was also a local resident here. When he died most tragically in a travelling accident, we decided to use more unorthodox methods.

'You will find that in this house we are dedicated to herbs and vegetables, to natural food that can be grown and gathered on the estate. Wait until you have tasted Mrs Robson's mushroom soup, a splendid example of what nature can produce for us.'

And with a glance at Wolf, he added, 'Mr Rider is a witch doctor, a shaman in his own native land, where we are aware that the

51

American Indian tribes have excellent results with herbs. He has made good progress with Kate. A last resort that seems to be working,' he added, as Collins put in rather anxiously:

'There seemed little to be lost in the circumstances.'

They both regarded Wolf who said dryly, 'Witch doctor is not a very flattering description, but I agree with Hubert that nature's cures have always been with us, to hand for the picking, one might say, older and more reliable than dangerous drugs invented by civilisation in search of health and longevity. We believe that as good is an antidote to evil, so too for all sickness there is a herb that can cure, and if that is not possible, then it can alleviate pain.'

'You are certainly succeeding with Miss Kate,' I said, echoing Hubert's remarks. 'She certainly does not look like—' I paused, realising my lack of tact too late as Hubert moved uneasily in his chair and Collins glanced at him, biting her lip.

'I thought she looked reassuringly well,' I stammered. 'And this might well be the explanation. Well done.'

I beamed at Wolf Rider across the table, who bowed his head in modest acknowledgement of the compliment, while I was considering it strange indeed that Hubert Staines, with wealth and doubtless influence, should put his beloved stepdaughter's

52

remaining days into the hands of a shaman.

Vegetable soup was succeeded by poached salmon, and the talk turned to estate matters. In particular, the white cattle and the possibilities of new-born calves being lifted from the herd and shipped to the wealthy Texas rancher to begin breeding a new strain.

I learnt again that this was a dangerous business, for cows in calf would not hesitate to attack humans, and it was not always possible to predict when and where a calf would be dropped. The cow usually found some secret, isolated place, well away from the herd and particularly the king bull who, in common with many wild animals whose interest ceased with the mating, lacked all paternal feelings regarding his offspring.

'Only Mr Rider has the remarkable gift of moving freely among the cattle,' said Hubert. 'They seem to trust him.'

'Whether they will continue to do so when I steal their calves is a different matter,' said Wolf. 'The cow I am watching now is unusually large. In sheep we might expect twin lambs, and if the mother is unable to feed both, she might abandon the weaker. Unfortunately twin births are not frequent in the white cattle.'

As our empty plates were removed and there was, regrettably from my point of view, no offer of dessert, I decided to excuse myself.

Thane was waiting patiently in the hall and we slipped into the garden, my intention to go downhill and investigate the village. At the Saxon church, now an abandoned ruin, Rider caught up with us, his approach greeted with Thane's usual delight.

'I have to collect from the post office in Alnwick some of the more unusual herbs not readily available in this part of the country. Expensive too, but Hubert buys from a well-known and trustworthy firm in the south of England.'

I looked around. Apart from grass and stately trees, there might have been an occasional mushroom born to blush unseen, unless one was out sharp enough in the morning dew, but nothing that I would recognise immediately as a herb like basil or thyme or wild garlic.

As our ways parted, Wolf said, 'I can recommend the teashop. They serve excellent cream cakes,' he added with a grin.

I looked at him sharply. Had he read my mind again and recognised my disappointment at the lack of a pudding after an otherwise substantial lunch?

Suddenly he turned back and said: 'I go to Holy Island—over there off the coast,' he pointed to the horizon, 'to collect sea herbs. Perhaps you would like to come with me sometime. It's a place well worth a visit.'

I thought I would, and said so.

Climbing back up the hill, I found an ancient and dilapidated rustic seat, no longer very secure and doubtless installed by a late Staines overlord to keep an eye on his village far below. I sat down, acutely aware that I needed time to think, for, unless I was grievously mistaken, I had been brought here with Thane under false pretences regarding Kate's tenuous grasp on life.

If that was the case, then I needed most urgently to discover the truth, to return to Edinburgh, and safely return Thane to Arthur's Seat.

The facts made no sense. A child who was a beautiful young woman. And Thane, whom her stepfather claimed she needed to comfort her in her last earthly days, had shown as little interest in her, his former beloved owner, as she did in him.

So what was behind it all?

Suddenly the peaceful scene before me erupted into activity as two black Labradors rushed down the path, followed by Hubert, who greeted my appearance with the warmth and cordiality of one discovering a long-lost friend. Meanwhile his dogs seemed unaware of this other canine presence as Thane remained stolidly at my side.

'Ah, here you are, my dear Mrs McQuinn. My dogs flushed you out, did they? Do you mind if I join you?'

Even if I had objected, it would have been too late, and I made room for him on the seat never meant to accommodate two persons who were not on very cosy terms, especially when one was of Staines' girth.

He stretched out a hand, patted my arm, and smiled into my face, just inches away from his own.

'Ah, my dear, how I wish that we had met when I was in Edinburgh three years ago. The day I lost Roswal.'

Pausing to sigh deeply, he went on: 'Just imagine, all these wasted years when we might have become—' and, searching for a word, 'friends.' That choice did not please him. His hesitation, the shake of his head as he gazed deep into my eyes would have hinted even to a woman of little perception that he had more than friends in mind.

'You are a truly remarkable and a very lovely woman, Mrs McQuinn.' Suddenly he laughed. 'Mrs McQuinn—Rose, the most beautiful of flowers. Might I call you Rose?'

Even had I wished to do so, I could hardly say 'no'. I remembered my painful, early days alone in Solomon's Tower and knew I would have been extremely vulnerable had I met Hubert Staines then.

Jack Macmerry had been just a pleasant young police constable. There was no bond between us until he saved my life and infatuation was not one of my failings. From twelve years old, my eyes had always been steadily fixed on Pappa's Sergeant Danny McQuinn who had snatched my sister Emily and me from kidnappers. I had vowed to marry him and, against all odds, had done so.

Even when Jack and I became lovers, I was uneasy, unwilling to commit myself to marriage, somehow sure that Danny McQuinn would one day walk back into my life.

But a meeting with a handsome stranger on Arthur's Seat, in search of his lost deerhound, with an invalid stepdaughter and the weight of past tragedies on his shoulders . . . It was a scene out of a romantic novelette indeed! And with the experience of ten years of marriage behind me, I might have reacted less conventionally than my favourite fictional heroine Jane Eyre.

But now the situation was different. And for me, there was no better opportunity than the present for prying deeper into Hubert's motives for bringing me to Staines.

'What I would be most grateful to know is why . . .' I hesitated. His physical closeness bothered me. I moved as far away as the rustic seat would allow.

I never got to finish that question, as out of the corner of my eye I saw Collins rapidly approaching from the direction of the house.

We both heard her footsteps and a moment later she was gazing down at us, her face scarlet, murmuring something inarticulate about Miss Kate.

Hubert sprang to his feet. I was overcome with embarrassment, as if by sitting on that tiny seat together we had been apprehended in some indelicate situation.

I was certain of one thing; the atmosphere she had come into was charged with emotions. Hubert's, not mine, although I found myself blushing and stood up so hastily that I stumbled. Hubert steadied me and, excusing myself hastily, l left him to deal with Collins' ill-suppressed anger.

As I hurried up the path with Thane trotting at my side, they remained within earshot. I heard protests, murmurs, sharp words, denials, as I hastened towards the house.

In my bedroom, I closed the door thankfully, with no wish for an embarrassing encounter with Collins. Seated on the bed, I considered Hubert's extraordinary conversation. Had he seemed remotely a flirt, I would have laughed, but there was something deep and serious and even sincere in his manner. His behaviour towards me had changed in this short time to that of a man utterly captivated, which I found very difficult to understand.

I have no illusions about my appearance. I am no beauty, just a woman in her early thirties, small with very average looks, and a cloud of unruly yellow curls—the bane of my life. Surely, I told my mirror, no man would ever pause to give me a second glance.

Yet, looking out of the window, for a moment I allowed myself to imagine a future as lady of the manor, floating down the grand staircase in a beautiful gown with Thane at my side. Would that be a happy ending for us both . . . ?

Stop this! Stop this nonsense, Rose McQuinn. It isn't you and what is more, it never could be you. Be sensible, remember your mission in life—Lady Investigator, Discretion Guaranteed. And I suspect if you keep your eyes open there will be much in Staines to investigate.

I was right. Dangerous matters involving life and death and, as I was to discover, much need for that discretion, too.

CHAPTER SIX

I met Mrs Robson in the hall. 'Is he', she asked, indicating Thane, 'to go to Miss Kate? I'll take him upstairs, Collins isn't around,' she added, a fact I already knew.

As he followed her into Kate's room, Thane's woeful look hardly fitted his role as her beloved pet.

Alone again, I sat by the window and, while trying to read, my thoughts drifted longingly to Edinburgh and what had been my normal daily routine. Did the situation I had found myself in at Staines, with its baffling undertones, suggest an extended stay? If so, then I was going to find the days very long indeed.

I had not long to wait for an answer.

Mrs Robson tapped on the door. 'Sir would like a word, Mrs McQuinn.'

Hubert was waiting in his study. As he told me to close the door, I hoped this was not to be a continuation of our conversation on the rustic seat. To my relief, he indicated a chair and took a seat behind his desk.

Studying me for a moment, he seemed to come to a decision. 'I am afraid I have not been completely truthful with you, Mrs McQuinn—Rose, may I call you?' he added.

My smile was all the answer he needed and, with a sigh, he went on: 'I have to confess that when I asked you to bring Roswal to Staines I had a dual purpose in mind.' Pausing he regarded me sternly, pointing a finger across the desk. 'What you may even decide to call false pretences.'

So I was to get the answer to my speculation at last.

He smiled. 'Of course, Kate and I are delighted by the coincidence that our long lost Roswal should have been found with you and have been adopted, as we might say, by the stepsister of my good friend Dr Vincent Laurie.'

His speech sounded suspiciously theatrical and well-rehearsed, I thought, as he continued:

'We were delighted that Roswal should have been taken such good care of by you and now at last to have him home again with us, but . . .' he paused, emphasising the word, 'but I am also taking advantage of what Vince has told me regarding his truly remarkable stepsister.'

A frown, punctuated by a rather pained smile. 'It may surprise you to learn that I happen to be very interested in your other role. That of Mrs McQuinn, Lady Investigator, Discretion Guaranteed.'

With a sigh, a heavenward glance of despair, he added softly, 'Especially the latter,' and, opening a drawer in his desk, he took out a wad of bank notes and pushed them across the table. 'Especially the latter,' he repeated. 'I am hoping most earnestly that I can persuade you to take on a rather difficult and delicate assignment.'

A gesture towards the bank notes. 'You will find one hundred guineas there. This is in the nature of a retainer as I am not certain what your usual fee might be, but I hope this will make you feel that my little problem is worth your while—whatever the result,' he added gloomily. 'Should you be as successful as I hope, then I will give you the same amount again.'

Two hundred guineas. More than the yearly wage most Edinburgh working men had to feed and clothe a family and keep a roof over their heads. My mind was already racing ahead, thinking of what I could do with such a sum, as he asked, 'Well, will you undertake this

61

investigation?'

'Yes, of course I will,' I stammered. *Sight unseen?* whispered a shocked conscience. *Don't be a fool, Rose McQuinn. First of all, find out what you're letting yourself in for.*

Hubert looked pleased. 'To begin at the beginning, as Vince will have told you, Her Majesty has graciously commanded my services to photograph members of the Royal family, particularly the children—my speciality.'

Folding his hands together, he said dreamily, 'Capturing the innocence and radiance of childhood, having them behave at their most natural. Not an easy matter, especially with young Royals who, not to put too fine a point on it, are often quite spoilt and can behave very badly indeed.'

He paused, his frown saying more than any lengthy explanation. 'Her Majesty has looked favourably on my efforts. Indeed, they seem to please her and she looks forward most eagerly to seeing the results after each engagement. As I expect you are aware, Her Majesty is a devoted grandmother. She has been most generous.'

Another pause and, as Hubert took a deep breath, I remembered that Vince had hinted at a knighthood in the offing.

'However, some years ago, as an apprentice in the art of photography, I had experimented in capturing some artistic images which were

62

only for my own pleasure and not for general contemplation.'

I guessed what was coming as he went on: 'Alas, they fell into the hands of a thief during a break-in. He had access through the window here in my study. The photographs were kept in a locked drawer—' Pausing he indicated the desk. 'And they are now being used as a means of extracting sums of money for his silence.'

Blackmail was something I had experience of in my profession. Indeed, it was the main root of several of my most successful investigations. There were a number of routine questions I had to ask, firstly: 'Have you any idea of this thief's identity?'

'Alas, no.'

'When did this break-in occur?'

He shrugged. 'I cannot tell you precisely what time it took place.'

'Quite recently?'

He shook his head. 'Six months ago.'

Rather a long time to elapse before tracking down an anonymous thief, I thought, and said, 'Were the police alerted?'

'No. Since nothing else of value had been stolen. Only the photographs.' An uncomfortable shrug. 'And I had good reasons for keeping silent considering their content.'

'How did this intruder get in? Was the window glass broken or had the latch been forced?'

'The glass was unbroken. As regards the

latch, however, checking that windows are locked each night would normally fall into a servant's duties. I am afraid that we are careless about that, especially in warm weather.'

As he spoke I went over to inspect the window. It was a few feet above ground level with a tree almost touching the wall; almost an invitation to access.

'The key to the locked drawer. Where was it kept?'

'Here,' he said, pointing to the desk's long central drawer. There was a pause, then he added, 'Well, what do you think?'

From his information I had already decided that this was no casual burglary. Just a step away across the hall there were rooms containing many portable items of considerable value; silver, clocks, ornaments— any of which would make a thief's daring break-in well worthwhile.

The clues so far indicated that the thief knew precisely what he was looking for, and I doubted that he had sneaked in at night by the window. The location of the key, so readily to hand, suggested someone who was familiar with the house's layout. The photographs, I decided, were most probably stolen during the day.

'When did you discover they were missing?'

'Not until I had received the first of these notes demanding payment for their return,' he said, taking out an envelope from the desk drawer. Opening it, he thrust across the table a sheet of cheap note paper with letters cut from a newspaper. I read:

'Your time has run out. Pay up or the newspapers will get the photographs.'

'This is the third note,' said Hubert. 'I was so angry, so outraged, that I destroyed the earlier ones. Each demanded £500 and, to prove he had the stolen items, each one contained a corner of one of the photographs.'

'You were able to recognise them?'

'Indeed, yes,' he said grimly. 'They contained enough to leave no doubt of that.'

'May I see the envelope please?'

'All three were posted in Newcastle,' said Hubert, anticipating my next question. Regarding the postage stamp, I thought cynically that the Queen would not be impressed by the contents relating to her favourite photographer.

While I was unsure what the term 'artistic images' meant, if, as I suspected, Hubert was referring to naked or indecently clad females, then Her Majesty would most certainly be shocked and outraged. Prudish in nature, she had commanded that grand pianos were to have their curvaceous legs packed in covers, and if the contents of such photographs became known, then Hubert would also be sent packing. No knighthood there, alas.

With any criminal activities, whether

murder or mayhem, the first place for questions is within the family circle, the servants and close friends.

'Had you any unexpected visitors at that time?'

Hubert was silent, thoughtful, making me wonder if he had someone in mind.

At last he sighed, shook his head. No trail there.

'I have to ask you this again. Please be quite frank about it. Have you any suspicions about who this person might be?'

Hubert bit his lip, looked unhappy. 'The only stranger to the household, if he may be so called, is Wolf Rider. He knows the house well, comes and goes as he pleases.' His glance was loaded with reluctance, his manner implying that he would like to say more but could not conjure up the right words.

If that was so and he suspected Wolf Rider, why then had he kept him in his employ? Then I remembered Wolf's extraordinary story of their kinship through Miranda Staines, and I wondered if this might be of some significance as Hubert went on:

'I want you to track down as soon as possible whoever stole the photographs and retrieve them. I shall be most grateful to you, Rose.'

It was I who would be grateful, I thought, considering the fee I would be receiving should this investigation be successful.

He must have observed my wry smile as he added with a lofty gesture, 'The clue, of course, lies in the fact that all the letters have a Newcastle postmark.' And frowning, as if in afterthought, he added casually: 'In the absence of a doctor for Kate, Rider also makes frequent trips to Newcastle Central Station to pick up supplies of herbs.'

Ah, I thought, *an indirect accusation.* I asked, 'How many people are acquainted with your, er, present problem?'

He shook his head, said firmly, 'No one. I have not confided this unhappy business to anyone—except you now, Rose.'

Not even Collins? Well, well. I thought that was highly unlikely considering the intimacy of their relationship.

'I find it difficult to remain calm in these circumstances. Matters are hard enough to bear with a young girl so ill upstairs, without these added complications,' he added in a note of appeal.

I could sympathise but, as I left him, I felt helpless, wondering where and how to begin.

Little was revealed in the letter he had received. I had reached one conclusion, however. I believed the thief must be either the blackmailer himself or an individual being paid to steal to order. The Newcastle postmark I dismissed as a deliberate attempt to mask the blackmailer's identity. Such matters are fairly common. I knew from

67

similar situations in Edinburgh that blackmailers rarely use the postbox at the end of their own street, cunningly prepared to invest in a train journey and the safety offered by some anonymous area.

As evidence it was a waste of time, and I was fairly sure my search lay closer to home and could be safely narrowed down to the village of Staines, if not the actual household.

I considered the grim message again, and longed for Jack Macmerry and his access to the relatively new science of fingerprinting. But Jack had gone from my life. At least I now had a case to solve that would engage all my efforts and ease the melancholy of his desertion and the possible loss of Thane.

I had to admit Thane was showing precious little interest in his 'beloved owner' Miss Kate, and none at all in her stepfather, whose final words to me had been:

'I am sure it is not necessary for me to say that I have made you my sole confidant. I am in your hands and I am relying entirely on your discretion.'

At the door I turned and smiled reassuringly. 'Discretion Guaranteed, sir. Part of the contract.'

'One more thing, Rose. You are not to call me "sir".'

'Mr Staines, then. You are employing me—'

'No! Hubert—Hubert, I insist, if we are to be friends. I could never think of myself as your employer,' his voice softened as he murmured, 'dear Rose.' So saying, he made a sudden move from the desk and I took instant flight.

As I ran upstairs, I wished I could confide in someone—and that someone was Wolf Rider.

Hubert's silent eagerness to cast suspicion on him seemed idiotic. At that time I could not imagine Wolf stealing incriminating photographs or using them to blackmail his distant cousin.

From the little I knew of him, such an idea seemed utterly out of character.

And I thought then, right or wrong, that Wolf Rider was the one man I would trust.

CHAPTER SEVEN

When I collected Thane from Kate's room, he was lying on the floor near the door, as far away from her as possible. He immediately ran to my side, his expression one of almost human boredom—and relief.

Collins was at my heels. She looked round anxiously and gave the impression of being reluctant to let her charge out of her sight.

Kate laid aside a ladies' magazine and looked up wearily. 'Roswal is rather detached now. He was much livelier in the old days. Loved to play and he was so affectionate—'

I felt sorry. She sounded so let down and disappointed, especially as affection was the one thing Thane had in abundance.

'He used to sleep here, at my bedside, every night,' she ended sadly.

'That won't be possible now, Miss Kate,' said Collins sternly. 'Your father has given orders that he is to sleep in the stables.' And to me, perhaps with a note of triumph, 'Our two Labradors sleep in the kitchen; they are guard dogs, you know.'

They hadn't given me that impression, but I nodded. Thane looked at me as if he understood, and I wondered for a moment if I could have him in my room.

'You are taking him for a walk?' said Collins.

'Perhaps I could come with you,' said Kate eagerly. 'Poor Roswal must be weary of my long silences and I'm sure I could manage a short walk in the gardens while the sun is shining,' she added to Collins.

'Perhaps later, Miss Kate.'

'Why not today?' was the weary response, but her protests were cut short as Collins hurried me out of the room. In the corridor she said, as if this was not for Kate's ears:

'Quite out of the question, Mrs McQuinn. She is very frail, you know, thinks she is much stronger than she is, as is often the case with her condition. But you would need to take her out in the bath chair, make sure she doesn't catch a chill. That could be fatal.'

I felt sudden pity for Kate, an unhappy prisoner. 'Does she ever leave her room?'

'Sometimes she feels well enough to go downstairs and dine with Mr Staines. But such occasions are getting rarer.'

I thought about Collins as I walked with Thane. She did not seem at all happy, her nervous manner betraying her unease, yet she did not strike me as Hubert's blackmailer.

Just as I was dismissing her as not nearly confident enough and the first to be struck off my small list, I realised this was a hasty decision. No one was beyond suspicion and often the most surprising and unlikely person can turn out to be a blackmailer, or more often a writer of poison pen letters.

Collins' actions betrayed her love for Hubert. Had she seen the photographs by accident, then, jealous and angry, simmering with resentment that he had not asked her to marry him and made her mistress of his house, had she decided that blackmail was the answer?

But what had she to gain? Anger and instant dismissal if he ever found out, but she would still have the money which, I suspected, would be a great deal more than her salary. Could it be a last resort, an insurance for her uncertain future and that eventual rainy day when, no longer required as a nurse, their relationship came to an end?

71

That set me wondering if the payment for my investigation was the mark of an open-handed employer. It did strike me as odd in this large house with its vast estate that there were no other indoor servants. Perhaps a probe in the direction of Mrs Robson, who had been with him far longer than Collins, would provide some answers.

'Our needs are modest,' Hubert had hinted. Did this indicate that he shared, in common with many wealthy men, a tendency to be mean about paying servants and employees?

If so, his decision to pay me a substantial sum as a private investigator took on a new aspect and should be regarded with extreme caution.

There was a lot more I wanted to know about members of the Staines family, alive and dead, and my thoughts drifted towards Kate's mother, whose photograph in its silver frame occupied her bedside table.

And who better to supply some information regarding the late Mrs Staines than Mrs Robson, who seemed disposed to be friendly, I thought, as I drifted into the kitchen.

Sipping the cup of tea she offered, I remarked casually that having been at Staines for many years she must have known Kate's mother very well.

'Indeed. A charming lady she was, too,' she sighed. 'We all miss her.'

I said how sad it was for Kate to have been

orphaned so young, and, trying to phrase it delicately, asked how she had died.

Mrs Robson's eyebrows arched in surprise. 'Has no one told you about her?'

There had scarcely been time for that, I thought, as she continued: 'Madam was a bit older than Sir but fit as a fiddle, in her prime as you might say. Her first husband had left her very well off.' she added confidentially. 'A Durham colliery owner with a posh big house and pots of money.'

Pausing to sigh, she went on: 'Sir was her first cousin, and a struggling photographer, the last of a fine old family who had been here since the year dot. They'd fallen on hard times when the coal ran out at the Staines pit, and in those days taking photographs wasn't considered a worthwhile occupation, until the Queen's interest changed all that.'

Another pause for breath and to refill the teapot. 'A real love match. Would you fancy a piece of fruit loaf—or a scone? I make good scones—'

She beamed on me and gave a romantic sigh, and in order to prolong the subject I yielded to the lure of a tempting snack.

'Miss Kate was eleven when they married, but there were hopes of an heir. Sir was desperate for a son, poor man, the son who would have solved all his problems, but after a few false alarms nothing happened.'

Laying aside her cup with an air of

resignation, she returned to her darning. A pile of men's socks. Was this another indication that her master was a little on the mean side? Her sigh as she threaded the needle might have been taken as dismissal and a sign that the conversation was at an end. But not for me. Not yet.

'You were saying,' I reminded her with a sad smile. 'About how Mrs Staines died.'

'Oh, didn't I tell you?' Another sigh. 'A tragic accident. We could hardly believe it. Such a simple thing. You know yon big bay window in the sitting room, overlooking the garden?'

I nodded, and she went on. 'Well, it was a stormy day—we get awful storms up here sometimes, take the full force of the gales. That night there was a shrieking wind rattling the panes. It woke Kate and Madam went to see what was wrong. In the sitting room someone had left the window open. The wind had caught it and as she leant forward to seize the latch, she lost her balance—and—that was that!'

She shook her head. 'Poor lady, fell out head first, down onto the terrace. Broke her neck. Poor Sir, he was distraught, poor little Kate screaming for her mam. An awful business, Mrs McQuinn—none of us could take it in.'

Did that terrible moment still haunt the room, their cries, their anguish, linger in the air, clinging to the very stones? Was that why I had felt so uneasy?

'A terrible time, terrible. Poor Sir was beside himself with remorse, looking round the house, as men will, for someone to blame. Fortunately it had nothing to do with me, but we had a maid, a young lass just a couple of years younger than Kate is now, a bit slovenly and careless. Always breaking things in my kitchen—a nightmare she was. Anyway, Sir seized on her, blaming her for leaving the window unlatched. He sent her packing and, what was worse, refused to give her a reference.'

That sounded very harsh to me and I protested: 'That was hardly fair. She was very young, after all.'

'Lasses go into service here at twelve often enough, Mrs McQuinn. They don't need much wages, work for pennies at that age—'

Another sign of Sir's meanness, I thought, as she went on: 'And Lily's family—there were five other bairns younger than her—needed the few shillings she got each week. Their dad was an invalid, after an accident in the mine when he was a lad. Couldn't work again.'

I felt a rising sense of outrage against Hubert Staines, with his child labour exploiting the family of one of his injured pitmen. 'Surely Mr Staines could have given her a reference,' I said angrily.

Mrs Robson shook her head. 'No. Sir said

she was unreliable and that he couldn't in all conscience recommend her to anyone else after her causing his wife's death.'

'She didn't push her out of the window, Mrs Robson. It was a tragic accident,' I protested.

She shook her head. 'We all knew that. But Sir was beside himself at the time, said I'd have to do all the work myself, he would never trust another young maid in the house. Put a lot of responsibility on my shoulders, I can tell you,' she said, sounding ill-used. 'And all for two extra pounds a month, but beggars can't be choosers, can they? I had my living to make and I'd been a loyal trusted servant to the family for years.'

'What happened to the girl? Does she still live in Staines—I mean, did you keep in touch?'

She gave me a slightly offended look. 'Not with me. Sir wouldn't have approved. Sad for Kate, though, she missed her, they were very friendly. Lily might have been useless in the kitchen but she liked making things for Miss Kate, doted on her. Good at sewing, too,' she added with a reproachful glance at the pile of darning. 'Used to do all this sort of thing, even said she enjoyed it. Now it all comes to me, as if I hadn't enough to do running the house.'

My thoughts were with Lily. 'I hope she got another job in spite of everything.'

Mrs Robson shrugged. 'Couldn't say, but her father limped up to the house next day and went on something terrible, shouted at Sir, for taking away his daughter's character. I was at the door but I heard every word. Threatened to strike Sir with his stick, he did. It was awful.'

Shaking her head, she added: 'How it might have ended is anyone's guess if Lily's father hadn't been killed on the level crossing in the village—the one that divides us from the old colliery. You would have come through it when you came on the train.'

I nodded and she said, 'Last I heard of the lass was that she'd married a railwayman who was a chum of her father's. That must have been a comfort for her. They moved to Alnwick.'

I was making a mental note of Alnwick and bad feelings, trying to see if they might add up to someone with a good reason for blackmailing Hubert. A maid who had been familiar with the house might have seen those photographs, and if she didn't steal them herself, she might have gossiped about them. And that gossip could eventually have led to a burglary and Hubert's present unfortunate predicament.

Mrs Robson was saying, 'Sir really showed how kind he was and prepared to forget the past; he gave them a good wedding present.'

From someone who had refused Lily a character reference, that was a surprise. I asked, 'Something for their home?'

She laughed. 'No. Money! To help them set up.'

Perhaps I was misjudging Hubert and he had shown genuine remorse. 'A sad story indeed,' I said encouragingly. 'Do you ever hear of them?'

'Not I, Mrs McQuinn. They weren't my type of folks, if you understand. Lily was, well, a bit common and not really a suitable companion for Kate.'

'Has Kate a good doctor to take care of her?' I decided craftily to feign ignorance of what I already knew.

'Not any more. Old Dr Holt was a good man and all his patients—that is everyone in Staines since he was the only doctor—they all loved him. He was more like a friend, a father confessor, they all said, as well as taking care of their bodies, they could tell him anything, get his help with all their problems.'

The recipient of secrets, I thought. That could be dangerous.

She was saying, 'He looked after Kate, kept her spirits up. Refused to accept or let her accept that she might not get better. He was certain that her trouble might turn out to be some respiratory weakness, not that deadly consumption.'

A sigh and she went on: 'He took her into the hospital in Newcastle just a few months ago for tests, and when he was driving back home, his carriage went off the road at the level crossing and he was killed by an oncoming train.'

Shaking her head, she added indignantly, 'It ought to be got rid of, that crossing, especially with the pit closed. It isn't needed any more.'

I agreed but could not help thinking that it might also provide a convenient means of disposing of one's enemies.

I made a mental note that it would be well worth investigating, as I said:

'How tragic. Did he have a family?'

'No bairns. His widow still lives in the village.'

And I decided to put Mrs Holt high on my visiting list.

CHAPTER EIGHT

So my introduction to Staines drew to a close. I was not sure what I had expected when I left Edinburgh, filled with a sense of dread and melancholy, to reunite Thane with his owners.

Now the whole scene I had imagined had changed well beyond my expectations. Thane's owner was an attractive man with problems that made the arrival of a Lady Investigator, Discretion Guaranteed extremely useful, and I had already accepted a very substantial fee to find out who was blackmailing him.

Quite frankly, I did not expect this to be too difficult; from what he had told me the possible suspects were few in number and in a limited radius, compared to many similar Edinburgh cases recorded in my logbook. Blackmail was always my most frequent case. The victims were ready to part with substantial sums of money to keep some indiscretion from reaching the eyes and ears of a wife, husband or employer or the general public through the newspapers.

The photographs in question suggested risqué French postcards of naked females in provocative poses, doubtless quite naughty, the kind most gentlemen had access to in their clubs and would dismiss with an appreciative grin.

But in Hubert's case his employer was none other than Her Majesty the Queen, who would be outraged, shocked and scandalised at having such a wanton creature anywhere near her precious grandchildren. His anxiety was understandable; a promising career and a prosperous future with the possibility of a knighthood were all at stake.

I had promised to take Thane in to see Kate before bedding him down for the night. This was a matter of form only, since there was little evident rapport between them so far. Much to my relief, I might add, but I was curious. Did Kate suspect that this was not Roswal but have motives of her own for accepting him?

She was sitting by the window and hardly lifted her eyes from the book she was reading when we entered, as always pursued by a breathless Collins, whose sudden appearances suggested that she was permanently stationed in a nearby linen cupboard.

Glancing at Thane, she said, 'You're taking him to the stables. Mr Staines sends his apologies that he is unable to dine with you this evening. Perhaps you would like Mrs Robson to bring a tray up to your room.'

I said that would be agreeable. I was tired after my broken night's sleep in Wolf Rider's bothy and didn't fancy sitting at one end of a vast dining-table under the solemn countenances of bygone Staines in their gilt frames.

'Very well, I will inform Mrs Robson,' said Collins, holding open the door. I wasn't prepared to leave just yet, as if under supervision.

Taking Thane over to Kate, who patted his head dutifully, I pointed to the photograph on the bedside table. 'Your mother was quite beautiful, wasn't she? You must miss her.'

Kate jerked upright in her chair. 'That's not Mamma,' her voice quivered, and sudden tears welled up in her eyes.

I was aware of Collins' touch on my shoulder. 'That is Miss Kate's sister,' she whispered, and as Kate began to sob noisily I was bundled out of the room. Outside the door, she said: 'Amy was her older sister. She—died—and Kate can't bear to talk about it. Surely you understand that,' and emphasising 'that' she slipped inside again and slammed the door behind her.

Left in total embarrassment, I could hear their murmured voices, Kate protesting, Collins consoling.

What on earth was going on? A sister no one had mentioned; where did she fit into this untidy scheme of things?

*   *   *

As I walked Thane towards his night's lodgings, considering why Mrs Robson, so eager to impart the Staines' family history, hadn't mentioned Amy, I decided to give the unhappy subject an airing when I returned my supper tray later that evening.

At the stables a man leant against one of the stalls. Little more than a boy, with black curls tumbling across his forehead, the cigarette dangling from his lips seemed inappropriate, a defiant gesture against the grown-up world.

He watched us approach with a mocking bow and an insolent gaze that stripped me naked. 'Ye must be the new woman.'

I said nothing, concentrating on Thane as the boy patted his head. 'You're a good dog, aren't ye?'

Thane wagged his tail politely but made no further overtures of friendliness.

The boy turned his attention to me. A bold glance from large, dark eyes suggested that he might be a gipsy.

'Me auntie mentioned ye—I looked in to see her just now.'

'Mrs Robson?' I questioned.

'Aye, that's her.'

'Do you work here?'

He grinned. 'On and off, like. On and off. Give Mr Rider a helping hand when required. Ye can put yer dog ower there,' he pointed to one of the stalls. 'There's food and water for him, and fresh straw.'

I thanked him and received again that suggestive leer as he bowed and said, 'I'm away then. Be seeing you if ye're to be staying for a while.'

I watched him stroll away, the cigarette smoke trailing after him. He even walked with an insolent air and seemed a very inappropriate nephew for Mrs Robson. If he came to Staines 'on and off', was he a suitable contender for my list of possible suspects as Hubert's thief and blackmailer?

*   *   *

I returned to the house, wishing I could have had Thane's company. I was so used to having him in Edinburgh where he had become more of a domestic pet—happy at my fireside—than a wild deerhound whose home was on Arthur's Seat.

My hopes that another interview with Mrs Robson would reveal more about Amy as well as her nephew were thwarted. She was wearing her bonnet as she delivered my supper tray—steak pie and Scotch trifle—indicating that she was in a rush to leave. Later, returning it to the empty kitchen, I decided to have a walk in the gardens and take full advantage of a late summer evening.

The air was calm, very still with storm clouds building up in the west. Thunderheads, too, threatened the future and an end to this tranquil season. But there was with no hint as yet of autumn in the lush green leaves above my head as I sat on a wall overlooking the village, its chimneys wreathed in smoke, huddled far from the brooding disused colliery, a blot on an otherwise charming rural landscape.

Suddenly I was overwhelmed by a sense of isolation and loneliness, a longing for someone to talk to, and my thoughts turned almost immediately to Wolf Rider. I headed briskly in the direction of his bothy and, a short distance away, still concealed by the path that emerged close by, I heard voices.

I looked out cautiously and there were Wolf and the bold youth who claimed to be Mrs Robson's nephew, in fierce discussion. I was too distant to hear the words, but Wolf seized the other's shoulders in a threatening gesture. It looked as if I had stumbled on an ugly scene and I made a rapid retreat, glad that the exuberant Thane was not with me to rush over to his hero and reveal my presence.

Returning to the house, my footsteps echoed hollowly on the polished floor of the hall. Where was everyone, I wondered, climbing the stairs to my bedroom alongside Kate's. Gazing down into the silent regions below, I presumed she would be asleep and that Collins' duties were over for the day. Perhaps she was with Hubert.

Taking out *The Tenant of Wildfell Hall*, I sat at the window, distracted by what we call in Scotland 'the gloaming', the magic twilight between day and nightfall. Yawning, but not tired enough to retire, I was very surprised to open my eyes in total darkness and, still clutching my book, to realise that I had been asleep for some time. Wearily I crept into bed, sighed, and slept again until a busy rooster noisily summoning his harem announced that it was morning.

Mrs Robson was in the kitchen and greeted my entrance with the usual polite questions about whether I had slept well, was warm enough, needed more blankets, pillows, etc. Having reassured her on these vital matters, as she juggled pots and plates, scarlet-faced with the stove's heat, over her shoulder she said,

85

'Sir takes breakfast in his study; I've set yours in the dining room.'

I could hardly refuse as the time was not right nor opportune to engage her in lengthy conversation about Kate's sister Amy.

I said, 'I met your nephew last night.'

She stopped, spoon in hand. 'Cedric? So he claims, but that's as maybe,' she added darkly: 'You look sharp with him, Mrs McQuinn, he's a holy terror.' And flourishing the spoon again, she went on, 'Bone idle, works when the mood takes him, that is when he needs baccy money. He's a bad lot, a devil for the girls.' Pausing to draw breath, she said. 'His ma, my da's youngest cousin, told everyone she had him to a gipsy, married Romany fashion.'

Tightening her lips, as if there was a lot more she could say on that subject, she shook her head, leaving me hoping for more, and wondering if I might somehow lead her round to the topic of Amy. But as she turned away, spooning porridge into bowls, buttering toast and dealing with a whistling kettle, a bell clanged noisily above our heads, twice to denote urgency and impatience.

'That's Sir. Oh my goodness. I'm late.' And off she went like the White Rabbit in *Alice in Wonderland*.

Left to my own devices, I ate in lonely splendour in the dining room, where hard Staines' eyes staring down from mediocre portraits made me nervous as I planned my first day's sleuthing on the trail of Hubert's blackmailer.

With clues virtually non-existent, this would certainly task my ingenuity, I decided, pushing my bicycle towards the path overlooking Staines, where I had met Hubert yesterday. The street bordering the village green seemed oddly deserted at this hour, where I had imagined households would be busy with the usual early morning activities: labouring husbands and sons off to work, wives and mothers hanging out the family washing.

Where were the children? With Staines colliery closed, the village would now be too small to accommodate a school, so presumably they were sent to Alnwick for their education.

Instead there was silence, with none of those plumes of smoke that last night cast an air of homeliness over the village. Beyond the occasional cat or dog slinking across the road, the houses had a closed-in look, repelling any would-be visitors.

How did the villagers occupy themselves? I wondered. With the lord of the manor no longer eager to employ servants, did they all walk into Alnwick each day, or labour in neighbouring farms?

No doubt time would reveal all, if I remained in Staines long enough, I decided, as I bicycled along the street wondering what dramas were being, or had been staged behind those firmly closed doors, where only an occasional twitch from tightly closed curtains indicated that my progress was under observation.

But how to contact my few suspects I had not the least idea. And guessing which of the dull houses in that dull street harboured a hopeful blackmailer was quite beyond me.

From Mrs Robson's account, Lily sounded like a prime suspect. The maid had had access to his study, was unfairly dismissed, and would have been distraught at the death of her father.

The drawback to this theory was that, from what I had heard so far, I doubted that she had the education or the initiative—without an accomplice.

And then there was Cedric, Mrs Robson's would-be nephew. He had access to the house certainly but, bone idle, would he have the necessary ingenuity and the energy required for a blackmailer?

CHAPTER NINE

I entered the local teashop at ten o'clock that morning with not the faintest notion what I was looking for, and regretting that it was too early after breakfast to sample those delicious cream cakes recommended by Wolf.

Taking a seat at a quiet table near the

window where I could survey the scene of complete inactivity outside, I found I was not as alone as I had supposed. A group of women occupied one of the six tables. Evidently the teashop was the hub of female life in Staines.

However, as I tried to look interested in the book I was supposedly reading, I became aware that the shop was emptying of customers. Goodbyes were exchanged until only one middle-aged woman remained, reaching for her purse. Her resigned expression, I thought uncharitably, hinted that she had been left with the bill.

About to leave, she glanced over in my direction. I smiled and, accepting this as an invitation, she gave me good-day and stopped by my table.

'I was up at the house yesterday and saw you with Mr Staines' dog, the one he lost a few years back.' I said nothing and overcome with curiosity, she added: 'How did you come by it?'

I did some quick thinking. So she knew the deerhound; was she simply a dog lover or perhaps some connection with the family?

'I found him in Edinburgh.'

Her eyebrows raised. 'Well, well. What a coincidence. A bit of luck that.'

'So you know Roswal?'

She shrugged. 'All dogs look alike to me, but my late husband was their doctor, treated the little girl. He thought a lot of her.'

This was my turn for a piece of luck. 'I was

sorry to hear of your loss,' I said gravely.

She looked at me wide-eyed and laughed out loud. 'Save your sympathy, lass. Fergus and I were separated. A right bastard, he was. Never a great marriage, ashamed of the fact he had married a servant and felt I wasn't socially acceptable, as he called it. So whatever happened to him, I had another fellow by the time he was killed.

'Got married since,' she added with a happy smile, touching her wedding ring. 'I'm Mrs Sloan, now.' Her face clouded for a moment, the smile banished. 'His accident was the kindest thing he ever did for me. Made it easier for us. Folk don't look kindly on divorces hereabouts. And I still have the house—till they find a new doctor, if ever. Folk now have to call on the Alnwick ones.'

I wanted to know more about that accident, hear her side of it, so pretending ignorance, I said, 'When you just said "whatever happened", er, to your late husband, was there some doubt?'

'They said he didn't get off the level crossing in time. Train hit him. Peter—my man—saw it all. He works on the railway—'

And he was in love with the doctor's wife. Well, well, I thought grimly, was there a murder enquiry that had been carefully swept under the carpet? Perhaps not seeing many strangers in these parts and my connection with Staines made her eager for a gossip.

Certainly her frank manner suggested that she was either innocent or else a very good actress.

She had stopped speaking as a shadow loomed over us, a man in a railway guard's uniform, smelling strongly of drink.

'Hello, love.'

So this was Peter Sloan.

'Thought I'd find you here, Grace,' he said, supporting himself on a vacant chair. Did I detect a reproach although they smiled at each other?

His questioning glance indicated that I introduce myself. He grinned and Grace said, 'Pete, Mrs McQuinn is staying with Staines. She brought his dog back from Edinburgh.'

The grin turned into a scowl, a look of dislike that indicated Hubert Staines was no friend of his. 'Have you told her about the accident?'

Grace looked uncomfortable. 'Well—'

He laughed and said to me. 'She hasn't told you that her brother-in-law Derek Sloan is in the police at Alnwick and that he was all for a proper investigation as he called it—'

Grace took his arm. 'For heaven's sake, Pete. Leave it be.'

Peter swayed a little as he laid both hands on the table. 'That was no accident, Missus, mark my words. I can say that freely although it did us a good turn, the one thing we have to be grateful for to the Lord of the Manor.'

I shook my head. 'Surely—?'

'Aye, surely. Stands to reason, he should have got rid of that level crossing when the pit closed. Death trap, it is. And how's the wee lass doing?'

I didn't know what to say, shook my head and took refuge in: 'I feel very sorry for her, so young.'

Peter looked mockingly at me. 'Feel sorry for her living with Staines—all alone, just the two of them in that big house,' he added. There was something very unpleasant about the way his tone was loaded with meaning.

'Miss Kate has a very good nurse looking after her.'

Ignoring that, he was looking hard at his wife. 'Grace's man was a good doctor, I give him that,' he added reluctantly. 'Aye, and he could have told you a thing or two about the two lasses—and what went on in that house—'

'Pete!' Grace's hand was on his arm. 'That's enough.'

'More than enough, some would say. A lassie under age.'

'Pete, there was no proof.' And to me. 'Only rumour, villages are like that.' She stood up and said firmly, 'Look, we must go.'

Her husband was swaying unsteadily and she smiled at me apologetically. 'Sorry, Mrs McQuinn, this fellow needs to get to his bed.' And so saying she marched him towards the door.

I watched them go, disappointed and

frustrated by the termination of what had promised to be a very interesting interview. At the door, Grace turned and came back.

'I wouldn't stay over-long in that house if I were you. Do take care.'

There was no mistaking the warning.

'Grace!' bawled Pete. 'Where the devil are you?'

'Look,' she said, 'come and see me, anytime. We'll have a proper chat. You can't mistake the house; it's the last one back there on the main street. High wall and a garden.' She gave an uncertain smile, 'Don't take any notice of Pete—he's an old gossip.'

Old gossip or not, I was aware again that Staines was not quite as I had imagined, nor how Vince had depicted it. Apart from the feudal lord of the manor, which sounded deceptively romantic, I had to bear in mind that Vince had only visited Staines briefly and, as was his nature, was prepared to see only the best in his friends, in whom he could admit to no fault. His one weakness, he had absolutely no discernment and regrettably tended to be unduly impressed by anyone remotely connected with Royalty.

I had also to remember that he had never met Kate.

Deciding that Wolf Rider might have some valuable information, I was heading in the direction of the bothy when a large shadow hovered above my head.

A bird of prey. Alarmingly it swooped down. I leapt from my bicycle and felt the swish of wings as I yelled, shielding my face from that murderous beak.

'Rose!'

Wolf was hurrying towards me and I felt like an absolute idiot as he said, 'Kokopele recognised you.'

As I dusted myself down, my face scarlet with embarrassment, the falcon settled on Wolf's gloved fist, ruffled his feathers and regarded us solemnly. An enigmatic bird indeed. At close quarters he looked innocent and rather merry as if he was hearing a funny story. His beak half open ready to laugh outright, watching us both eagerly, he looked as if he had some amusing anecdote he was dying to tell us.

I shook my head, thinking of Thane. If only animals could talk!

'Sorry he alarmed you. His social manners leave much to be desired. He's on patrol for the white cow. She must be ready to drop that calf any time now. At least with Kokopele here, I will know where to look.'

'But it's still very dangerous.'

He shrugged that aside, stroking Kokopele absent-mindedly, as if walking into the midst of wild cattle to steal a calf was little more than assisting at the birth of Daisy the dairy cow.

'How long are you staying?'

'I am not certain. I am afraid I have been

94

seriously misinformed.' I could hardly tell him, as one of Hubert's prime suspects, the real reason for the invitation and the uncertainty of my departure date.

He frowned. 'How is that?'

I took a deep breath. 'I was given to understand by Vince—my stepbrother—that Kate was on her deathbed and wished to see Roswal once again.'

He smiled. 'And instead you find an apparently healthy young woman.'

'I am glad of that—' I interrupted.

He nodded. 'Glowing complexions are often part of the condition, alas. I have seen many die tragically young with this disease that claims so many in our present-day society, but I have to admit that my herbs, about which Hubert has so much faith and reliance, could not really save her, or prolong her life, if she was in truth suffering from tuberculosis.'

Pausing, he frowned and shook his head. I asked: 'What do you think—what is your diagnosis?'

He shrugged. 'Some pulmonary weakness which exhibits the same symptoms as a more serious condition. But I would confidently predict that with care and attention Miss Kate may have a normal life span, marry, have children, although childbearing might bring a return of the symptoms.'

'I thought she was an only child. What happened to her sister? Was she ill too?'

'Amy?' He sighed. 'A bad business. Amy was Kate's elder sister and Kate adored her.' He paused, looking up at the sky, in the manner of one in urgent search of something to change the subject.

'What happened?' I insisted.

His sad expression as he faced me again told all. 'She died before her mother had that tragic accident. Amy was a great beauty, very wilful, very indulged. She had an ill-advised love affair with a local boy. Hubert threw her out of the house and she walked into the pond over yonder.'

'How dreadful.'

'She was eighteen—and pregnant.'

My imagination could cope with Hubert's anger but not with such a violent reaction. He was only her stepfather after all. I asked the obvious question.

'Why couldn't they marry?'

'Hubert absolutely forbade it.'

'What about her mother? Surely she had a say in that?'

He shrugged. 'Mary was shattered and Hubert was no doubt trying to protect her from further distress. Amy's death was too much for her to bear.'

A moment's silence and I asked: 'Do you think that her death—falling out of the window—wasn't accidental? That it was suicide?'

He looked thoughtful. 'I doubt that she

would have chosen that window. Twelve feet high? A broken arm or leg. No, she would definitely have chosen something higher.'

Another pause. 'Are you hinting that she was hit on the head first and then pushed out?'

Wolf stared at the horizon, shook his head. 'We will never know the answer to that.'

'What about the young man? What happened to him?'

'Dave was a bit wild. Hubert said he was after their money, and he could have been right about that. It was one good reason for not wanting him in the family. A friend of Cedric, Mrs Robson's nephew.'

'I've met him.'

Wolf nodded. 'They were two of a kind. Soon after Amy's death, Dave was cleaning a gun—he had been drinking—nothing unusual about that—but it went off and killed him.'

'Oh really!' How very convenient. And my mind immediately signalled: Murder.

My rueful expression was not lost on Wolf. 'I know what you are thinking, Rose. The same as the village did. But there was no proof, these kind of accidents—' he made a gesture, 'a young man in a highly emotional state, heartbroken by his lover's suicide . . . But unfortunately no one who knew Dave believed him capable of such a reaction. Girls to him were "take them and leave them"—like Cedric.'

'Holy terrors, as Mrs Robson would say. But

you don't think it was an accident.'

He shook his head. 'Dave was good with guns, best shot in Alnwick, won all sorts of competitions. I don't think he would have been careless with one, or loved any girl so much that he would want to destroy himself—'

'And so—'

'I think—someone—fixed the gun. But it was smoothed over. It can never be proved. The coroner's verdict accepted and recorded. A tragic accident.'

Or was it? To my mind, that made four—or was it five? possible murders.

CHAPTER TEN

As we talked, a steady stream of smoke headed in our direction. A train had paused at the level crossing, then the earth vibrated as it gathered speed and headed south to London.

'I heard about the doctor's accident; spoke to his widow in the teashop. His death must have been a great loss to Staines.' I decided to omit its benefits regarding her second marriage.

Wolf said nothing, intent on putting a cute tiny leather hood on the now somnolent Kokopele. I added the obvious, 'Level crossings can be very hazardous unless they are well manned.'

'That is true and as it is no longer needed as access to the colliery, it should have been closed. The coal seam died out several years ago and as well as taking the fortune of the Staines family it left behind shaky ground. Last year there was a great rumble, like an earthquake, and what remained of the old colliery workings collapsed.

'The whole village flew out of doors, terrified of losing their houses and all their possessions, and gathered on the village green. Engineers arrived from Alnwick and said that the search for coal over so many years had damaged the understructure and that this was, in fact, a minor earthquake. Every time a train passed by after that, we expected there to be another tremor.

'Hubert was very upset, feared for his fine house up there on the hill. Pictures had fallen off the walls, ornaments slid off tables. Everything has been quiet since, but it was close to the time of those other tragedies in Hubert's life, losing his wife and Amy. He went through a very difficult time,' he added sympathetically.

Raising his hand to shade his eyes, he looked at the sky. 'Weather's going to change.'

'Looks perfect to me.' There wasn't a single cloud, just a vast canopy of azure blue above our heads and stretching away to infinity.

Wolf shook his head. 'Don't be fooled by appearances, Rose. Believe me, there's a storm, a big one, brewing up just over the horizon.'

'How on earth can you tell?'

He shrugged again, the gesture becoming so familiar that it seemed to sum up the man himself. 'Let us just say that I belong to a world where such knowledge still exists. We have not yet been veneered over completely by what the white man calls "civilisation". We still retain some of the feelings, the affinity with nature, that Thane and his kind still possess.'

'So that is the answer. Nothing supernatural,' I said.

'Rather the opposite,' said Wolf. 'Predicting weather is easy if you are attuned to nature. Look around you, Rose.' He put an arm about my shoulders, and his physical closeness didn't bother me at it had with Hubert. It was completely natural, avuncular, the way he would have tried to teach a young child.

'Observe the trees. See how still they are, drawing into themselves as a man does his coat as the storm approaches. They have sent the signal to the leaves—have you ever seen leaves so still, as if they were alerted to danger?'

That was true, they looked as lifeless as a painted picture, frozen in time, although I would have sworn that only moments ago, they had been moving gently above our heads.

Giving me a gentle push towards my bicycle, he said, 'Get yourself into sheltering walls, Rose. You can warn them up there, of course, but they probably won't believe that there will be storm, a wild destructive storm before many more hours have passed.'

As I headed back I had more things on my mind, I must confess, than Wolf's predicted storm. I was thinking of those five deaths and not one of them that might truly be classed as 'natural causes'.

Amy's suicide, then her lover, Dave, encounters a faulty gun and her heartbroken mother falls out of the window. Dr Holt's carriage encounters a train on the level crossing, which also accounts for the accident to Lily's angry father.

Collecting Thane, who gazed rather resentfully at my bicycle that had deprived him of a walk, I took him inside to see Kate who again hardly looked up from her book. Thane made no joyous attempt to interrupt her and sat down grumpily near the door.

As I patted his head, he gave me a reproachful look, sank his head upon his paws, and with an almost human sigh, closed his eyes.

Back in my room, I knew I must direct all my concentration and energy towards the main issue: Hubert's blackmailer.

At this stage I thought it extremely unlikely that there would be any clue to link the five unfortunate deaths with the stolen photographs, but I was, after all, being paid handsomely to think positively.

Regretting the absence of my logbook, still in Edinburgh with all its cases written up, I used instead the back pages of the sketchbook which accompanied me everywhere. It seemed extremely unlikely that I would find time to sketch rural scenes on this particular assignment.

So I began my list of possible suspects:

First, Lily the maid and friend of Kate, whom I had already decided was an unlikely blackmailer unless she had an accomplice. But from Mrs Robson, I knew that Lily had married a railwayman who, no doubt familiar with the main line, would have ample opportunity to post blackmailing notes from Newcastle. The couple now lived in Alnwick, information that was useless unless I could discover his surname.

And then, as always, what was the motive? Mrs Robson said the couple had been given a substantial sum by Hubert. Had Lily's husband decided that it wasn't enough?

To build further on this picture, I imagined Lily's husband, armed with information from his wife, a former maid in the house, breaking in and stealing the photographs, simply intent on making some money out of them. Or was it possible that Lily had posed as a model in some of Hubert's revealing photographs? If her husband had seen them, with or without Lily's knowledge, jealous and angry, had he decided to have his revenge?

The letter Hubert had shown me was not one of those ill-spelt pencilled notes I had encountered in two similar cases in Edinburgh, but suggested the hand of someone with cunning enough to cut out the letters from a newspaper, making it all the more impossible to identify the sender.

And that led me to the second name on my list: Collins, who seemed certain to have ready access to the required ingredients. I could see her diligently cutting out letters and sticking them on paper.

Was she desperate and angry that her position as Hubert's lover was not likely to end in marriage after all? She had a lot to gain financially but also a lot to lose—Hubert, if he ever found out.

I would need to know a great deal more about Collins than our brief acquaintance had revealed so far. All I knew was that she was unable to disguise her feelings of dislike and fear that I was trying to steal her lover.

A ridiculous idea, but I would be wise to discover her background. How she had met Hubert, what of her family, if any, and so forth.

Third was Wolf Rider. This I could not take seriously even though he and Hubert were distant cousins—family relationships were so often a reason for murder, where inheritance was the prize. Did Wolf, despite what he had told me, nurse secret yearnings to become lord of an English manor? Perhaps he needed money if he wished to return to Arizona or wanted to buy a home here in Britain. But since he claimed to like Scotland and seemed totally disinterested in material possessions, I could not imagine him taking such a bizarre action.

I felt I could safely cross his name off my list.

Fourth was Grace Sloan, the doctor's widow. Before meeting her, I had wondered if she had borne an unknown grudge against Hubert Staines, possibly relating to her husband's untimely death. But when we met, she was candid enough to reveal that she had been glad to be rid of Dr Holt so that she could marry again. And though she and her new husband, Peter, clearly disliked Hubert, they were both unlikely candidates for the role of blackmailer—unless they knew of the photographs and were chancing their luck. Unlikely, was my comment.

I was left with the remaining permanent occupants of Staines Manor: Kate, whom, of course, I could dismiss—apart from being an invalid, she was also Hubert's indulged stepdaughter, with everything she desired.

Mrs Robson was an even more unlikely suspect. Although she perhaps had more chance of finding the incriminating photographs as she had free access to Hubert's study for cleaning purposes, I doubted

104

whether she would have considered them worthy of more than a brief and perhaps shocked glance. I was fairly certain it would never have entered her mind, had she even desperately needed the money, to imperil her immortal soul by challenging her master, a member of the class she venerated as so much above her.

But there was one more suspect on my list. The ne'er-do-well Cedric, whose character Mrs Robson reluctantly admitted left much to be desired. Suppose she had mentioned the photographs in a hushed and scandalised voice, and that gave him the idea that they were worth taking a look at. He had access to the house and in Hubert's absence he might have seized the opportunity to steal them.

I decided that, so far, Cedric was the most likely candidate for the role of blackmailer with the best motive, a lack of moral conscience and a constant need of money.

So I put a star against his name and closed my book without the least idea where to begin. There were no clear roads into this labyrinth. I had hoped initially that meeting Grace, the doctor's widow, would start peeling the onion, leading to the next layer and so on. But I now realised that I had no leads to follow. Except Cedric.

How to question him? Could I start by asking him to tell me about the gun incident and the death of Amy's lover, events that had little to do with Hubert's blackmailer? I winced away from any closer acquaintance with that knowing leer, his eyes crawling all over me like black beetles.

I did not doubt that this was going to prove a very difficult case, and I had a shrewd idea that I was going to earn every shilling of that handsome fee, those two hundred guineas.

I suppose I should have felt heartened that my role as Lady Investigator, Discretion Guaranteed was the main reason Hubert had been so anxious to bring me to Staines, since Kate's reactions to her 'beloved lost deerhound' indicated that she instinctively recognised that he was not her Roswal.

And I had a certain impetus for solving this case: the sooner I apprehended Hubert's blackmailer, the sooner Thane and I would be free to return home to Edinburgh. I resolved to start immediately.

In that my instinct was correct, for by the next morning, when the clock had moved forward twelve hours, the scene had changed dramatically. The stage was set and, like the storm steadily approaching but still mercifully veiled, there were terrible events lying in wait.

The first attempted murder . . .

CHAPTER ELEVEN

The sky was still cloudless and I decided to clear my mind with a visit to Alnwick, where I was certain the leads in my investigation lay in wait. With luck I might find someone employed at the railway station who knew Lily and her husband and their present whereabouts.

Locating the library would be useful. In Edinburgh, the library had always proved an invaluable source of information, and back-copies of newspapers could be relied upon to provide more graphic accounts of local events, like those accidents on the level crossing.

I decided to leave my bicycle and have a brisk walk, which Thane would enjoy. We had accomplished most of the journey when I was hailed by Cedric.

He had been occupying my thoughts so much as prime suspect that I felt a blush riding up from my neck which, I hoped, would not be regarded as a quite different emotion.

Getting smartly into step alongside me, he looked down into my face and treated me to one of his atrocious leers. 'Goin' into the town, are we?'

I said yes a little coolly but he was not to be put off by my somewhat obvious lack of enthusiasm for his company. 'Goin' to the shops?'

In response to my non-committal shrug, he laughed. 'Auntie'll give ye a great list of things to bring back if she knows. She's like that, never misses an opportunity for a body to fetch and carry for her, lazy old cow.'

If he expected some comment, there was none, except that I hastened my steps to increase the distance between us.

'Thinks a lot of hersel' does Auntie, being with the gentry all these years, shaken the hand of Royalty in her time. Visitors they aren't allowed to talk about too.'

I felt mildly interested and he went on. 'Guests of the lord and master.' He put his finger to his lips and looked round with an elaborate air of secrecy. 'Shh—not supposed to talk about that. Very proper is Auntie, knows her place and the side her bread's buttered on, if ye get my meaning.' And with a mock shudder, he added, 'She'd skin me alive if I telt anyone—'

His skin was saved by a shrill whistle, his name hoarsely shouted as a lad about his own age emerged from a cottage and approached us. 'Comin' to the pub for a jar, Ceddy?'

'Right by me, Jock.' Cedric grinned and with a mock bow added, 'If ye'll excuse me, that is.'

I nodded coldly, and as he left me I heard his friend remark: 'Is she not coming too?'

He sounded disappointed and Cedric's

answer was indistinct, but it was greeted with a roar of laughter, as his friend thumped him on the shoulder. 'You don't say. Thought ye'd got yersel' a right classy fancy woman.'

I hurried on, cutting across a rough path where the towers of Alnwick Castle were visible above the trees, when Thane suddenly sat down.

'Come along, Thane.'

He did not move. I looked at him. Such behaviour was odd, since he loved a walk and distance never bothered him.

'Oh, for goodness sake,' I said rather impatiently, 'It's not far now.'

He was staring straight ahead. Then he turned slowly, shivered, and regarded me with that imploring look, almost human in its intensity, that I knew so well.

Something was wrong. But there was nothing in sight, just that well-worn path across scrubland leading into the town. 'What is it?' I asked, touching his head.

He remained quite still. And then I saw it, what I took to be a milestone just yards away. I went for a closer look. The stone was to commemorate a battle if the crossed swords were any indication, but only a few letters of the inscription remained, the rest having been worn away long since by wind and weather.

'Is that it, Thane?' I asked softly.

He shivered, stood up, and shook himself.

'I didn't realise you could read.' I walked on

a few steps, expecting him to follow, but when I turned and said, 'Come on, everything is all right,' he remained stubbornly unmoving, as if rooted to the spot, a living statue.

What was I to do? I didn't feel like continuing, nor could I do so and leave him here. Besides, I knew Thane well enough not to disregard his warnings, and as danger had seemed obvious, I turned back.

There was no sign of Cedric and his friend and the road was almost empty apart from an old gentleman, perched on a large stone and smoking a pipe.

He was reading, and at closer quarters he had the look of a scholar. Saluting me gravely, he gave me good-day and pointed at Thane, who had raced ahead.

'A fine hound you have there, miss. Gave me quite a shock when I saw him. Lovely old chap, aren't you, let's have a look at you,' he said holding out his hand to Thane, who, always polite, with a swift look in my direction, allowed his head to be patted.

The old gentleman smiled. 'You gave me quite a turn, old chap,' he repeated and to me: 'Don't see many deerhounds these days, miss. Thought I was seeing a ghost.'

'A ghost?'

'Indeed, yes.' Seeing my frown, he went on: 'Stranger in these parts, are you?' I nodded and he smiled. 'Then you won't have heard the old legend. Place hereabouts, all this area,' he

110

gestured with his pipe, 'was where the English defeated the Scottish army long ago at the Battle of Alnwick. Year 1093 it was. The Scottish King Malcolm, the son of Duncan and the defeater of Macbeth, was slain and his devoted hound, who had followed him into battle, leapt upon the armoured English knight and tore out his throat. The soldiers tried to catch him but he was too quick for them, just disappeared, vanished.'

He paused and added, 'Never seen again, but some say his ghost haunts this road, baying at the moon, mourning his lost master.'

'Have you ever seen it?'

He shook his head, grinned. 'Not I. Not until this evening, miss,' he chuckled. 'Thought I'd have a fine tale to tell my grandbairns when I got home. My daughter, of course, would scold me and say I'd been at the brandy again.' He paused. 'Where do you live, miss. Have you far to go?'

'Just to Staines.'

He frowned, 'Oh, that's where the pit was. Knew it well once upon a time. Worked down there as a young lad, before my lungs gave out and I had to seek more congenial employment. Never liked the pit—too many accidents.' He grinned. 'Teaching was vastly preferable—and safer.'

He stood up with a groan and an arthritic creak. 'Good to talk to you and meet this old chap,' he said giving Thane a final pat. 'I'll bid you both goodnight.' And looking up at the sky he pointed in the direction of Alnwick. 'See you get home before the rain, I fancy we're in for a storm.'

I watched him go and quickened my steps, Thane trotting eagerly by my side. Now his reluctance had an eerie explanation. Did he see that other ghostly hound? Was that battle still taking place in some other segment of the circle of time to which Thane—and Wolf, I suspected—had access? Access that was denied to most other mortals, myself included?

Or, another uneasy thought struck me. Was Thane reliving his own past? This 'creature of heaven'—according to Sir Walter Scott's description—where had he come from that day three years ago when I met him on Arthur's Seat? His coat shiny, so groomed, well fed and clean, he was certainly no stray. That was one mystery still unsolved, especially as his behaviour each passing day clearly indicated that he was not Roswal, Hubert Staines' missing deerhound.

When we reached the back door, Mrs Robson was taking the washing off the line outside the kitchen. As we exchanged greetings, I remembered Cedric's remarks about a mysterious visitor no one was allowed to talk about.

Did I have another suspect to add to my list, this person or persons unknown, that not even

Hubert had been prepared to discuss? Was that the vital piece of information, the missing piece of the puzzle? And if so, why he was reluctant to confide in me?

*   *   *

Wolf's predicted storm blew up two hours later, out of that hitherto cloudless sky. The earth took on a strange stillness; the distant hills had a dazed look too, as if all life held its breath. In the garden, the trees stood starkly against a sky wiped clean of all colour, their burden of leaves shivering gently although there was as yet no wind, like spinsters whispering an improper story.

A blackbird asserting his territorial rights and sparrows going about their business of noisily pursuing domestic matters were suddenly watchful. In human terms they would have been described as peering apprehensively over their shoulders, alert to danger. Somewhere a solitary robin gave voice, an eerie sound piercing the silence.

Near at hand I heard Mrs Robson in the corridors busy checking shutters and closing the first rattling windows. A moment's respite to batten down hatches and then the gales began, great swooping winds, so strong it seemed impossible that such noisy elements should remain invisible. In some ruthless pursuit, they gathered momentum and violence, penetrating every nook and cranny, howling down chimneys and along corridors, an army of trapped demons.

Rain followed, crashing waves of water, hurling themselves against wall and window. Mrs Robson looked into my room and said, 'Just wanted to make sure you're all right. We're in for a right storm, so stay away from the window. There'll be lightning as like as not. Not scared of thunder, are you?'

I said no, that I rather enjoyed storms, at which Mrs Robson looked worried. Obviously she regarded taking pleasure in storms as very odd indeed. She shook her head. 'You wouldn't if you lived in the country, lass.'

I did not add that I had witnessed tornados in Arizona that would make an English storm look like a mountain mist as she went on: 'In towns it's different. High buildings to protect you, but here the elements can do so much damage. Like that earth tremor when the colliery workings collapsed.' And she repeated the story of how there had been an outcry when the colliery was closed.

'Sir's father wouldn't give permission to keep it open. He was right, too, and just in time. The seam ran right under us here and he'd have lost the house too.'

As she bustled off to check the other rooms, I was aware that darkness had come early, riding on the storm. Heavy black clouds were billowing across the horizon, like some monstrous fleet of ships in full sail. The trees and bushes in the garden below were no longer still; they were now swaying to a wild dance, their leaves shiny, bright emerald in the gloom.

Wind and rain increased, thunder rattled the windows and jagged flashes of lightning ripped across the garden, where everything that grew was suddenly united in a wild dervish dance.

Thane didn't like storms. I knew that, like many other lesser canines, he hated the loud noise, so I had brought him back into the house with me rather than abandoning him to the stables. I thought of all the animals and birds out there that took storms as a matter of course and instinctively knew the tricks of survival.

I lit a candle against the growing darkness and, with Thane at my side, prepared to sit out the storm, watching its progress from the window and daring the lightning to do its worst.

CHAPTER TWELVE

I never heard the crash of the falling tree that caved in the roof of Wolf Rider's bothy, one of several ancient elms that went down like matchsticks.

The commotion downstairs alerted Thane. I

got out of bed and looked over the banister to see a bedraggled figure framed in the doorway. Thane's exuberant tail-wagging identified this new arrival as Wolf Rider, of course.

Hubert was saying: 'Come in, man. You're soaking wet. Of course you cannot stay there. You must move in here until we can get the roof fixed. No arguments, please. We have plenty of spare rooms.'

A murmur, perhaps of protest, then Hubert's voice: 'Get them later. For heaven's sake, come in and take off those wet clothes. Mrs Robson will fix you up with some of mine.'

Wolf Rider stepped inside. A wild figure indeed; his long black hair plastered against his skull, he looked strangely alien—a savage contrast to his surroundings, his dripping clothes making pools on the marble floor of the handsome and very civilised Georgian hall.

Thane was all for dashing down to greet him and I said firmly: 'No, Thane. No.'

With a little moan Thane obeyed and we went back into my room, where we remained for half an hour until Mrs Robson rang the bell for dinner. There we were joined by Wolf, Collins and Kate, who had been terrified by the storm. It had now faded away leaving behind a trail of destruction, which was the main topic of conversation.

Hubert went into a long explanation, presumably for my benefit, about the bothy and the trees and how dangerous these storms

116

could be. I heard for the second time that where coal had been discovered, the land was very fragile—some sort of a geological fault which had caused an earth tremor that made the pit workings collapse.

Listening politely and hoping my expression was intelligent enough to indicate interest in the conversation, I wished that my knowledge of geography and, more important, geology was not so primitive.

When Hubert reached the end of his little lecture he looked at me, smiling, awaiting comment. I told him how, long past childhood, I had believed what our gardener in Sheridan Place, Edinburgh, had told me. When I asked about the hole he was digging, he had solemnly said that if he dug down deep enough he would come out in Australia.

Everyone laughed. During dinner Wolf said little. He was wearing, presumably from Hubert's wardrobe, a cast-off smoking jacket. Ill-fitting, it was curiously at odds with his Aztec warrior image.

Seated next to Kate, he had an air of preoccupation. Detached from the rest of the company, he evaded all her attempts to engage him in whispered conversation. She darted him almost childlike looks of adoration, but he ignored her, staring anxiously towards the window.

Strangely, Kate's behaviour and his reactions struck a chord, reminding me of childhood days and forlorn attempts to get Danny McQuinn's attention on the rare occasions when we met at Pappa's dining-table in Sheridan Place. No doubt as Danny had once been absorbed by important police matters, Wolf was preoccupied by the damage to his bothy and wishing that he could escape and inspect the roof now that the storm had died away.

I was seated across the table from Hubert, who seemed to be directing his geology monologue mainly towards me. During the meal I was acutely conscious of his regard. Each time I looked up, his eyes were upon me. The first time I thought it was an attempt to start up a conversation, but he quickly averted his gaze to concentrate on Mrs Robson's roast lamb. Later I looked up—same again—and, embarrassed, I avoided eye contact, aware that someone else was not paying full attention to the talk, which had swung to white cattle and the shooting party tomorrow.

And who was watching Hubert very carefully but Collins. When our eyes met, her look was venomous, clutching her fork fiercely as if she would like to use it on me as a weapon of destruction.

I had no wish to cause friction between the pair but I was beginning to realise that the sooner I found Hubert's blackmailer and returned to Edinburgh the better for all concerned.

Hubert said, 'I hope your cow doesn't decide to drop her calf tonight, Rider.'

'I was thinking the same, sir,' said Wolf and, as if this was the moment he had waited for, he rose from the table.

'If you will excuse me, I'll take a walk round and do my evening inspection.'

'Later. It's still raining,' said Hubert. 'Have some more wine,' he added, refilling his glass.

Wolf shook his head. 'I'm used to rain, sir. I won't melt away.'

Hubert looked at him doubtfully. 'Take Roswal with you then,' and to me, 'Save you having to take him for a walk. Everything will be so wet and muddy.'

I knew that Thane, lying in the hall with the two Labradors, would be delighted at the prospect, as Hubert continued:

'Timing couldn't have been worse for the shooting party. Remember your gun, Rider. I'll expect you to carry an extra one for me, just in case.'

Wolf looked at him. 'I understood I was to be with the beaters, sir.'

Hubert grinned. 'Not this time. Consider yourself upgraded. We'll need picnic lunches,' he said to Mrs Robson, who was removing the dessert plates. 'Thank goodness, the weather should have settled down and dried up in time for the Duke's garden party next week.'

'Yes, sir, he is so proud of his lovely garden.'

Hubert looked at me. 'We have been invited

and, of course, you must come along, Rose.'

I heard the clatter of cutlery from Collins' direction. Obviously this did not please her. She helped Kate to her feet as if she was made of Dresden china while Hubert bowed in my direction.

'Allow me to escort you to your room, Rose.'

As we approached the stairs, he took my hand and tucked it into his arm in a proprietary manner. I didn't like it. There was something intimate in the gesture, as if we were a couple, for so I have seen married people behave at the end of a party, happy to be retiring to their bedroom.

Outside my door, my hand still captive in his arm, he leant forward and, putting his hand behind my head, he kissed my mouth firmly and deeply.

'Goodnight, sweet Rose, sleep well.'

I was taken aback. I had not expected a goodnight kiss. It was a pleasant experience, I admit. He had what one of my school friends had often sighed over: Thick, well-shaped, warm lips, 'a mouth made for kissing'.

He smiled, stroked my hair. 'I think I am falling in love with you, Rose,' he whispered.

I did not know what to say or even what to think. I realised that gratitude, flattery, should be expressed, but somehow this confession did not please me. It made me feel uncomfortable and a vague smile was my only response.

As I pushed him away I was conscious of a

shadow along the corridor. Collins had emerged from Kate's room and had witnessed that goodnight kiss.

And this was the night none of us were ever to forget. Someone—perhaps that same person or persons at present still unknown who had stolen Hubert's photographs—tried to murder Kate.

*　　　*　　　*

The scream woke me from an amorous dream about Jack Macmerry, which had turned into a nightmare. I thought I had cried out but when I opened my eyes and sat up in bed, the room was filled with the dusky gleam of sluggish moonlight.

There were raised voices from the floor below. I threw on a robe, opened my door and looked over the banisters.

Hubert was there. He looked up at me and said in exasperation, 'It's only Kate. She's been sleepwalking again—go back to bed, Rose.'

The scream had now turned into noisy sobs and regardless of Hubert's instructions, I ran downstairs.

The door to the sitting room was open, admitting an icy blast from the open window from which Mary Staines had fallen to her death. Mrs Robson, hastily dressed, cradled Kate and threw a shawl over her nightdress. Wolf Rider, still wearing his borrowed clothes,

121

was closing the window with some difficulty, as it creaked back and forth in the rising wind which was billowing heavy rain into the room and forming a pool on Mrs Robson's nicely polished floor.

Collins was there in a nightrobe, shivering and wringing her hands in a fair imitation of Lady Macbeth, while Hubert, in a handsome brocade robe, surveyed the scene with remarkable aplomb.

It was a tableau etched on my mind, something I was to try to recall in detail later when it was important to remember exactly what I had seen and where everyone was stationed in the room.

Kate screamed again. 'Can't someone do something? He tried to kill me.'

'For God's sake, all of you, do sit down. Now, Kate, my dear,' said Hubert, a flick of his fingers indicating the sofa. Seated, he drew her down beside him and put an arm around her shoulders, smoothing down her tangled hair.

'There, there. You are quite safe. No one is going to harm you.'

'He—he tried to kill me,' Kate wailed.

'Do try to be calm. Tell us exactly what happened and we will soon sort it all out,' Hubert said gently.

Mrs Robson, always practical, came forward with a glass of water from the carafe on a side table. Collins thrust it into Kate's hand. Gulping it down, she sat up straight, stared round as if aware of us for the first time.

'You were sleepwalking again, Miss Kate. It's all those drugs you've been giving her,' Collins said with a spiteful glance at Wolf, who was standing by, silent and watchful. He shook his head, gave a helpless shrug.

'Now, Kate, what's all this about?' demanded Hubert patiently.

'A man—he tried to kill me, that's all I remember,' said Kate.

Hubert gave an exasperated sigh. Humouring her, he said, 'So that we can all get back to bed, tell us all about this person you think you saw—'

'I don't think, Hubert,' Kate said defiantly. 'I know. He was here. I awoke and he picked me up, carried me to the open window over there. He thought I was still asleep, tried to push me out. He didn't expect me to struggle and start to yell.'

Taking a deep breath, she added in a whisper: 'It was going to be another accident—like—like—' A sob.

Mrs Robson and Hubert exchanged worried glances that finished the sentence for her: 'Mamma!'

Hubert sighed deeply, patted her hand and insisted patiently: 'All right, my dear. Perhaps you can at least tell us what he looked like.'

'How can I do that? It was dark.' She shook her head. 'I think he was wearing a mask. But when I was struggling, he felt—velvety—like

123

one of those fancy costumes, the ones we wore that last Christmas before—before Mamma—'

Hubert's brow darkened momentarily, the pain of remembrance of happier days. He nodded briefly and said, 'I think you should go back to bed now, my dear, and forget all this.'

'But—'

Hubert cut short the protest. 'Mrs Robson will give you a warm drink. Something to calm her, Rider, if you please. We'll soon have you back to sleep,' he added, unduly hopeful in the circumstances, and Kate gave him a bewildered look.

'I'm afraid this was one of your nasty nightmares again, my dear.'

'But it seemed so real, Hubert, so awful. I can still feel what his arms were like. I was sure I could feel it and that I was awake.'

Hubert shook his head. 'Just a horrible dream, and dreams can seem very real to us at the time,' he added as if speaking to a small child. 'Now, off to bed with you.'

Kate looked at us all as if we were owed an apology. Collins held out a hand and she took it obediently, gave a bewildered backward glance and left, not unwillingly, but obviously still shaken.

Hubert stood up. 'Kate has suffered from nightmares and been walking in her sleep ever since—ever since—' he shook his head and sighed, leaving us to fill in the details about their two tragedies.

124

I looked round the room. The lighted candle fluttering on the mantelpiece. Who had put it there, since Kate said it was too dark to recognise her attacker but there was enough light to see his masked face?

Something wrong about her appearance taunted me, but I was not to recall what it was until later. Meanwhile, Hubert was waiting for me at the door. He smiled and I wondered if he was about to escort me upstairs and kiss me again. I considered how I should react. A dignified and firm rejection was called for. Let him know I did not encourage that sort of behaviour.

This time it was not needed. He merely bowed. 'Sleep well, Rose,' although how any of us would manage to fulfil that wish after the night's events was utterly beyond me.

I must have looked surprised as he turned, came back and, taking my hand, said: 'Don't concern yourself, my dear, over the rather distressing scene you have just witnessed. There is an explanation. I had reason to believe that Kate had an assignation. I disapprove—she is much too young, you know. I was awake; she heard me approaching and invented the entire story in order to distract everyone's attention so that—he—could make his escape.'

'You know this fellow.'

He smiled wryly. 'I do indeed, and I shall be keeping an eye on them both.'

125

Bowing, he again whispered goodnight, and I suddenly realised what had been troubling me about the scene. Despite the rain that had blown into the room from the open window where her attacker had supposedly attempted to throw her out, Kate was quite dry.

As for the candle, that was a necessity to guide her downstairs to her would-be lover.

CHAPTER THIRTEEN

Closing my bedroom door in the now pearly light of dawn, the drama over, silence all around me once more, I lay awake with my thoughts tumbling like rats trapped in a cage.

Had I imagined Hubert's declaration of love? I felt a little embarrassed remembering a kiss too wickedly passionate to pass for mere politeness. Was I making too much of where it might lead? And more to the point, would Hubert remember, or had it been due to an over-indulgence in brandy after dinner?

Despite Hubert's explanation regarding Kate and her sleep-walking drama, I wished Thane had been in the house, instead of being securely locked away in the stables. Not, of course, that he would have been much use. He had certain limitations as a bloodhound.

I slept uneasily and went downstairs next morning after nine to a solitary breakfast. The night's events seemed like a bad dream. The house was again deserted—not even the bustling Mrs Robson was in evidence and, apart from the porridge kept warm in the oven, there was no indication of whether Hubert and the others had yet put in an appearance.

I went to collect Thane. The storm's destruction was evident in the abundance of fallen branches and here and there was an uprooted tree. I decided to have a look at Wolf's bothy. Even from a distance I could see an ancient elm, with a tangle of broken branches, was sprawled across the roof, which had caved in leaving the two cable ends reaching up into the sky in a gesture of pathetic surrender.

Wolf was up a ladder—with Cedric giving him a helping hand—sawing off the branches to ultimately remove the tree. Cedric gave me his cheeky leer and jumped down onto the ground, obviously glad of a diversion.

'Keep on working,' was Wolf's stern rebuke. 'You can't slope off yet.'

'Just having a smoke, boss. Have to see Auntie,' Cedric added with a grin.

As he turned towards the house, Wolf called after him: 'Don't forget you are to be a beater at the shoot tomorrow.'

'Aye. Auntie'll need to pack some extra grub.'

Wolf watched him go and, with a despairing

heavenward sigh, ruefully considered his damaged roof.

'Plenty to occupy us here without having to go out and shoot over the Duke's estate. I dare say they didn't escape damage, although there isn't much to blow down on the moors. His main concern, of course, will be if the number of grouse have been affected. His guns cheated and his guests disappointed.'

His tone sounded bitter and disapproving but, turning to me, he smiled. 'We do not shoot to kill as a sport—only for food. That is built into our psyche. We believe that we are all of the same earth and we share it with all other living creatures. Of necessity we kill to eat, as animals in their turn also do to survive. But we do not kill for pleasure and after we kill a deer, we ask for its pardon. Call it Brother, say that we honoured its speed and grace and that, in killing it and eating its flesh, we are honoured to be taking those qualities into our being.'

Was that why Thane, sitting at his side, was so comfortable, so in tune with this new friend? For despite Wolf's outward trappings of civilisation and Thane's recent conversion to domesticity, both were creatures of the wild.

I found myself remembering again something less pleasant from my first meeting with Chief Wolf Rider.

I was still curious. Because it concerned Thane, it continued to haunt me, try as I might to put it from my mind, so I decided to broach the subject.

'When you were in Edinburgh, one of your Ghost Dancers, Wild Elk, had an accident and died on Arthur's Seat.' I paused. 'You told me an extraordinary story.'

I tried to sound casual, amused, and was conscious of having failed as Wolf gave me a mocking look. 'And what was that? I have many.'

But I was sure he knew what I was talking about even as I reminded him. 'Wild Elk believed that the spirit of a white man he had killed by mistake had entered into the soul of an animal, possibly a dog. He had seen it several times, and told you of his fears. You thought it was this animal that made his horse throw him and so by his death was avenged.'

Wolf listened carefully, nodded. 'An extraordinary story for your culture, but we believe that in dying our spirits can take refuge in the body of an animal.' As he spoke he smiled, patting Thane's head.

Thane looked up at him, also listening, and I could have sworn that he understood perfectly what Wolf was saying. Their affinity was uncanny and I felt scared and angry too. I didn't like the idea any better now than I did three years ago of my Danny's spirit inhabiting Thane, protecting me as he could.

The uncomfortable silence deepened and I said: 'Talking of extraordinary things, what did

129

you make of Kate's outburst last night? Someone trying to kill her indeed!'

Preoccupied now with the broken roof, I wondered if Wolf had heard me. Then he said, 'Sleepwalking can be dangerous. Hallucinations can seem quite real,' and his action of picking up the saw Cedric had left, indicated that he had work to do.

As I turned to leave, he said, 'I often go to Holy Island to gather seaweed that contains a special ingredient I need for some of my herbal remedies.' Hesitating for a moment he smiled, 'You said you would like to come along.' I nodded agreement and he looked pleased. 'It is associated with one of your more eminent saints and has tremendous spiritual qualities. A place where the soul of a non-Christian is refreshed—that is if you don't get cut off by the tide. Thane would like the sea too, I am sure.'

Escaping from Staines for even a few hours was something to look forward to, I decided, as I walked back to the house to deliver Thane to Kate for the day—a rather reluctant Thane, who would much rather have stayed with his hero.

We went in by the front door and, as the hall was empty, I seized the opportunity to have another look at the scene of last night's events.

The sitting room door was open and Thane seemed to know my mind. He sniffed around and suddenly darted behind the sofa and returned with a piece of black material in his mouth.

I took it from him.

A very dusty velvet mask. Although it fitted Kate's story of a fancy dress costume, it appeared to have lain there, overlooked, for some time. I thought back to the meal earlier that evening and to Kate's apparent attraction to Wolf. Again I tried to reconstruct the scene in the sitting room. The open window, the rain streaming into the room.

When we all arrived in response to her screams, Wolf was there already, closing the window. Hubert seemed confident about the would-be lover's identity. Could it be Wolf?

I felt suddenly chilled, remembering her words. The feeling of velvet 'like a fancy dress costume'. In the darkness, perhaps she hadn't realised what she was touching was a velvet smoking jacket. Like the one belonging to Hubert that Wolf Rider had been wearing while his own clothes were drying in Mrs Robson's kitchen.

I didn't care for my suspicions. If I needed an ally to help me find Hubert's blackmailer I would certainly have chosen Wolf and it was unimaginable that he could be capable of seducing the young girl who was his patient, taking advantage of her hero-worship for an older man.

For all our actions there has to be a motive, something to gain. It always came back to that.

131

This one was obvious, but unpleasant to contemplate. Kate was an heiress and would bring Wolf closer to inheriting Staines to which, I was to learn from two independent sources, he had a stronger claim than Hubert.

*   *   *

In the kitchen Mrs Robson was eager to chat about poor Miss Kate and all her 'troubles', as if the consumption wasn't enough, poor lass. The room smelt of scorching irons as she stacked up the pile of drying clothes from last night's storm.

'What do you think really happened?' I asked.

She paused with the iron raised in her hand and frowned. 'Sounded to me as if she was having one of her nightmares about someone trying to kill her. When she woke up in the sitting room, what with the storm and all that, she thought it had really happened.'

And shaking her head: 'I couldn't say, lass. But she does walk in her sleep quite often.' She blew briskly on the hot iron indicating that she had wasted enough time.

I looked at her sternly, sure that 'couldn't say' might be correctly interpreted as 'wouldn't'.

'You've been with the family a long time,' I said. 'You were here when her sister and her mother died.'

'So I was. Awful times, they were.' She gave me an enigmatic look. 'Families are not always what they seem like on the surface, you know. You shouldn't be taken in by appearances.'

'Meaning, Mrs Robson, meaning?' I said eagerly.

She shook her head. 'None of my business, lass, nor yours either. But yon Indian chap, Mr Rider, I hear tell he's got a stronger claim on Staines than the master. If anything should happen to Sir, that is,' she added darkly.

'Really? Tell me more.'

'That I will not, lass. None of my business to spread village gossip.'

'I know, of course, that his grandmother was a Staines,' I said encouragingly. 'So they are related distantly.'

But closing her lips firmly, with a stubborn shake of her head, she began rearranging the ironed garments on the clothes-horse.

I was to get no more information that day, but I had enough to establish a motive for Wolf to woo and win Kate. Between them they stood to inherit all, should Hubert die.

On my way out of the kitchen, over a chair by the fire, there was a moleskin jacket. I touched it, and she said:

'That's Cedric's, his best. He didn't want it ruined when he was clearing up the storm damage.'

I looked at it, touched the sleeve. It was damp but felt like velvet, and Cedric was a

133

suspect I welcomed as infinitely preferable to Wolf Rider.

CHAPTER FOURTEEN

Hubert was to shoot over the moor a mile away, part of the Duke of Northumberland's vast estate where specially invited guests—and others who paid a large fee for the privilege—gathered to bring down game birds bred for the purpose.

There were two rooms in the house that I had never entered. One was the door near the kitchen with the warning notice 'Photography. Keep out!' It led to the sacred precinct in the cellars where Hubert developed his photographic plates, made prints and no doubt stored valuable equipment.

The other was the gun room near the front door, similarly labelled, from which Hubert was emerging, carrying two weapons.

Indicating them, he smiled. 'We don't have many guns these days, I'm afraid. Different matter in Grandfather's time. He kept an armoury of weapons, including ancient swords and old blunderbusses dating back centuries.'

He pointed back into the room. 'A fine selection of animal trophies. Something of a big game hunter, he was also an amateur archaeologist and an expert taxidermist. One or two of them are my own handiwork,' he added proudly. 'I was quite interested in the art in my younger days, but alas I no longer have time to spare for such demanding activities. Photography is my entire life now. Do go in and have a look,' he added, holding the door open for me. As I entered, he bowed and headed towards his study.

I was quite intrigued. Hubert had obviously inherited many of his grandfather's talents, I thought, facing a semi-circle of stuffed dogs—obviously beloved family pets. Labradors, retrievers, and spaniels, all faced towards the door, poised to welcome visitors with a glassy stare. Once beloved pet cats and wildcats alike, stared down from shelves while, safely above them on inaccessible branches, perched brightly plumaged exotic birds.

All were very lifelike and the more exotic creatures were quite alarming. There was a crocodile and, most impressive of all, a huge grizzly bear—eight feet tall, propped up on a pedestal. Its mouth hung open showing fierce yellow fangs and its claws were extended, ready to grip the unwary in a death hug.

Against one wall in the gloomier depths of the room there were three Egyptian mummy cases with elaborately painted masks, whose eyes also seemed to follow me.

As a domestic museum, it was a collector's dream, but something about those staring eyes fixed hard in my direction gave a feeling of menace to the heavy silence. The air still retained an unpleasant dead animal smell which had evaded all the taxidermist's skills.

I had no desire to linger and went back to my room thinking about Hubert. We had been alone on two occasions but he had made no attempt to kiss me again. I realised that I was expecting some reference to that extraordinary declaration of love and whilst I was a little relieved, I recognised in the depths of my secret heart that marrying Hubert—if he should ask—would be the perfect answer to the problem of losing Thane for ever.

Such a marriage, romantic as any novelette, was every young girl's dream. But I was no young girl. I was not in love, I hardly knew the man and I knew what marriage involved.

It would be the end of my career. I could not imagine that Hubert, any more than Jack Macmerry, would encourage or even consider allowing my role as Lady Investigator, Discretion Guaranteed to continue. Besides, once I had solved the mystery of Hubert's blackmailer, there would be little scope for such activities in Staines. It was unlikely to offer as many opportunities for solving domestic crimes as a great city like Edinburgh.

*   *   *

I had hoped to spend some time in Alnwick, obtaining information that would lead to tracking down and interviewing the disgraced housemaid Lily and her railwayman husband. However, as I was leaving the house, the heavens opened; I retreated to my room and watched the rain pour down the windows. The atrocious weather continued unceasingly all that day but did not deter activity in the rest of the household, as I realised, sitting at the dining-table to eat alone, under the watchful gaze of the dismal family portraits.

Kate was obviously bored with Roswal/Thane and Collins brought him down to me. Glad of his company, I retreated upstairs once more and, considering my list of suspects, I found myself once again wishing that Jack and I had not parted.

Indeed, I valued his love more now that it was absent than I had latterly at home in Solomon's Tower. I had never pretended that I loved him (or could love any man) as I had loved Danny, whom I had loved passionately and unwaveringly from the day when he entered my life and became my hero.

Our ten years of marriage, despite all the hardships and constant dangers imposed by pioneering life in Arizona, would remain the happiest in my whole life.

Jack had entered as a saviour, too. In my first Edinburgh case, just months after I had arrived back in Scotland, he—and Thane— had saved my life from a vicious killer. I knew he loved me, but although accepting him as my lover, I had always declined marriage—the total commitment he desired. My excuse was that Danny, as far as I was concerned, remained still officially only missing, not dead.

Sadly, I now knew that I should abandon any hopes of Danny walking into my life again, and any excuses I had for not marrying Jack were invalid. But marriage was important to him, a necessity. He wanted a proper home life and children, and of equal importance, it meant that he was more likely to be promoted to chief inspector. I could only blame myself that I had lost him. My refusal to come to a decision had sent him into the arms of a more accommodating lover.

My thoughts turned again to Hubert; a wealthy middle-aged widower, strong and handsome, with the look of a medieval Border warrior—Harry Hotspur, to the life, I thought. Was he what my destiny intended? Aware that the reason for upper class marriages had less to do with love than the Biblical begetting of children, considering my own disastrous history of miscarriages, could I provide him with that essential—the heir he needed for the future of Staines?

I read a little, talked to Thane, and with the misery of rain streaming unceasingly down the windows, I decided that if this was the outlook for tomorrow's shoot then I would not be the only person within a radius of some miles, including the elite guests at Alnwick Castle, as well as the humble beaters, who would be retiring that night with similarly dismal thoughts.

*   *   *

I woke the next morning to misty, pale sunshine framing my window and Mrs Robson's tap on the door telling me it was 6.30 and that the shooting party would be leaving within the hour.

'Sir wishes to see you.'

I presented myself in the dining room. I had never imagined going voluntarily to a shoot, sharing as I did Wolf Rider's aversion to a sport that killed for pleasure. I had been close to death too many times, a witness to guns fired in deadly earnest, their intention to maim and kill fellow human beings. Any desire to participate in the mass slaughter of innocent birds bred for the table was not for me.

Hubert indicated the seat opposite. 'Roswal will be coming with us today.'

I made a protesting sound and he smiled indulgently. 'He always accompanied me on the shoot—'

'But he hates guns,' I said.

'Then he must *un*learn to hate them if he is to be part of this family.'

Did that endearing smile hold significance, a personal message for me alone, I wondered? My decision was now clear; where Thane went,

139

hating noise, then I must go too. I did not want him bolting away in the general direction of Edinburgh and his home on Arthur's Seat at the first gunshot.

As Hubert spoke, the commotion outside announced Cedric's arrival with the two Labradors and Thane. His friend Jock lurked, grinning, in the background, presumably also to be a beater.

A collar was produced. As I fastened it around Thane's neck, wondering how he would tolerate this, Hubert said, 'Sometimes hounds get very excited and can get lost, as we know, do we not?' He cast a tender smile in my direction.

While the docile and now collared Thane and I exchanged pitying glances, I patted his head reassuringly, resolving to stay close to him, and I declined Hubert's rather mocking offer to carry a gun myself.

He seemed to think the idea might strike terror into my heart, but I was pretty certain that I could shoot straighter than most men, having used that ability to survive in a violent and often brutal society in America's Wild West.

Now outside the house, I found that Collins was to accompany us and, most surprisingly, so was Kate. Yesterday's persistent rain had vanished, leaving some dripping trees and muddy pools as evidence, while a beautiful calm sunny day had arisen from a sleepy

140

morning mist.

Hubert had decided that a day in the fresh air would be good for Kate, and I suspected that Collins had persuaded him; no doubt she wished to keep a close eye on us both. A witness to that goodnight kiss, she was not prepared to take the risk of letting us spend the day together. I could have told her that it was a waste of time and misgivings, as I suspected, knowing men better than she did, that Hubert would have more important manly activities that day than allowing his blood to boil in hot pursuit of me.

Kate, armed with book and parasol, would remain safely in one of the pony carts, watching from afar, with the picnic prepared by Mrs Robson. Much to Collins' ill-concealed chagrin I was to accompany Hubert in the second cart, which had space for the day's kill to be carried back to the larder at Staines.

I caught a glimpse of Wolf Rider and knew by the twitch of Thane's ears that he had spotted his hero. Wolf's long black hair was tied back with an Indian-style sweatband and, despite the uniform gamekeeper's outfit, he looked more like an Aztec warrior than ever.

I patted Thane's head firmly. 'You stay with me.'

But Hubert had other ideas. 'Roswal will come with me; he will be needed to assist in retrieving the birds.'

I shook my head in despair. He hadn't

141

listened to my warning. Whatever Roswal might have been, Thane was no retriever and after that first volley he would be off like a shot himself to the far horizon.

I chose my words carefully, tried to explain as tactfully as possible that Roswal had changed during the past three years.

Hubert listened gravely, shook his head, and said sadly that it was a disappointment, but now that he thought about it, he realised that Roswal had always been a bit of a house dog. He had allowed Kate to indulge him, make a lapdog of him.

Eyeing Thane sternly he said, 'You had better take him back to Kate.'

I was delighted to do so, but as I was about to leave, there was a new commotion: a lot of bowing, straightening of shoulders, removing caps and tugging of forelocks, all indicating that the Duke's party had now arrived.

Hubert also bared his head, bowed, but received no acknowledgement from the Duke's carriage as they swept past us, a handsome youth with bright auburn curls at his side.

I was surprised, having expected them to mingle, but it was now obvious that they intended keeping themselves to themselves. Even in sport, there was no taking down of the barriers that generations had erected to divide the aristocracy from the tenants.

Presumably everyone was waiting for the

142

Duke to declare the event open and fire the first shot. They had settled about twenty yards away. A few words, some cheering and a barrage of shots followed. Someone misfired and swore loudly. The sound carried and so did the reproof:

'Ladies present!' Although the Duke's ladies were hearty-looking females, tweed-clad and businesslike in their efficient handling of the guns, and looked well able to take care of themselves. For one wild moment, I am ashamed to admit, I longed to hold a gun again, not as a frantic device to save my own skin as in past days, but to demonstrate and surprise these sportsmen and women by my expertise. I was certain I would be better than any of them.

It was an unworthy thought and I dismissed it quickly. Why should I care what they thought of me anyway?

So I took Thane and headed back towards the carts, interrupting an earnest conversation Cedric was having with Kate. He seemed to be pleading with her and I wondered what was going on between them, since he should have been in place with the beaters.

At my approach, he looked guilty and, pretending he hadn't seen me, he cleared off.

'Shouldn't Cedric be with the beaters?' My attempt at innocent curiosity failed to draw any response or explanation beyond a shrug from Kate, who didn't question why I had

143

brought Thane back.

'Where is Collins?'

She shrugged again and, looking rather flustered, said, 'Gone to see a friend, over there with the Duke's party, I expect.'

Later, it did occur to me to remember that Kate was an heiress and that perhaps Cedric had hopes, however unlikely, as a suitable candidate for her affection. But, remembering the damp sleeve of the moleskin jacket in the kitchen, was what I had witnessed a secret understanding?

If so, then it also had to be fed into the puzzle of Hubert's mysterious blackmailer, a role that was already fitting Mrs Robson's would-be nephew uncommonly well.

After the first noisy barrage of shots, Thane lay down with a bored sigh while I tried to engage Kate in conversation. I directed it somewhat craftily towards Roswal as a puppy, but her answers were vague; hardly what one would expect of a devoted and proud dog-owner, heartbroken by his loss and overwhelmed with joy at his return.

As we spoke, Collins returned, gave me a sour look and, seizing one of the guns, headed towards Hubert again, doubtless intending to stay as close to him as possible.

It was going to be a long hot day. Making my excuses to Kate, who obviously did not mind the prospect of being deprived of our society, as she retreated beneath her parasol with her book, I took Thane up to a small mound well behind the guns.

Here the few sheltering trees would be welcome when the sun got higher and I was glad of my sketchbook, though I didn't have much notion of what to draw, apart from quick images of men and their dogs. Looking towards the horizon, the brooding image of the magnificent castle and a wide vista of attractive countryside. Far below, tiny figures with raised guns, the echo of their dogs barking excitedly, bounding ahead to retrieve the fluttering shapes of birds as they fell from the sky.

Where was Wolf Rider in the mêlée?

Kate and the picnic carts were still visible and I noticed with considerable interest a young man heading in her direction, his bright auburn curls identifying him as the Duke's travelling companion.

Suddenly my attention was diverted by a shout followed by a flutter of activity, not from the terrified birds this time but from the Staines shooting party.

I knew what the distant shouts were about, although I couldn't distinguish voices.

Someone had been hit.

Men I recognised, among them Wolf Rider, and Grace Holt's new husband Peter, were heading rapidly in the direction of the Staines party. I could not see Hubert clearly, but with a chill of horror, an ominous dread certainty, I

145

knew that he had been the victim . . .

CHAPTER FIFTEEN

I ran back down the hill.

The Duke's party were also heading towards Hubert, including the youth whose conversation with Kate had been cut short.

'Anyone hurt?'

'An accident.'

'No damage done,' I heard someone shout.

I passed close to Kate, who was now standing up in the cart. Collins had returned to her side to see that she was safe.

'What's happened?' Kate asked.

Out of breath, Collins gasped, 'Someone took a pot shot at Hubert.' She put a protective arm around Kate's shoulders.

'No!' Kate wailed.

'It's all right. Just missed him. Stop it, Kate. Look, he's fine.'

And so he was, striding towards us, unharmed though obviously shaken.

'You're not hurt, are you?' cried Collins wringing her hands.

A man rushed over from the Duke's party. 'His Grace wishes to know if anyone was injured.'

Hubert bowed: 'Thank His Grace for his concern. Please tell him that I am quite well.'

The man continued to regard Hubert dubiously and, gesturing towards the sportsmen staring in his direction, said apologetically, 'One of the novices, I fear. Poor shots. Some of our party are first guns, young and reckless.' And touching his cap politely, 'Could have been a nasty accident, sir.'

Collins was still clinging to Hubert's arm whispering: 'Thank God you're not hurt.'

I watched his grim expression as the man returned to the Duke's party. 'Nasty accident, indeed,' said Hubert shortly. 'Someone tried to kill me.'

'Surely not!' said Collins.

Hubert shook off her hand, straightened his shoulders, and looked towards the men who had resumed their stances with the guns.

'This was no accident,' he repeated. 'It was deliberate—someone tried to kill me.' As he spoke, he directed a look at me that was so significant it was impossible not to recognise the unspoken message: he believed this was an attempt on his life by the blackmailer.

Wolf Rider appeared, so swiftly that I did not see him approach, aware that he was at our side only by Thane's greeting.

'Where the devil have you been?' Hubert demanded.

Wolf looked guilty at the question, gave the familiar shrug as Hubert shouted at him: 'Don't you know that someone has just tried to kill me?'

Wolf looked suddenly alert and I guessed, perhaps wrongly, that, hating shooting, he had followed my example and strolled away some distance from the main range.

'You did not see your attacker?' he asked Hubert.

'I did not, but I heard the bullet whizz past me. I threw myself to the ground, yelled out a warning. I thought he might try a second shot!'

Wolf shook his head as Hubert went on: 'I looked round and saw him duck out of sight.'

'Which direction would that be?'

'I don't know. I wasn't concerned with directions,' Hubert said angrily. 'Just with keeping alive.'

Wolf considered this, frowning and thoughtfully regarding the landscape as if it might provide some clues. 'Perhaps if we could find the bullet, it would identify this man.'

Hubert laughed harshly. 'And how are we to do that, pray? There must be dozens using the same guns, hundreds of identical bullets thick on the ground all around us—'

'What I mean,' Wolf interrupted, 'is that this was probably an accident, the very reason why the person didn't want to be seen and identified. A very natural reaction.'

'Hmph,' growled Hubert, picking up his gun again.

'Are you sure you want to continue?' Collins piped up, that hand on his arm again.

'Of course,' was the short reply. And to

148

Wolf. 'You'd better stay at my back, just in case.'

'You think he might attack again?' asked Collins in a shocked voice. 'I really think you—'

Hubert whipped round on her. 'And I really think you should shut up, Collins. Look after Kate, that's what you're paid to do.'

It was cruel of him, and poor Collins visibly wilted at this harsh statement. As Hubert marched off with Wolf, she darted a murderous glance at me and said, 'As you can see, Kate is very distressed.'

I hadn't seen anything of the kind but realised this was a ruse to get rid of me as she added, 'As I am in charge of the picnic, I must remain here, but perhaps you would be so good as to take Kate back to the house in the spare cart. Take Roswal with you.'

Kate did not demur. I was curious about the Duke's young companion but all my attempts at conversation were met by a sullen silence.

I gave up as I had a lot to think about.

Was it possible that Hubert's blackmailer had made an attempt to kill him? As for his attacker's identity, this clearly indicated a man. But who?

My possible suspects—Wolf and Cedric— were both present, the latter among the beaters. But there was always the possibility that I was wrong and that an unknown man from Staines or Alnwick had found a way into the shooting party.

I have to admit I was baffled. I was inclined to lean towards Wolf's theory that this was an accident and that the culprit, from the Duke's party with its acknowledged first time guns and bad shots, had sneakily ducked away, afraid of retribution.

And then there was Collins, of course. I must not forget Collins, who had a gun with her. This might have been an attempt to scare Hubert, but in her present emotional state she might well have been tempted to turn that gun on me. Perhaps I would be wise to watch my own back.

*   *   *

Matters were not helped in that direction when, after dinner that evening when Collins left to put Miss Kate to bed and we were alone together, Hubert produced another note from the blackmailer.

You had a lucky escape this morning. Pay up or you may not be lucky next time.

It was written in heavy black pencil on a piece of brown parcel paper, identical to that used by Mrs Robson in the kitchen to wrap the picnic sandwiches. The blackmailer had obviously seized the opportunity that Hubert had been badly frightened by the accident.

'What do you think of that, Rose?'

'When did you get this?'

150

'It was in my jacket pocket when I went to hang it up in the gun room. I always check pockets for handkerchiefs and so forth.'

'Which means it was put there before the shoot ended.'

He nodded and I did not add the thoughts that we were both sharing. That this was a clear indication that the blackmailer had been one of the sportsmen—or women, whether he or she had fired the gun or was merely taking advantage of the situation and Hubert's terror.

I said, 'This certainly narrows down the field.'

Hubert again nodded and sighed in weary agreement while I let my thoughts go unspoken.

The note had been hastily written on paper torn from a pack of Mrs Robson's picnic sandwiches. Who had the opportunity to do that?

Opportunity? Collins had been in charge of the picnic cart and there would be plenty of samples of her writing in the house, but I wasn't hopeful. It looked like a man's hand to me.

'Did many come to the picnic cart for sandwiches?' I asked, sorry now that I had not stayed.

'Everyone in our party, mostly tenants from Staines.' And I remembered Grace's husband, Peter Sloan was at the shoot. Could he have thrust the note into Hubert's pocket? If so, what were his reasons for those earlier threatening notes?

'Were the beaters there too?'

'Of course.'

That would include Cedric and his friend Jock. Collusion perhaps? Had they organised the burglary and the theft of the incriminating photographs together? It was a thought not to be ignored. It fitted well. Two reckless lads on the make, both desperate for money.

'And Wolf Rider, of course,' Hubert added dryly. He let that sink in for a moment, and then asked, 'Have you any suspicions, Rose? I should like to hear them. I fear my time is running out.'

And in the next breath, he leapt from his chair, seized my hands and was asking me to marry him. I wasn't sure that I had heard correctly. He smiled at my bewildered expression and repeated the offer.

I was taken aback, quite unprepared for this proposal. I had not been a week in his house, yet Hubert had fallen in love with me and, what was more, on the strength of one kiss, now asked me to be his wife! I could not believe all this was happening, aware that we were certainly not moving on the same plane.

I wrenched my hands away. He was attractive enough for me to toy with a fantasy 'what if?', but in the real world, I did not believe that I would ever fall in love again or ever have the slightest desire to marry. And what did I know of this man? Handsome and strong, yes, but there were unknown depths of character still to be explored. What had we in common? Did we view things in the same way and, most importantly, did he make me laugh? Jack did, and there followed an unworthy thought—that accepting Hubert would be such a slap in the face for him.

I had remained silent so long that Hubert, watching my face anxiously, sighed and said, 'I thought I had reason to believe that you felt the same as I did.'

'Really?' I said shortly. 'I have given you no cause for that assumption.'

'Don't you believe in love at first sight?' he asked in wounded tones.

Frankly, one love, one life, could have been my motto. My first love.

'I don't want to rush you, but I hope that your silence stems from the modesty that I find so charming in your character.'

I fought back indignation. He really didn't know me in the slightest. A feminist who abandoned man-trapping wiles long ago. I have neither time nor patience to indulge in the hypocrisies of hiding maidenly blushes—as well as my ankles—from prying male eyes.

'You have had children, have you not—during your long marriage?' He paused. 'Vince told me there was a child, a boy.'

'He died of a fever.'

He nodded. 'How sad. I love you, but please

153

don't wait too long, Rose,' he said earnestly. 'I want this marriage soon, as soon as it can be arranged. I want to give you a child; I need you to bear me a son—our son who will one day inherit Staines.' And with a gesture. 'All of this will be his!'

I was surprised and a little embarrassed by his frankness. Although the begetting of an heir was the main reason for many marriages in his class, I had expected the fact to be disguised in a sentimental flourish. And Vince obviously hadn't told him the whole truth regarding the several miscarriages that had haunted my marriage to Danny, or of the fact that the Faro women had been notoriously unlucky in childbearing. My mother died giving birth to a third child, a son, who also died. My sister Emily had also suffered multiple miscarriages before producing a healthy little boy.

Hubert was living in a fantasy if he expected me to be a breeding machine of Staines children.

I said the usual things about being flattered and so forth, but that I couldn't possibly marry him. He looked so let down and disappointed, shaking his head, determined not to take 'no' for an answer, his eager smile transforming this man of the world, many years my senior, into a lovesick, hopeful boy.

'Please think it over.'

Evading a possible goodnight kiss, I left him

154

pouring a drink and made my way upstairs. *There is so much to gain by this marriage*, a voice whispered in my head. *This lovely house and, more importantly, Thane's future as well as your own.*

What was I thinking? Most women would say I was idiotic to even hesitate. But then I wasn't like most women. I had an inbuilt sense of caution and, in this case, more urgent matters faced a Lady Investigator, Discretion Guaranteed.

Matters that must be sorted out, the puzzle solved. I must discover why someone had tried to kill Hubert, my present client, and the identity of the blackmailer, before his life could be further endangered.

First things first. I must go to Alnwick immediately.

CHAPTER SIXTEEN

I had a disturbed night, as I was woken by a succession of banging doors and raised voices. Alarmed that this was another of Kate's sleepwalking activities, I jumped out of bed and opened the door to see a dim figure emerging from Hubert's room. It was Collins, shouting at him angrily and tearfully, for all the house to hear.

The door banged shut behind her and I

heard her footsteps marching past my room. There had obviously been a bitter quarrel, there was no doubt about that. I hoped that I was not the cause, and that Hubert had not told her that he had asked me to marry him.

Eventually I got to sleep again but awoke feeling weary, and went downstairs to my usual solitary breakfast in the dining room. When Mrs Robson bustled in to greet me with porridge, toast and a pot of tea, I wondered if she would be offended by a suggestion that I ate in the kitchen on the occasions when I was alone.

Setting down the tray before me, she said, 'A message from Sir. Miss Kate is not to have Thane today; Mr Rider has requested that he stays with him—something to do with this cattle business and the new calf they are all so excited about.' She sounded faintly disgusted. 'I thought you'd better be told.'

Thane would be pleased to spend a day with Wolf and I had little wish or intention of taking him to Alnwick with me, aware as I am of his aversion to towns and remembering his extraordinary behaviour when he sat down at the outskirts of the town and refused to go any further.

Gathering my bicycle from the barn, I rode through the grounds past the fenced-off province of the wild cattle. There was no sign of any of the beasts. I would have been surprised to find it otherwise, as Wolf had said it was rare to see them during the daylight hours, but in case I ever felt like taking a short cut across the fields, he had warned me, they would be watching from over there among the trees.

I wondered if and when Wolf would get his calf. The only indication that he might also be somewhere in the vicinity was a mere dot hovering in the sky far above—Kokopele keeping vigil.

Today I was glad to be alone, especially as I expected to spend some time in the library and the local newspaper office, but my first port of call would be the railway station, trying to track down Lily's husband and their present address.

It was good to be bicycling again, flying down the hills on an exhilarating sunny morning with the summer laden trees just tipped with gold as they began their dramatic change into the glorious shades of autumn. Soon I was toiling uphill, on the outskirts of the town dominated by the magnificence of the castle. There were interesting landmarks on the way, delightful ancient houses and inns as well as a busy market place, all of which I hoped to have an opportunity to explore.

My bicycle, oddly enough, excited fewer curious stares in Alnwick than in Edinburgh's Princes Street. As I rode through the Hotspur Gate for the second time, I thought how greatly my fortunes had changed. When I had first come through this way, I had little expected to find Harry Hotspur personified, alive and well, reincarnated in the person of Hubert Staines. A man with whom I had become involved in less than a week and, quite against my will, to the extraordinary extent that he has asked me to be his wife.

Entering the railway station, I remembered my arrival in Alnwick with Thane, full of misgivings and trepidation, wondering what Staines would be like. All that seemed to belong to another world, for I had soon discovered that my usually reliable stepbrother had been seriously misinformed concerning the state of affairs at Staines. The dying child, whom he had never met, pining for her lost deerhound was in fact a pretty young lady who, to outward appearances at least, looked far from her deathbed.

I had little guessed that I was riding into a complex case of blackmail and would soon once again be donning my role as Lady Investigator, Discretion Guaranteed, and returning to this town, certain that here the truth was to be found and the identity of Hubert's blackmailer revealed.

And then there was my unexpected encounter with Wolf Rider, that enigmatic Sioux Indian whose sinister insinuations regarding Thane I still regarded with fear.

What did it all mean? I was sure sometimes that I had all the facts and was on the right road, only to find that each path I took led further into the labyrinth.

As I was riding through the Bondgate towards the station, the sun disappeared and a hovering black cloud erupted into a heavy shower of hailstones. I dived for cover and found that I was just steps away from the local library.

Parking the bicycle, I went inside, where my revised plan of action brought with it a much needed stroke of luck.

Enquiring at the counter for information concerning the level crossing and the Staines Pit, for an imaginary newspaper article I was writing, another mantle more or less skilfully assumed, I was conscious of being watched. Looking round, a hand was raised, and when the face came into view, I recognised, seated behind a mound of books, the old scholar who had told me about the Battle of Alnwick and the phantom hound of King Malcolm of Scotland.

As I acknowledged his greeting, the assistant emerged with a file of newspapers and indicated that I follow him to a vacant seat alongside the old gentleman.

'Do you mind if this young lady shares your desk, Mr Tetley?'

'Not at all. I will be delighted,' he replied with a grin.

As the assistant left he held out his hand. 'James Tetley, schoolmaster, retired.' And

159

indicating the pile of books, 'Amateur genealogist.'

I told him my name and he nodded. 'Ah yes, the owner of the deerhound that gave me such a scare. Are you enjoying your stay in Staines?'

I said yes and again he nodded, then putting on his spectacles, he resumed his reading, pausing only to switch volumes and make copious notes.

I tackled the newspaper cuttings, which turned out to be hardly a mine of new information regarding the history of the level crossing, for which a former Duke had graciously extended the necessary permission to give access to the Staines Pit.

I had almost given up hope when, at last, I found what I was looking for: an article about how the crossing had been the sad cause of two tragic deaths. The local doctor, Fergus Holt, got a good spread; there was a full account of his funeral, mourners who included Members of Parliament and a representative of the Duke himself. He had obviously been a popular figure in the neighbourhood, with a moving tribute from Hubert Staines.

Curiously, I could almost hear Hubert's voice as I read his eulogy to this man who had been his family's doctor for two generations. He praised his work and said how sadly he would be missed, both at Staines and by his many friends in Alnwick.

Less space—a mere paragraph—was given

to Lily's father, who had been crossing the line in the dark. There was an obvious hint that his death was due to lack of vigilance and intoxication. No requiem from Hubert or anyone else this time.

I had little idea of the exact date of the deaths of Mary Staines and her daughter Amy, or of the gun-cleaning accident that killed Amy's lover Dave, and I felt that asking the assistant for such information might be regarded as ghoulish.

However, the young assistant was keen to help since I was on friendly terms with his former schoolmaster (as I gathered). He came over and said, 'If you are interested in material for your article, miss, there are some cuttings on Staines House. It is well worth a visit, if you have the time to spare.'

Disregarding Mr Tetley's wry look, I thanked him and was soon in possession of a file relating to the Staines, which contained an account of Mrs Staines' death fall 'from a window carelessly left open during a storm by one of the young servants, who has since been discharged.'

All of which I already knew. As I sighed and laid it aside, Mr Tetley abandoned his notebook and said, 'An interesting family; rather too inbred. Some of them went insane and tragedy has certainly stalked them in recent years.'

Hoping for more, I gave him an eager look

and he continued: 'I notice you were reading about poor Mrs Staines. Her daughter, you know, committed suicide after an unhappy love affair—we got that information not first hand, of course, but through the village grapevine.'

He shook his head gravely. 'I fear that first cousins marrying each other is not particularly healthy—in body and indeed, in mind also—for their offspring. Such unions are often motivated by money and dynastic aspirations rather than the demands of the human heart.' And throwing down his pencil, he added grimly: 'Property and money, money and property, the ruin of the human race.'

A bell rang somewhere and he took out his watch. 'Ah, time for a little refreshment. Would you care to have a cup of tea with me and we can continue our discussion?'

I followed him out and a few moments later we were seated at a window table in the Swan Hotel, a coaching inn in the days before the railway opened up new prospects for travellers passing through Alnwick, north and south.

As we waited to be served, he told me of his passion for local history and how he had made a lifetime study of the Staines family, whose roots predated the Dukes of Northumberland.

'There was a time when de Percys and de Steyns had equal status and, if truth were to be told and records went back far enough to be deciphered, the de Steyns should be the

162

present incumbents of Alnwick Castle, since the de Percys died out and the present family are descended from the distaff side.

'Genealogy has become my hobby since I retired and I have helped many people to discover their roots. My efforts and a few published papers have extended my work beyond local history and Alnwick—it now extends south as far as London and north into Scotland, particularly Glasgow and Edinburgh,' he said proudly, pausing to smile at me, perhaps hoping that I had heard of him.

'I had a most interesting encounter with Mr Rider—the gamekeeper at Staines, an American gentleman, perhaps you have met him?' I said yes and he went on, 'Ah, quite a fascinating and romantic story. He was searching for his grandmother who had been kidnapped by Sioux Indians when the rest of the safari party she was with were slaughtered. Mr Rider's grandfather fell in love with her.

'My background research revealed that the lady was not Scottish as he believed. Miranda was a member of the Staines family here, not only by marriage but by blood. There was a history of twins on her side of the family who had twice married first cousins.'

He shook his head. 'A very complicated heredity, which I have been studying for some time now, but the indications are undoubtedly that Mr Wolf Rider could claim to be the legitimate heir of Staines.'

His frown turned into a smile as he looked across the table. 'I trust that he never will do so, of course. If you have read Mr Dickens' *Bleak House* you will know that such claims can linger on unresolved for generations, costing not only fortunes but bitter grief and heartbreak to the claimants.'

'Is Mr Rider aware of these facts regarding your research and his possible claim to Staines?' I asked.

His eyes widened. 'Of course. Yes indeed he is.' A sigh as he added: 'I doubt whether Mr Rider would have enough money to initiate such a search in the courts of law. I sincerely hope not, anyway, for the bad feeling it would cause in these parts where Mr Staines and his family are held in high regard. I doubt whether the substitute of a—' he searched for a suitable word and said 'a gentleman from a savage part of America would be held in high esteem by the Duke either.'

He had certainly given me food for thought, and a damning reason for Wolf Rider to dispose of Hubert Staines without going through the intricacies of a legal claim. Whether this tied in with the blackmailer was another matter.

As I prepared to part company with Mr Tetley and thanked him for the tea, he handed me his card and extracted a promise that I would call upon him if I needed any further material for my level crossing article—the subject that, I confess, had been completely obliterated by the unexpected revelations regarding the Staines and Wolf Rider.

I remembered my mission and said that I was keen to interview some of the people whose lives had been upset in any way by the presence of the level crossing.

'Such as one of the servants from Staines, a young maid called Lily. I am told her father was killed by a passing train. Does she still live here?' I asked innocently.

Mr Tetley thought for a moment. 'Indeed, yes. I meet her husband, Will Craid, quite regularly. One of my former pupils, we play chess together in the Diamond Inn. A most intelligent young man, very bright indeed. Works for the railway.'

He shook his head regretfully and added, 'But had he been born above the labouring class, I believe he would have gone far academically. I tried to persuade him into clerical work, perhaps for a lawyer. Writes with a splendid hand, and he's an excellent shot, too. Wins many competitions. He had to miss our game of chess yesterday, as he was shooting with the Duke's party.'

'How interesting,' I murmured faintly, as indeed it was.

'If you would like to talk to his wife, I am sure I could arrange it for you.'

Thanking him, pleading urgency and shortness of time, I said, 'If you could give me her address, I might take a chance on her being at home.'

He laughed. 'At this time of day, you are most likely to find her up at the castle. She is a sewing maid to the Duchess.'

Following his directions, I made my way up to the castle, wondering if I had found another suspect to add to those persons unknown who might have stolen Hubert's photographs and were now blackmailing him for their return.

Mr Tetley's revelations about this highly intelligent chess-playing railwayman suggested that Lily's husband might also fit perfectly the role of Hubert's blackmailer.

CHAPTER SEVENTEEN

My interview with Lily Craid was something of a let-down. It was heartening to know that the lack of a reference from Hubert had not put off the Duchess, who presumably had better latches on her windows, but my hope that this visit would provide an excuse to see something of the Castle's grand interior was not to be.

I was being passed through a series of long narrow corridors by a series of high-nosed retainers—very lofty in countenance—before my bicycle, which had received some hard looks, was removed to be parked outside. It was handled very gingerly, in a manner that suggested that it might be a carrier of the Bubonic plague.

At last we reached the servants' quarters, where I was finally unceremoniously pushed rather than ushered into Lily's presence by a stout downstairs maid with the words; 'Woman to see you, Lil. Don't let her keep you from your work, mind, or Her Grace will give you whatfor.'

Lily was seated at a well-scrubbed table in one of the kitchens, the surrounding walls bristling with gleaming copper pots and pans. Invited to take a seat, I soon realised that her position of sewing maid to the Duchess related to an overflowing basket of linen, presumably containing torn petticoats, dropped hems, garments to be altered, mended or patched, and buttons to be replaced.

Seeing her engaged in this activity recalled Mrs Robson's laments over her loss. I wondered if this was one of her noble employer's socks she was busily darning, and whether His Grace shared in common with the humbler members of the male sex a tendency to thrift, not to mention downright meanness, concerning undergarments and socks.

She greeted me nervously after the ample housemaid left us, obviously not used to receiving visitors. I introduced myself, saying that I was writing an article on the dangers of level crossings for a Newcastle newspaper.

This explanation seemed acceptable, but I

had a feeling that Lily was either shy or reluctant, or both, to recall the past and, indeed, looked most uncomfortable when I asked what her feelings were on the subject?

'I knew it was dangerous, all the Staines folk thought so, and they all said it should be better guarded or done away with altogether when the pit closed down.'

Trying to phrase my words carefully, I said, 'I realise it is a painful subject for you personally, since your father met with such a tragic accident. You must have been terribly shocked.'

She gave me a wry look. 'Shocked yes, but not surprised. Not really. My pa was a firebrand, always talked too much and drank too much as well,' she added bitterly. 'He could be an interfering old so-and-so and he certainly made things worse for me, not better, up at the house—when I had to leave.'

Although I knew already, she obviously wasn't going to elaborate on the reasons why, so I said, 'You were happy there. Were you not the personal maid to Miss Kate?'

At the mention of Kate her face froze. Looking away from me, she concentrated on her darning.

I persisted. 'No doubt being near in age, you were good friends.'

She thrust aside the sock, clasped her hands together, and said indignantly, 'Whoever told you that, missus, was quite wrong.' Nodding

168

vigorously, she added: 'I was only a servant and I knew my place.'

'Perhaps I got it wrong.'

'You certainly did that.'

I changed my tactics. 'How did you get along with her sister Amy?'

'Never knew her sister. She was older,' was the sharp response.

I knew I could not stumble on in this clumsy fashion so I returned to the subject of the level crossing, made some more notes and left her. I felt she was relieved to see me go.

As I recovered my bicycle and headed back to Staines, I was disappointed, unsure of what I had expected regarding Lily, but one thing was clear. She accepted her father's death as an accident. It had certainly never occurred to her, knowing her father's fiery nature, to think that someone might have wanted to be rid of him. And for a man known to drink too much, the level crossing seemed to provide an admirable assassin.

I decided my next step would be to see how best I could engineer an interview with her husband, the chess player.

*   *   *

A fine smell of cooking greeted my arrival in the Staines kitchen. Mrs Robson was making soup.

'Mushroom,' she said, holding up the ladle.

169

'Sir loves it—a special treat, his favourite. What a morning we've had. The mushrooms are at their best at this time of the year. We all turn out with our baskets. There's a special place in the wood over there. Mind, you have to be up early for the best ones.'

So that was the explanation for why I had breakfasted alone.

'Even Collins came and gave us a hand. And she doesn't like leaving her bed early. A right sleepyhead she is in the mornings.'

And remembering the angry sounds of quarrelling that had awakened me during the night, I felt Mrs Robson had a point. After such a disturbed and distressed night, Collins must have felt dreadful plunging out into the morning mist to collect mushrooms.

Thane had spent the day with Wolf and was now back with Kate, who sat by the window with Collins. When Thane greeted my arrival like a prisoner on reprieve, they were jolted from their earnest conversation, their guilty expressions giving me the uncomfortable feeling that I had been the subject under deep discussion.

As I left with Thane to take him for his long-awaited walk, Collins followed me out. At the top of the stairs she said, 'I hear that Hubert has asked you to marry him.'

I was taken aback by her blunt statement. Who had told her? It must have been Hubert himself, and I think I blushed furiously, but words failed me and I could think of no denial or indeed of any response.

She seized my arm, and for a moment, I panicked. I had a horrible feeling that she was going to push me over the banister, for her face was livid with fury.

'Don't fool yourself that he is in love with you and that's why he wants to marry you. He's only marrying you because you're young and he thinks you will be able to give him a son, to cut out Kate.'

And pausing to give me a triumphant look, she sneered, 'That's all. A son is what he needs most in all the world. Remember love hasn't anything to do with it. He could never love a woman like you. But anyone would do.' Her look as she said the words reduced me to something she had trodden in on her shoe.

'Once you have given him a son, he'll be off again, leaving you stranded. Don't say I didn't warn you,' she added shrilly. 'I know him well; I know what he's like.'

I was suddenly angry. This was none of her business, or was it? 'Then why doesn't he marry you?' I said.

She laughed. 'That's easy to answer, Mrs Clever McQuinn. It's because I can never have a child. We've both known that for long enough,' she added bitterly.

I pushed away from her and went downstairs with her leaning over the banister, watching me. Still trembling as I left the house

171

with Thane, I was furious, but tried putting myself in her place. As Hubert's discarded lover (and had I not suffered a similar fate all too recently with Jack Macmerry?) her venom and spite were understandable, especially realising that had she become pregnant, he would have married her.

It didn't do Hubert any credit, though, that they had had a showdown last night and he had told her what he intended. I felt pity, too; a woman's pity for Collins. I knew all about loving blindly. And I was furious at Hubert's presumption that I would change my mind and marry him.

Thane didn't seem eager to go to the stables after our walk, which was shorter than usual. He seemed tired, possibly the effects of spending all day with Wolf, trailing the white cow about to drop her calf. When I returned to the house for dinner, he had followed me, a little distance away. As I walked up the steps he rushed forward and his eyes begged to stay.

'What's wrong?' I patted his head. 'You've missed me today, is that it? Very well. Stay in the hall with the two dogs while we have dinner. Then I promise you another walk together.'

He wagged his tail delightedly, his mouth open in that strange approximation of a human smile, and as I entered the dining room, he sat down obediently beside Hubert's Labradors.

As I took my seat at the table there was an uneasy feeling in the air; a strange atmosphere brought about by the darkening sky, a room colder than usual and those unforgiving eyes trapped for ever in the Staines family portraits.

Suddenly I wished with all my heart that this interlude in my life and this assignment that had been forced upon me was ended. I longed to be free of them all, and most urgently wanted Hubert's blackmailer apprehended so that Thane and I could head back to Edinburgh, myself richer by two hundred guineas.

The events of the day had upset me, especially that scary meeting with poor Collins. I hadn't the heart to be angry. I could feel only sympathy when I thought of her broken-hearted by her lover's cruel revelation. Especially when I looked at Hubert, so complacent and uncaring, talking to Wolf Rider as if the white calf and estate finances were the most important things in the world. Which they probably were, to him at least, at that moment.

Mrs Robson came in to light the table candles, followed by Collins with bowls of soup on a tray. Kate had remained in her room, so Collins was giving Mrs Robson a hand in the kitchen, which was probably an unusual occurrence as she would normally be preparing her charge for bed.

She set a bowl before Hubert with a more

restrained hand than might have been expected, in the circumstances, which to anyone knowing the full facts would have better suited her flinging it in his face.

'Well done, well done, Mrs Robson,' he said without thanks or even a glance at Collins. And, holding up his spoon, 'My absolute favourite soup.'

Collins placed another bowl beside Wolf, one for herself, and the last was for me. All in silence, then she took her seat at the table.

Hubert murmured something about *bon appetit*.

I had just raised the spoon to my lips when Mrs Robson, opening the door to leave, was almost knocked down by Thane, who rushed in past her.

'That dog!' she screamed, staggering against the door. 'He has no business—'

Thane ignored her, bounded towards me, leapt up and, his paws on the table, sent the bowl of soup crashing to the floor.

I jumped up unscathed. It had all happened almost in the twinkling of an eye, and none had spilt on me. I grabbed Thane, yelled at him, looked at the others helplessly. I didn't know what to do.

Such behaviour was quite out of character, and was to be expected from an untrained puppy, not from Thane, who always knew his manners.

'I can't understand it,' I was apologising, as

Hubert said shortly, 'Roswal was never like this in the past. He should be better controlled. We can't have dogs leaping at the table, knocking plates on the floor. Very unseemly behaviour. Not at all what we expect,' he added, hinting that Thane's sojourn with me was to blame.

Shocked by this scene of chaos, Mrs Robson rushed out and reappeared flourishing a mop. Wolf, meanwhile, was gathering up the fragments of broken china.

'Not one of our best sets, Mrs Robson,' Hubert said wearily as, looking flustered and cross, she pushed Wolf aside and said, 'I'll do that, Mr Rider,' and looking up at Hubert, she added, 'No, Sir, not the best, but it does still make one short. I don't like that. It spoils the setting.'

Hubert flung a reproachful glance in my direction, hardly able to restrain his anger at this disruption of his normally tranquil supper.

'Do take Roswal away, Mrs Robson. When you've finished mopping, that is.' And to the rest of us, he added wearily, 'I can't think what has come over him.' Another stern glance indicated that I had been a bad influence on his lost deerhound and that such shocking behaviour might be the norm in Edinburgh dining rooms but not in Staines.

'Shall I take him back to the kennels?' Wolf asked.

Hubert made an irritated gesture. 'Later.

175

Mrs Robson will put him in the hall with the other two. Now, let's get on with our meal, for heaven's sake.' And placing his hands on the table, he said, 'Come along, it's only a broken bowl, not the end of the world.'

That endearing smile appeared again as he patted my hand. 'You all right, my dear?' As I said I was and began to apologise, I saw Collins glaring at me from across the table, her eyes full of hatred. Her hands trembling, she picked up her spoon while I tackled the soup Mrs Robson had replaced before me.

I still couldn't understand Thane's eruption into the dining room. It was so unlike him, and could not be excused by his having missed me all day. I shook my head. It was as if he had reverted to a moment of reckless puppyhood.

I got the explanation, however, when I went out to the stables later, wanting to reassure myself that he was all right. Wolf was with him.

'Just as well you didn't take that soup, Rose.'

'What on earth do you mean? Was it poisoned or something?' I asked with a laugh.

In reply he shook out the contents of a table napkin. 'This is Destroying Angel, one of the *Amanita* species, the deadliest kind of mushrooms. Had you eaten these tiny pieces, you would be dead by now.'

What he held out looked as innocent as the white of a hard-boiled egg. I stared at them in horror. 'You mean someone tried to poison me

176

with these?'

He nodded. 'I mean exactly that.'

'That can't be true! What about the others?—all of us were having the same soup.'

He shook his head. 'I cannot answer that. But I know all about poisonous mushrooms and I can tell you that no one experienced in gathering the edible kind would have made that mistake. There is no doubt that this was put in your bowl deliberately.' He turned and patted Thane's head. 'But you knew, didn't you, clever Thane. You knew with that extra sense of yours that the soup was poisoned and someone was going to kill your beloved Rose.'

Thane wagged his tail, gave us a look of triumph, and opened his mouth in that almost human smile.

'Who—who do you think . . . ?' I asked

Wolf shrugged. 'Examine your conscience, Rose.'

'What do you mean? Who could hate me that much?' Then I saw it all; Collins putting a bowl before each of us, mine last of all, and Mrs Robson saying how Collins had risen early to help her gather the mushrooms. And I knew she had tried to kill me that night.

'I believe you know the answer, Rose. Hubert has made it very plain—his feelings for you. And anyone in the house who heard the angry voices outside his bedroom last night could have made a shrewd guess as to what was going on.'

He smiled. 'I have the guest room across from Hubert's until my roof is fixed, so I got the full benefit of their argument.'

'He has asked me to marry him.'

Wolf looked at me sharply. 'And you have agreed?'

I shook my head.

His sigh was of relief. 'That is good. Do you love him?'

Again I shook my head and he laughed softly. 'You are bewildered by this proposal, are you not?'

'I haven't been here a week, I hardly know him!'

'Then I would advise you to get to know him much better before you give him the answer he wants.'

'Perhaps I never will give him the answer he wants.'

He gave me a shrewd look. 'Then I am sure you have also assessed how much there is to gain. You are not a greedy young woman, Rose, but think of it.' He made a wide gesture around. 'All this would be yours and his Roswal, your Thane, would be safely yours for ever.'

Pausing, he repeated, 'You have much to gain and you have been far from happy. This coming to Staines was—how do you say—the last straw, was it not?'

I could only surmise that this was an inspired guess, but as I desperately needed a metaphorical shoulder to cry on, I decided to tell him about Jack, that we had been lovers and my refusal to marry him had sent him off into the arms of another woman.

Wolf heard me out, sitting on his heels in the typical manner I had seen in so many Indians in Arizona, a stance that our white hamstrings find extremely painful after a short while, and unbearable to retain for hours on end. He made no comment.

As he listened he took a stick and idly drew patterns on the ground. It jolted me back into the past, to memories of the only other man I had ever seen do that: Danny McQuinn.

When I came to the end of my story, he said, 'You didn't marry him because of Danny, although you now have reason to believe he is dead. Is that not so?'

I looked at him eagerly, hoping that his psychic powers might still tell me the truth. But he said nothing, merely nodded towards Thane, stroking his head.

I didn't want to be reminded again of that first encounter and his theory. It was too ridiculous as well as too terrifying to contemplate the transmigration of a human soul into an animal.

This time our talk was ended by a whoosh of wings. I gave a scream—I still wasn't used to the unexpected entrances of Kokopele.

Wolf leapt to his feet. 'Ah, I think this is what I have been waiting for.' And turning to me excitedly, he said, 'He has news for me. Our calf has arrived. It is almost dark, we should be safe now. Come along, Thane.' For a moment he hesitated, about to say something and changing his mind.

This time I did the interpreting. 'May I come with you?'

He frowned and gave me a searching look as if he was rapidly weighing up whether or not I was fit to be trusted on such a dangerous mission.

'The fewer humans the better.' Again that consideration. I felt suddenly naked, for it seemed to assess not only my physical reliability but to reach into my soul too.

Finally he nodded at Thane. 'He will protect you. Promise you will move only when I tell you to—when it is absolutely safe.'

I agreed and the two of us, with our escorts of Thane and Kokopele, set off towards the fenced-off pasture.

Wolf carried no lantern this night. Presumably he was used to finding his way around in the dark, and on this occasion we were blessed by the presence of a cheerful, bright full moon. Like a lamp held by a guardian angel, speeding from cloud to cloud, to see us on our dangerous journey into that no-man's land, the domain of the white cattle.

CHAPTER EIGHTEEN

We had climbed two fences and reached the first copse of trees when the first rumbling sounds reached us.

Wolf held up his hand. 'Stampede,' he whispered.

We froze, the two of us and Thane, the falcon, our vanguard, no longer visible hovering far above.

The rumbling got louder, nearer. My heart thundered in unison as the very earth beneath our feet began to shake.

Were they coming our way?

My fear communicated itself to Wolf who took my hand, held it firmly as if I might rush off in terror.

Then suddenly all was silence around us. Not even a breath of wind. 'Have they gone?' I whispered.

'Yes. It's all over,' said Wolf sadly.

'I'm glad of that. We're safe to move.'

'Yes, we're safe. Nothing will touch us now.' Again he sounded sad, detached, defeated somehow. But, still holding my hand, he led the way, running swiftly to the next clump of trees twenty yards further afield.

Kokopele became visible; the bird and the moon were still with us. As we took shelter, the area exuded a choking animal smell of excrement and blood. I could hardly breathe and, releasing my hand, Wolf said, 'Wait!'

He went forward a short distance into the clearing, leaving me with Thane, who never moved from my side. It was as if he had been doing this sort of thing all his life, a complete contrast to his extraordinary behaviour an hour or two earlier.

At last Wolf returned. I expected that he would be carrying the calf. He was empty handed.

'It's all over now.'

'The calf—and its mother?' I asked.

He shook his head, looked around vaguely. 'I expect she's gone—back to the herd.'

'And left her baby?' I said.

His eyes were bright in the moonlight. 'Yes. Come and see. I think you have the stomach for this, Rose.'

I followed him to the patch of ground with that awful smell.

'The calf?'

He pointed to the ground. 'All that is left of him.'

I didn't understand, but looking closer I could see the trampled earth and nothing to indicate that there had ever been a newborn calf. Nothing but a few bones, bits of skin—and blood. Lots and lots of blood.

Kokopele was there, inspecting or perhaps, I thought with a shudder, looking for a free supper. Whatever it was, he looked satisfied as he flew onto Wolf's wrist and ruffled his feathers.

'What happened?' I asked.

'We had better get out of here, fast,' was the grim reply. 'Make no noise.'

Breathlessly, we reached the first clump of trees. We were about to move towards the still-distant fence and safety when Wolf held up his hand. 'We wait.'

'Tell me what happened. That stampede—did they kill the calf?'

Wolf shrugged. 'It was probably born dead, and the stampede is their usual way of disposing of their dead, beat them back into the earth from which they came, until no trace of them remains. More efficient and tidier than many human methods.'

'What of the cow—the mother?'

'She will have gone back with them.' He sighed. 'Hubert will be disappointed. He had set his heart, and I suspect his pocket too, on a calf for his rich rancher in Texas.'

'Surely there will be other calves?'

'Ah, there's the problem. There hasn't been a newborn for a couple of years and that really troubles Hubert. You see, there are a dozen cows but only one bull.'

'Only one male?'

He shook his head. 'Only one bull, Rose. One king bull who alone serves all the cows. And if there are no calves then the indication is that the king bull is either old or is sterile.'

We moved on across the pasture. 'You understand? No one can go close enough to inspect the cattle, but it looks as if Hubert's hopes are in vain and we will have to get another young bull from the original Chillingham herd. And that will not be easy.'

Suddenly there was a noise, the sound of hooves, and out of the dim light, a solitary white shape hurtling towards us.

I knew instinctively, before Wolf shouted out, that this was the cow, returned to search for her lost calf.

For us, there was no place to shelter. We were trapped in the open.

Wolf threw me to the ground, threw himself on top of me. 'Don't move. Play dead. Our only chance.'

But something was happening. The cow had come to a slithering stop, her impetus dislodging chunks of earth and throwing them into our faces. I looked up, trying not to cough.

Thane? What of Thane?

He was standing a few feet away from the cow, facing her. Her head was lowered, pawing the ground, snorting, her horns glistening, ready to charge.

Thane, oh dear God, she'll gore him to death.

And then that miracle happened again. She raised her head, considered him, her tiny eyes gleaming. Another snort, less angry this time, and then a final flourish of horns and, turning slowly, she raced back the way she had come.

Wordless, we rushed forward, and with Thane at our heels we leapt the fence. Once we were safely on the solid ground of Staines again, I put my arms around Thane's neck and hugged him, very near to tears. What is the appropriate thing to say or do for an animal that has just saved your life?

Wolf watched us. Enigmatically. For he alone knew the answers that were beyond me.

After I gave Thane a final hug, we left him somewhat unwillingly in the stables. Walking towards the house I asked: 'What will happen now about the calf?'

'Hubert will insist that I find him a new young bull without, of course, telling me how I am expected to achieve this minor miracle.'

At my expression, he laughed. 'Now I am exaggerating. There are guardians of the famous Chillingham herd and with their help and experience as well as, I imagine, a purse from Hubert, a young bull will be extracted and brought to Staines. I doubt whether he will be left to challenge the king bull as would happen in the wild. Someone will just get rid of the old one, efficiently, with a rifle,' he added bleakly.

'Poor thing. How sad.'

'But very efficient. Hubert will not tolerate delays, and with the new king bull he'll want to see some brave new calves for America.'

'And that is where you come in?'

'Yes. Once again.' He didn't sound very enthusiastic at the prospect.

We had now reached the front door, where Hubert was waiting. We followed him inside.

'The calf?'

'No calf, Hubert. I'm sorry,' said Wolf.

'What happened?' he asked shortly.

'Born dead,' was Wolf's reply, sparing him the details.

'Damn, oh damn. I had such plans. I had the next few weeks all worked out. A dairy cow from the village to feed it, and once it was strong enough—'

He left the rest unsaid. Wolf filled in the details later. The calf would have been sent with the dairy cow as its surrogate mother on the long hazardous sea voyage across the Atlantic and thence across land to Texas.

My imagination failed to provide a happy ending for the poor wee creature. A mad scheme, and the likelihood of its survival across America from east to west seemed beyond reasonable hope.

Now we both looked at Hubert, this man who expected the whole world to turn according to his bidding, and that included the birth of a white calf.

And, as if aware of my presence for the first time, he turned and said, 'You shouldn't have allowed Rose to go with you. It's far too dangerous.'

'I asked to go.'

He looked at me, shook his head as if I had said something quite idiotic. 'I think you should go to bed now, Rose. It's very late,' he added sternly, as if I was a little girl who had disobeyed him and stayed up long past her bedtime.

I was certain I would never fall asleep with the day's terrible images pursuing each other relentlessly across my mind, but welcome oblivion descended at last.

Which was just as well. When I awoke again it was to discover that I had not been the only one whose life had been in danger.

The Destroying Angel had claimed its first victim.

*   *   *

The kitchen was in uproar.

Mrs Robson was in tears. Wolf and Collins were there, the former trying to comfort her. There was no sign of Hubert, who was closeted in his study with the doctor, as the story was pieced together.

Cedric had staggered into the kitchen and collapsed in the housekeeper's bedroom at four that morning, being violently sick and screaming in agony. Mrs Robson rushed to alert Hubert, who had been somewhat difficult to rouse. I guessed that was because he had been drowning his disappointment over the dead calf and all those dollars invested in it.

He could have allotted the task of going to Alnwick for the doctor to Wolf, but had manfully ridden off himself.

By the time they returned, it was already too late. Cedric was dead.

The doctor took one look, a quick examination. 'Poisoned mushrooms, most likely.'

This raised a storm of indignation from Mrs Robson, who informed him indignantly that they were picked only yesterday morning and made into soup immediately.

'Excellent soup, Mrs Robson,' Hubert nodded vigorously. 'And we're all still alive and well, doctor. Everyone enjoyed it,' he added in happy reminiscence.

I exchanged a glance with Wolf, who shook his head, and I refrained from mentioning that far from enjoying Mrs Robson's soup, I had had an almost fatal encounter.

Hubert's reassurances, however, did not deter the doctor, who read us a stern lecture on the dangers of picking mushrooms for amateurs lacking scientific knowledge and then irresponsibly turning them into soup.

Mrs Robson, despite her distress, was outraged. She pointed out that she had been picking mushrooms since she was a child of twelve and had never poisoned anyone yet. She knew what she was doing all right, she added scathingly.

I listened, unimpressed. I could have told

them the whole shattering truth about my own experience.

I had not a moment's doubt that Cedric had been murdered.

But why?

Well, I was to find out the answer to that in time.

And by whom? That was still part of a larger, complex and dangerous puzzle. It swept aside all reason for interviewing Lily Craid's railwayman husband, now an unlikely suspect.

What I still did not realise was how far I was into the labyrinth, or that I had unwittingly passed the point of no return.

CHAPTER NINETEEN

Cedric's body was lying in Mrs Robson's room. He could not remain there or be buried from Staines Manor. When I asked why not, she said that it would not be proper, for his station in life. The hint was that his doubtful parentage ruled him out of such a privilege.

Maybe she was shocked by my expression. Besides, she said, there was no longer a church in Staines since the pit closed, and the Staines' private chapel had been disused since a disagreement with a previous incumbent. The church-going inhabitants now had to walk the two miles into Alnwick and back again.

189

However, there was a kirkyard still in Staines where many wished to bide their time until the last trump, and poor Cedric had to be taken to his own home in the village to await burial. She would make all the funeral arrangements.

'The old priest at Alnwick,' she continued, 'used to give services at Staines Chapel. Long retired, but I visit him from time to time and I'm sure he would say the words over poor Cedric. He would remember him as a little bairn.'

And with terrible realisation dawning once again, throwing her apron over her face, she began to sob noisily. Poor Mrs Robson. I put my arms around her.

I could sympathise. I knew what she was feeling. The guilt of not having cared enough for her would-be nephew who had met such a tragic end; who, now and forever, would be known not as 'that young villain' but, with all sins and misdemeanours wiped out by his tragic death, would be deified as 'poor Cedric'.

Wolf came in, asked if there was anything he could do. The situation was explained to him and he said, of course, he would take Cedric's body back in the cart to the village.

So it would all be arranged, his few drinking cronies notified as he had no relations. This brought new floods of tears from Mrs Robson. 'There's so much I could say, but I dare not—I dare not,' she moaned, in the manner of one beside herself with grief.

I offered to go with them down to Cedric's home, and I must confess that it was not only out of sympathy for the distraught housekeeper, but also because I had an idea that there might be some clues as to how Cedric had met his end.

Suddenly I wanted to see him.

'You're not afraid?' asked Mrs Robson. I shook my head, seeing no need to tell her or Wolf, who knew already, that dead people, whatever their race, were no novelty to me.

I followed her in and we both looked down solemnly on the young face I had never liked in life. Now death had taken away the mockery, the leering expression that had irritated me, and left only the marble effigy of a very handsome young man, almost noble in bearing.

A statue somewhere? The shooting party came vividly to mind, the glimpse of the Duke and his entourage—then just as quickly vanished.

'Would you like me to come with you?' I asked.

'Oh, Mrs McQuinn, would you do that? I'd be so grateful—that is, if you're not too busy.'

Wolf gave me an approving glance and left to talk to Hubert and bring round the cart, saying that he would deliver Thane to Miss Kate in his usual daily routine.

By the time I came downstairs, dressed and

ready to leave with them, Wolf was driving the cart and, in the back were the white-sheeted passenger and Mrs Robson who, with a sudden return to practical matters, was discussing undertakers and coffins and laying-out clothes.

The doctor had said the police would need to notify the coroner. They would have to be informed of the name of the deceased's next of kin. As Mrs Robson could not honestly claim that, she had told him she might come across something in his lodging—papers or letters that would reveal his parentage—a suggestion that also suited the purpose of my visit, but I hardly listened.

Something was worrying me, something that should have registered with Rose McQuinn, Lady Investigator. True, I was horrified and shocked by Cedric's death, far more than I would have imagined for a young man I had frankly disliked and avoided. Perhaps I was feeling guilty about that now, for whatever had been his real nature, that someone so young should have met with such a vicious and unnecessary end was an outrage.

But was it an accident? Always a greedy lad, ready to snatch up any food left lying in his auntie's kitchen, had he accidentally picked up the wrong soup? Or had he been deliberately poisoned, as would have been my intended fate had Thane not intervened?

Cedric's lodging looked little more than a derelict barn from the outside, but the sight that met us inside, as Mrs Robson pushed open the creaking door hanging by its one creaking hinge, was sordid in the extreme.

At first glance, we saw papers, clothing, piles of dishes, cracked cups and plates with the remains of food scattered everywhere. Added to that, a pile of unwashed linen and a rough unmade bed in the corner.

'Did he always live like this?' I asked.

'Like a rat's nest, isn't it?' Mrs Robson shook her head. 'I've only been here once before. He had a bad cold and I came to bring him some of Mr Rider's herbs. Didn't know the meaning of tidying or keeping a place clean, the poor lad. Knew no better. There's folks like that everywhere. He's not alone in his bad housekeeping,' she said, almost by way of apology.

But what Mrs Robson had not observed was that although there was little furniture, someone had been here recently and in a great hurry. True, Cedric's agony might well have accounted for an overturned chair and a table lying on its side, but he would hardly have been in a state to pull open drawers in the table, a cupboard and a decrepit sideboard and scatter their contents on to the floor.

All the indications were that his lodging had been visited by an intruder whose very hasty search had been interrupted.

Someone looking for something. And I could hazard a guess to what that vital something was. But had they found it?

I found part of the answer as, leaving Mrs Robson and Wolf to their sad task and deciding that I could be more gainfully employed with a sweeping brush and duster, I went into the tiny scullery, which had been adapted from a large cupboard.

There were no dusting cloths but in the dark corner of a top shelf I noticed a pot of glue and some newspapers, out-dated editions of *The Times*, surely odd reading material for Cedric. Removing them revealed a pair of scissors, and a substantial part of the solution to Hubert's problem.

As I reappeared, Mrs Robson snatched the sweeping brush from me. 'You're not to do that, Mrs McQuinn. I'll attend to what's necessary. Now, off you go.'

As I stepped out of the door, Cedric's friend Jock rushed over, looking considerably shaken.

'He was sick and in terrible pain when we were having a pint. Said he felt like he was dying and wanted his auntie, so I helped him over to the house. I didn't take it serious like.'

He looked as if he was going to burst into tears and I realised then just how young he was too. I murmured condolences and he said how greatly Ceddy would be missed, what great times they had together, particularly on a Saturday night when they took the train to Newcastle, where there was more life than in dreary old Alnwick.

And that, I decided, accounted for the postmark too. I was so deep in thought as I walked back through the village that I almost walked past Grace. With the speed at which news, bad and good, seemed to travel through Staines, she had already heard about Cedric. She made the usual hushed-voiced comments and put on a suitably sad face, the way people so often do about irritating persons suddenly transfigured and made noble by violent death.

'Bit of a lone spirit was Cedric. Got into bad company, like yon lad Jock. Tearaway, he always was, even as a bairn. Now he works for the gardeners up at the Castle—sometimes. Mostly he's bone lazy, lolling about and looking for fresh mischief to get into.'

She sighed. 'Poor Cedric, he was fond of his auntie, as he called her. Now she has the whole burden to carry. She won't be the only one to miss him, either. That young Kate, up at the house—he was quite gone on her.'

I must have looked surprised and she laughed. 'They didn't know what was going on under their noses. Not that Cedric had much hope there—Hubert would never have given his blessing. Not with her an heiress, if anything happens to him.'

I said I'd only met Cedric a couple of times. I had no idea there was anything between them.

She made a face, looked uncomfortable, obviously not wanting to say too much about the dead. 'Having no parents made a difference to them, drew them together, and they were both so young.'

'What of his father? I wonder if he's still alive.'

Grace nodded. 'No one had ever heard of Mr Smith, the surname he claimed. Most likely his mother was a servant in some big house in Alnwick and the master had his wicked way with her. Happens all the time. Cedric was a handsome lad, he had a look of the better class, I always thought.'

Those had been my thoughts too, seeing him lying dead.

As she made casual remarks about the weather and asked how long I was staying at Staines, I noticed, rapidly approaching, a tall, thin man, wearing a policeman's uniform and a purposeful expression.

'Ah, here you are, Grace. I went to the house, thought I'd missed you—'

She turned round. 'Derek! Your fault, you always descend on us without warning.' And introducing us she said, 'Meet Sergeant Derek Sloan, Pete's brother.'

I had noticed the stripes as he touched his helmet and bowed politely.

Grace asked: 'What brings you here today?'

Derek glanced at me and said: 'Police business, Grace.'

His voice held a note of warning, which Grace ignored as she said slyly, 'I know why

196

you're here, or at least I can make a good guess. Derek is investigating Cedric's death. He'll tell you all about it himself, I'm sure,' she added proudly, before giving an anxious look towards the teashop. 'I have friends to meet—I'm late—gossiping as usual.'

Dashing away, she turned and said, 'Look in on your way back, Derek, if you have time. And, Mrs McQuinn, do come and see me any time, if you have any problems I can help with.'

The sergeant smiled down on me. That wasn't difficult, as he was over six foot tall. 'Glad to meet someone from the house, Mrs McQuinn.' He put his head on one side in an interrogating manner that evoked memories of Jack Macmerry and made me wonder, do all policeman have such penetrating eyes? Was it part of the necessary equipment along with the uniform?

'Are you heading in that direction?' When I said yes, he nodded. 'Then perhaps I might accompany you?'

As we began walking, he asked how long I had known Grace. Saying we had just met, he looked surprised.

'You sounded like old friends. Of course, Grace is like that. Very caring. Some might even say a little nosey,' he added with a laugh. Remembering her parting remark, I wondered what problems she thought I had on my mind.

'Can you tell me anything about this

unfortunate accident?' Sloan asked.

I had expected the question. 'In what way, Sergeant? What is it you wish to know?'

'Did you, by any chance, witness the incident of Mr Smith's collapse?'

'Hardly, Sergeant. It was four in the morning and I was in bed, asleep.'

He sucked in his lower lip thoughtfully. 'Of course. I observed you leaving his lodging just before you met my sister-in-law.'

'Cedric was a stranger to me, Sergeant. I have only been in Staines a few days and encountered him a couple of times working in the grounds. I merely went this morning to support Mrs Robson. She was very upset.'

Sloan nodded. 'So I observed, poor lady, when I took a look around myself. Some kind of relative, I gather.'

'Cedric called her his auntie, but I believe that was more by adoption than by blood.'

A pause, then he asked. 'Might I ask, did anything strike you as unusual in any way?'

'Since that was the first and only time I had ever seen inside Cedric's lodging, I was taken aback by the general untidiness—a certain squalor, to put it mildly.'

He laughed. 'You are obviously far too young to have lads of that age about the house, Mrs McQuinn. I can tell you, boys take a longer time to house-train than our police dogs.'

I smiled. If he was hoping for information

198

regarding Cedric's accident from me, he wasn't going to get it. Discretion guaranteed; lady investigators didn't speculate—they kept their mouths closed until they were paid to open them.

The conversation turned to Edinburgh, which Sloan had visited on occasion. I refrained from asking if he had ever encountered Detective Inspector Jack Macmerry, or mentioning my own interest in crime, domestic and otherwise.

As we neared the house I left him to his official business, of getting statements from members of the household, so that Cedric's death could be filed away as accidental.

Or was it? And would he go back to Alnwick satisfied with the result of his enquiry? An enquiry that had only skimmed the surface of the terrifying truth lurking behind those smooth walls.

CHAPTER TWENTY

I took Thane from the stables and, as we returned from our delayed morning walk, I met Sergeant Sloan leaving the house.

'A splendid dog you have there, Mrs McQuinn,' he said, as Thane politely allowed his head to be patted.

Yes, he was mine, I replied to the next

question. Good-days were exchanged and I went round the back of the house to the kitchen door in the hope that I could avoid Hubert. There was no escape; he was at his desk with the study door open, obviously awaiting my return.

'Do come in, Rose. Close the door, please.' He indicated a seat opposite him but, apart from that intimate look I found so embarrassing, he made no attempt to walk round and kiss me.

'Where have you been?'

'I went to give Mrs Robson a helping hand.' He frowned at that. 'She was taking Cedric back to his lodging, with Mr Rider's assistance, of course.'

He nodded, then said sternly, 'Surely they could have managed without subjecting you to such a distressing ordeal.'

'Not at all. Mrs Robson was very upset and I offered to go with her.'

'Really?' he said vaguely. 'Do you know, I don't think I've ever seen her shed a tear in this house in all the years she's been with the family. Doesn't sound like her at all.'

To change the subject I asked, 'What do you think happened—about Cedric, I mean? Weren't you shocked?'

He came to life, saying sharply, 'Shocked, of course I was shocked—I still am—that something like that could happen in this house. I can't imagine Mrs Robson being so

200

careless with the mushrooms—that's not like her either. She's so meticulous. Mushrooms!' he repeated. 'My favourite! Now I don't think I'll ever feel the same about her blasted soup!'

And thumping his hands on the desk, he added indignantly, 'We could all have been poisoned. You are aware of that surely, Rose?'

I could have told him the truth then, about Collins' attempt on my life that would have succeeded had it not been for Thane's timely intervention. However, I felt that such a remark would be unworthy. She was not here to defend herself and she had suffered—and was suffering—enough without me heaping on the final straw in her deteriorating relationship with Hubert.

'Cedric lived in frightful squalor.'

'Did he?' Hubert didn't seem interested and said angrily, 'As for that policeman's visit, wanting to take statements from everyone! I wish you had heard him. As if that young villain was a part of the family and not just a casual labourer on the estate.' He paused, and then went on, 'And I could have told him a thing or two about being blackmailed too.'

'That would have been inadvisable, Hubert. Once the police are involved—'

'I know, I know—no need for any warning. That was precisely my reason for engaging a private investigator.' He paused to give me a tender smile, which was rapidly followed by an angry frown. 'But having a policeman waste my

201

time with all his damned silly questions . . . I shall put in an official complaint to the authorities—'

I interrupted. 'You might be interested to know that I believe I have solved your problem, Hubert.'

'What problem would that be?'

'The identity of your blackmailer.'

He leapt to his feet. 'You have! That's marvellous. Who—'

I held up my hand. 'This is just a theory, but I think it's a plausible one and worth further investigation.'

He sat down again and stared at me blankly.

'Apart from the general untidiness, it was obvious to me that someone had turned Cedric's place upside down, either before or immediately after his death, searching for something.'

Silent for a moment, he shrugged, and then said slowly, 'I don't follow. What has any of this to do with my—problem?'

I told him about *The Times*, the glue and the scissors. 'As for the last note you found when you got home from the shoot—'

'Yes, yes,' he said eagerly. 'He was with the beaters at the picnic and they came back here to deliver the birds. My jacket was lying over a chair.' He gave me a look of triumph. 'Well, well, he had ample opportunity.'

'I believe he was your blackmailer,' I said. 'And his friend Jock mentioned that they went into Newcastle regularly, which suggests that they might well have been in the plot together.'

There was no response from Hubert, so I went on:

'I considered Cedric a prime suspect from the moment I heard that he had access to the house when he came regularly to see his auntie, Mrs Robson.'

'She should never have allowed—' he began indignantly.

I cut him short. 'Well, let us suppose that he came while she was absent in the village, or was working in another part of the house, and that he took the opportunity to see if there was anything besides food that might be worth pocketing.'

'You mean that little ruffian stole things from my house!' Hubert sounded shocked and furious.

I ignored that. 'Let's just suppose he also walked across the room to your study here, found the locked drawer and, in the hope of finding money perhaps, searched for the key and found those interesting photographs instead.'

Even as I said the words I wondered, not for the first time, why Hubert kept such dangerous photographs in his desk drawer when they could have been safely locked away in his dark room.

I asked him as delicately as I could.

He frowned, shrugged. 'I don't know. Must have had them out for some reason, meant to replace them. And forgot all about it. It wasn't until I got the first threatening note with the clipped-off corner that I realised they were missing.' He shrugged again, saying shortly: 'I'm a busy man, Rose.'

A careless one as well, I thought, considering the cost of that moment's forgetfulness. It now seemed probable that Cedric would have wanted to share his secret with one of his cronies, like Jock, especially when they had downed a few ales. If that was the case, then with his partner-in-crime dead, Jock had seized the opportunity of returning to the lodging and removing the photographs.

I decided that it might be worthwhile finding out who else had been in Cedric's drinking company that last night.

I would need to enlist Wolf's aid since ladies could hardly, with any respectability, present themselves at the bar in the local inn.

For the present, however, I would keep my suspicions to myself, but I said, 'I think I should warn you, Hubert, that Cedric might not have been acting alone and that you may not have heard the last of the blackmailer.'

'You don't think that young blackguard was working alone?' Hubert looked quite scared at this new peril.

At least this new evidence seemed to clear Collins of suspicion. I remembered Cedric talking to Kate at the shoot. Had Collins been aiding and abetting Kate in her secret dalliance?

'As a matter of interest, was Cedric the man you disturbed with Kate that night?'

He stared at me, then said shortly, 'I don't know what you're talking about.'

I persisted. 'You said that the whole episode had been a charade. That Kate was pretending to be sleep-walking to meet a lover.'

He laughed. 'Oh, did I? Well, well, I made it up. Just trying to impress you with my detecting abilities.'

This was too much and I was about to tell him what I thought of that behaviour when sounds in the hall indicated that Mrs Robson and Wolf had returned.

Hubert stood up. He seemed glad of the interruption and said hastily, 'We'll talk of this later. I have to speak to Rider and I want a stern word with my housekeeper regarding her soup.'

'Don't be too hard on her, Hubert. She's suffered enough for one day.'

'Hmph,' he said as I left him.

Thane would be with Kate now for his daily dose of boredom, so I wandered out into the grounds. Glad to be free of the house, I found that rustic seat with its bird's-eye view of the village including the tiny kirkyard where Cedric would be buried.

Still angry with Hubert, I wondered if Kate

had been telling the truth. She seemed so genuinely scared. Had she really been in danger from a killer? And why had I allowed myself to be taken in by Hubert's explanation of a would-be lover?

So taking out my sketchbook, the back of which had become my case logbook, I brought it up to date with the dramatic events of the last twenty-four hours.

How cold they seemed in practical, casual words. How different to the stark terror of reality.

*   *   *

I had just closed my book when Hubert approached, the last person I wanted to see.

'I thought I would find you here. My favourite place, too. Isn't that extraordinary?' With that endearing smile, he indicated that I make room for him. I could hardly refuse, and he sat down beside me, too close for comfort.

Before I could resume our interrupted conversation and express fully my annoyance, he said, 'I am going across to Holy Island to take some photographs for a magazine article. I must seize the chance. This mellow weather is perfect, the lighting so dramatic. Would you care to come with me, Rose?'

The question was wistful and without waiting for my reply, in the manner of a grown up addressing a small child, he went on, 'This

206

has all been so distressing for you, my dear. I am sure the change would do you good.'

Pausing for a moment, he continued: 'I have another reason. There is an old clergyman I should like you to meet, Rose. He was a friend of my father's, fell on hard times, and I heard recently that he is now living on the island. My informant alerted me to the fact that he has been in poor health, so I have decided to offer him a refuge here with us, as winter can be severe on the island. Do you agree?' he added anxiously.

I did not see how his old friend's winter quarters should concern me as I intended that Thane and I should be safely back in Edinburgh long ere the first snowflake fell on Staines, but I said I thought it was a good idea.

'Excellent. I thought I might even give him a living and a small pension.'

Looking at Hubert then, I decided this was a new caring side to his character.

Wolf Rider was also to accompany us to Holy Island. He had invited himself along to bring back herbs for Kate's medicine.

I didn't think Hubert was best pleased by this arrangement, but I remembered that Wolf had made the suggestion earlier that we should go together. I confess that I was glad he would be with us to divert Hubert's amorous intentions, if intentions there were, since I also learnt that it was very easy to be cut off by the tide on the island if one didn't look sharp. And if that happened, there was no alternative but to stay overnight. That was the last thing I wanted.

Hubert was saying, 'We should go directly. I shall need to find out about the tides. But I believe Rider has a tide-table. We don't want to be cut off—stranded.'

The look he gave me hinted that nothing would suit him better as he added: 'There is nothing urgent to keep me here. I have Rider's assurance that there are no new calves imminent. When we return I shall have to negotiate with Tankerville at Chillingham Castle for permission to extract a new young bull from the herd.'

I presumed he meant for Wolf to extract a new bull calf, as I could not imagine Hubert undertaking such a dangerous task.

*   *   *

Later that day I collected Thane from Kate's room. She looked sadder than ever, staring out of the window, and hardly turned her head to acknowledge my greeting. Collins gave me an angry look and I didn't linger.

Wolf had almost finished repairing the roof of his bothy, and today he had a helper. 'This is Tom,' Wolf shouted, as he leapt down to talk to me.

'Tom is putting on the final touches. He is a great improvement on my last assistant,' he said sadly, remembering Cedric. 'Used to work down the pit here in his younger days. Can turn his hand to anything, the whole village is constantly at his door. His fame has spread as far as Alnwick too. And look, Rose,' he said, steering me round the back. 'What do you think of that?'

'That' was a bicycle, older, shabbier than mine. Held together here and there with pieces of wire, it had once been pride of possession to someone in its early days.

'Belongs to Tom. He has been teaching me to ride,' he added proudly.

Hearing our voices, Tom looked down from his perch on the roof, hammer in hand. 'My trusty steed, miss. Mr Rider needs no teaching from me, goes like the wind already. Seen you on your machine in the village, miss. Made quite a stir, it did. Not many women in these parts have bicycles—scared of them, they are.'

'Don't blame them,' Wolf whispered. 'I'm better on a horse.' And, looking back at the roof, he said he was hoping to move back within the week.

When I told him that Hubert had invited me to go along to Holy Island, 'A good idea,' was his only comment.

* * *

Kate did not appear at dinner that evening and when Holy Island was discussed, it became quite obvious that Hubert could not conceal his disappointment at the prospect of Wolf's presence.

Collins leant over, whispered something urgently to Hubert, doubtless asking him if she could come too, but he said shortly, 'Of course you cannot come. Who would look after Kate? We might even be gone for a couple of days. Who knows?'

At the mention of a possible stay overnight, she looked narrow-eyed at me, as if it was my fault—part of a plan to seduce Hubert, high tides and all. She was very subdued and even tearful for the rest of the meal. I couldn't help being sorry for her obsession with Hubert, which I felt was driving her to the threshold of madness.

'We can take Roswal with us,' said Hubert, and to Wolf: 'Are you sure you want to come? Can you spare the time?' he added weakly.

In reply, Wolf assured him that this visit was necessary. In fact, he should have gone a week ago as his herbs for Kate were getting low. They did not last indefinitely. Once their freshness was gone, so did their restorative powers diminish.

Kate's welfare was the one indisputable matter that Hubert could not counter. He knew he had no argument but I guessed that he gave in with mixed feelings about having Wolf with us.

As for me, I had no misgivings.

I was just glad that I wasn't going with Hubert alone. I had the feeling that Wolf read my mind and was making sure that I would not be compromised.

CHAPTER TWENTY-ONE

We set off early the next morning, with Wolf's guidance on the tide-tables. It was a beautiful, crisp, early autumn day, still sunny and warm, and we travelled in Hubert's carriage, with Wolf driving. Thane was in the back, alongside the bulky photographic equipment and my bicycle.

Hubert was a little taken aback by my insistence that it accompany us—I thought secretly, but did not put into words, that it might come in handy for a hasty departure.

We left the carriage outside the local inn, where Hubert was to meet his reverend friend that afternoon once the good light he needed for photography had faded. Shouldering tripod and camera, he set off towards the Priory and seemed disappointed when I declined his offer to accompany him, saying that I intended to make myself useful by helping Wolf gather his herbs, which had been left in the sea-wrack by the ebb tide at the shore.

At the shoreline, Wolf kicked off his moccasins and I removed my boots, carrying them strung round my neck. I wanted to paddle, to feel the sand in my toes. I hadn't touched the earth barefoot since my days with Danny in Arizona and I had forgotten how good it was. So exhilarating to feel free again, at one with the world of nature.

As Wolf gathered the sea-wrack he needed and I put it in a basket, he placed a small black bead in my hand.

'St Cuthbert's beads,' he said. 'The fossil remains of tiny sea creatures from prehistoric times. A link, so we are told, that rooted the starfish to the sea bottom. Legend says that the saint could work miracles and, during storms, his wraith could be seen among the storm clouds. There's a poem:

'"On a rock by Lindisfarne,
St Cuthbert sits and toils to frame
The seaborne beads that bear his name."'

We sat down on a rock to eat our picnic, such humble fare from Mrs Robson scorned by Hubert, who preferred to eat in style at the inn. Looking at Wolf, another holy man, telling me the story of a saint who could work miracles, and observing the devotion in Thane's eyes as he regarded his hero, I thought all three would probably have understood one another uncommonly well.

'From this small island, Rose,' Wolf concluded as he unwrapped a beef sandwich, 'from this very place, sprang all the elements of your Christian faith in Britain.'

212

And suddenly it would not have seemed at all remarkable had I looked up to behold the saint striding across the sands, staff in hand to give us a smiling blessing.

This hour of benediction was to stay with me; the tranquil sunshine, the glittering silver waves gently lapping against a boat moored alongside, sheltering us from the breeze, the seabirds' eternal cry above our heads. In harmony together and with nature. If only it could last forever and the world we had left never intrude again.

At last it was time to leave the crumbs to the sea gulls and head towards the inn to meet Hubert. As I stood up, Wolf gently dusted the sand from my skirt.

'Can't have you all dishevelled,' he smiled. Turning, my face touched his by accident and he smiled again, then kissed my cheek so gently it was almost an illusion, as if I had been touched by a feather and it wasn't a kiss at all, just another benediction.

Upright, the wind blew my unruly mop of yellow curls over my eyes and he brushed them back with a gentle hand, a gesture that I would have firmly rejected had it come from Hubert.

Then the moment was over, just the blink of an eye, yet sealed in that place in which memories remain forever young and never grow old or stale or bitter.

He gave me a helping hand, so warm and strong, over the sand dunes, laughing as we stumbled while Thane raced ahead, leaping over the rough grass, his mouth open, joyous, almost laughing too; glad to be with the two humans who mattered most in his strange world.

At the inn, that other world, harsh and real, awaited us.

Hubert and his old friend were seated by a table in the window. The room, drably brown with a spittoon and sawdust on the floor, smelt of spilt ale and stale pipe smoke.

Wentworth Sandeman was introduced.

His appearance—unshaven, unkempt,—did not suggest a man of God and I had a feeling that Hubert had arrived just in the nick of time, since his friend's shabby clothes, stained and dirty, gave forth an unpleasant odour of unwashed linen.

When I looked at him closely I realised that the smile, the slightly unfocussed stare, spoke of a recent over-indulgence in wine or spirits. When he stood up to shake my hand he almost fell and Hubert, with an embarrassed laugh, steadied him.

I hoped the reverend would improve on knowing and that I'd soon overcome my first misgivings, which were not helped later by another encounter with Grace in the village.

'He won't be welcome back here,' she said, having met him heading for the local inn that he had wrecked and left under a cloud—of alcohol fumes—some years earlier.

Far from the respectable clergyman as reported by Hubert, who had fallen on hard times, it seemed those hard times came not from his devotions but from a devoted adherence to the bottle.

Hubert was announcing that we were ready to leave and he would be taking Reverend Sandeman to Staines.

But I wasn't ready to leave yet. I was enjoying my day.

'I would like to do some sketching in the Priory.'

'The Rainbow Arch is worth drawing,' said Wolf enthusiastically, 'and I still have more plants to collect.'

Hubert didn't seem at all pleased by this decision and, regarding us both sternly for a moment, he said, 'Then you must please yourselves. But let me remind you it is a long walk home if you miss the tide.'

He had presumably forgotten the existence of my bicycle in his carriage parked outside.

Wolf handed it down to me silently and we left them, Hubert escorting Sandeman, who was hanging heavily upon his arm and swaying quite a bit.

We parted at the Priory and I began to draw, entranced by the architecture, the arch still so imposing despite its ruinous condition. Soon I was completely absorbed in my task and lost to the world—and to Staines in particular—but at last a shadow fell across the page.

'That is very good, Rose.' It was Wolf.

'Must we go?'

'I'm afraid so. I must drag you away if we are to get back before the tide comes in.'

At that moment I would have happily settled for being stranded on the island that had so captivated me.

'Ride your bicycle, Rose. Thane and I will keep up with you.'

And so they did, and a pretty unusual spectacle we must have presented to the few people we passed by. A woman on a bicycle—surely a rare sight on the island—with a huge deerhound the size of a pony trotting ahead and Wolf Rider running alongside in that easy, tireless pace that I had seen Indian warriors maintain, hour after hour, day after day, in Arizona.

*   *   *

Supper was already on the table when we arrived back at Staines. Hubert gave us dark looks. At his side sat Reverend Sandeman, beaming, but looking remarkably untidy, a blot on the elegant surroundings. Collins seemed very subdued, and there was no sign of Kate.

Wolf produced some St Cuthbert's beads and shells he had collected for her. Collins said she would pass them on as Kate wasn't feeling particularly well today and had decided to have dinner in her room.

Was Kate distraught over Cedric's death? If this was a case of first love, oh, how that hurt! And I wondered if Hubert was remotely aware of the reason for her grief? Angrily, I thought again of his trickery, that he had made up the story of her assignation and had hinted maliciously that he knew the man's identity.

With so many questions still unanswered, so ended my one and only day at the seaside, while the storm brewing up on the horizon and whipping the trees into a frenzy was also the end of my calm.

*   *   *

I slept well that night and the next morning a letter arrived for me. It was from my stepbrother.

Hubert hovered, unable to restrain his curiosity since this was the first communication I had received during my visit. I told him that Vince was on an overnight visit to Newcastle and wondered if I could possibly meet him there. At such short notice, I was surprised that he had not sent a telegraph, until I saw the Royal seal and learnt later that it had been dropped off at Alnwick Station and delivered to Staines by special courier.

'Why can't he come here to see you?' Hubert demanded.

'I imagine it's because he's on Royal

217

business, as usual.'

That seemed to placate as well as impress Hubert. As for me, Newcastle seemed impossibly far away, but Hubert, now mollified by Vince's important role, came to the rescue.

Wolf Rider would drive me to Alnwick where I could pick up a train to Newcastle.

I murmured about the bicycle to Alnwick but he said sternly, 'Too undignified, quite unseemly for a young lady off to meet a member of Her Majesty's household. I am sure Vince would not approve.'

Despite the friendship Vince told me existed between the two men, I felt certain then that they were mere acquaintances bound only by the fact that both were in Her Majesty's service.

CHAPTER TWENTY-TWO

Although I had become quite accustomed to Vince's surprise visits in Edinburgh, when the Royal train paused on its way back and forth to Balmoral and Her Majesty released him for an hour or two, a meeting in Newcastle would be an exciting new experience, an unexpected treat well worth the two changes of train involved.

Fifty years ago such a journey would not have been undertaken lightly, but the railway line linking Scotland and England had opened a new era, a boon to major cities, and Newcastle had seen a rash of Royal visits to open new institutions, launch ships, open bridges, hospitals and the like.

Vince's brief message informed me that he was to accompany Mr Windsor on a journey from London to Newcastle, and that he hoped we could meet in the Station Hotel, where he would be staying overnight to address a learned society while Mr Windsor, having done his duty at a launch, would be paying a private visit.

After consulting Wolf's timetables, I bicycled into Alnwick, bought Vince a late birthday gift of slippers, and sent him a telegraph care of the hotel regarding my arrival. Meanwhile, Wolf decided that I should be taken in the carriage to Morpeth, where trains were more frequent.

And so it was that half an hour after leaving Wolf, I found myself staring out of the window at the approach to Newcastle. I watched out for the ancient castle, called the Black Gate, the great sweep of the Cathedral and Pilgrim Street—tramped many centuries ago by those on pilgrimage to St Mary's Chapel, in Jesus Mount, the holy place that was now a crumbling ruin, tucked away in the wealthy city suburb renamed Jesmond.

I stepped off the train, and emerging from the wreath of smoke I was most impressed by

219

the station's cathedral-like magnificence. It had been built in celebration of Stevenson's steam train, which replaced, with what seemed like unbelievable comfort, the long tedious journey by stage coach to York and, with several other stops at coaching inns, along the way to London.

I looked for that familiar face in vain. Vince was not there to meet me. Before uncertainty could extend into panic a gentleman, obviously a station official by his impressive gold-encrusted uniform, was heading rapidly in my direction. Bowing, he glanced around in some confusion. I realised his problem. I was the only lady travelling without even a maid.

'Mrs McQuinn? You are alone.' His eyebrows rose in surprise. 'Dr Laurie has requested that I escort you to your hotel.'

A somewhat menial task, I felt, to be imposed upon him, and quite at odds with his elegant attire.

'Your luggage, ma'am?'

More shocks for the poor gentleman as I handed him a rather shabby leather container, which was considerably battered by its usual sojourn in my bicycle's saddle bag. With an ill-suppressed sigh of disapproval, he took it from me. Obviously this was not the quality of luggage that he had expected, nor was I quite the lady of quality his duty as escort had anticipated. He led the way through the station and into the entrance of the hotel, where eager faces in reception followed our progress up well-carpeted stairs to the first floor.

At either side of the door sat two very large, solemn-faced gentlemen. Despite lacking uniforms, they had the undeniable look of guards.

One tapped on the door.

It opened and there was Vince. As always he grinned, gave a whoop of delight, seized me in his arms and swung me into the air. A breathless return to childhood and, despite my giggling protests, it was no difficult achievement for a now rather stately middle-aged man whose little sister was less than five feet tall.

He closed the door, with a word of thanks. No tip, of course, was expected by the uniformed railway official. Such a gesture would have been undignified and an insult, especially when I took in my surroundings.

This was no ordinary hotel room but a luxurious suite of rooms. Now I understood the air of excitement in the reception lobby. It was not for Dr Laurie or his guest: a door opened and Mr Windsor emerged.

I had seen photographs and there was no mistaking that this was the heir to the throne. I beheld a vast, portly, well-corseted figure, with uncommonly small feet. Bearded, and with a port-wine countenance redeemed by remarkably fine deep blue eyes which were already surveying me in an expression I had previously despised in humbler males elsewhere.

An expression that any woman would immediately recognise, to put it crudely, as a question whether or not the lady might be bed-worthy and willing. For that, according to well-founded rumour, was still Bertie's chief concern. After all, he had little else to do with his life, as Vince subsequently explained by way of excuse, but open bridges, hospitals and institutions or launch ships.

All these activities were organised and briskly put into operation by a despairing Government to keep him in the public eye, since it was unlikely that he would ever become king. Especially as his imperial mamma, who led a much healthier and virtually cloistered life, seemed likely to outlive her eldest, reprobate son. Again according to hearsay, she had a reputation for keeping Bertie on a very tight rein where government prospects or important decisions were concerned.

Introduced as Mr Windsor, he took my hand and held it warmly, as I inclined my head graciously. The pseudonym dispensed with the necessity of a curtsey. However, as the Royal eyebrow twitched, I wondered if he found my reaction disappointing.

At my side, Vince shuffled uncomfortably, gave that suppressed cough that always declared embarrassment. He had not expected this sudden appearance from the inner chamber, lured by curiosity and, as I later learnt, the tales he had been told about me.

Young, attractive widows had long been considered the best Royal game; less dangerous than married women with irate husbands to be fended off with yet another Royal appointment, to Mamma's extreme displeasure.

Young virgins were equally, or perhaps even more, desirable, and were chosen strictly from the classes where an unfortunate pregnancy could be dealt with by a small favour or a hastily arranged marriage to some Royal menial—a footman or some fellow in the kitchen servant class. All very tiresome, of course.

And at that moment it was as if I could read the Royal mind, especially knowing the reputation that had gone before him. He was anxious to put me at my ease—make a conquest, for heaven's sake—a necessary escape from the boredom of another dreary Royal engagement at the local, rather dirty and smelly shipbuilders' yard.

I looked sternly at Vince, hoping I was mistaken—that Mr Windsor was not under the misapprehension that Dr Laurie had brought his young stepsister as an appetiser for His Royal Highness. But as I was being interrogated, quite pleasantly and genially, regarding my journey, an almost imperceptible shake of the head from Vince indicated his innocence of such a monstrous idea, as he later confirmed with many apologies.

It so happened that he had been as surprised as I was by the intrusion, since Mr Windsor was allegedly resting, having commanded that he was not to be disturbed and banished his valet to wherever hotel servants were kept until required.

'So you are residing with my old friend, Hubert Staines. Takes great photographs. Have you seen his ladies?'

He paused, head on side, with a wicked look in his eyes. 'Probably not, though I fancy you would not be as easily shocked as my dear mamma. After all, the good Lord gave us bodies to be admired and give pleasure to one another.'

A suppressed cough from Vince's direction and Mr Windsor threw back his head and laughed. A rather loud, coarse laugh, the kind one would associate with the hunting field or the gaming tables, rather than with Royalty.

He wagged a finger at me. 'I knew your father, Inspector Faro. We had dealings in his official capacity some years ago, y' know.'

'I did not know, sir.' Pappa was most particular about observing rigid confidentially and never discussed with us cases involving any of the Royal family.

Mr Windsor grinned. 'Is that so? He never mentioned me. Very commendable indeed. A stickler for truth and honesty. Mamma thought the world of her inspector, y'know,' he added, as if Pappa was dead, which he most probably was long ago to Bertie.

'Besides, you would have been too young to be interested in the goings-on of the grown-up world. Give my regards to Staines. Tell him, I haven't forgotten the incident at the card table, on my last visit—lost quite a packet.'

He bowed to indicate that the audience was ended and I felt Vince's hand on my arm.

'Enjoy your visit. Staines is a very fortunate man to have such beauty ready at hand. Ah, I see I have made you blush.'

I was not blushing but I managed a bow in return and as he made an exit, the 'Lady Investigator, Discretion Guaranteed' was already rapidly considering a new development.

Had I made an important discovery? Was 'Mr Windsor' the mystery visitor Cedric had hinted about? Was he the reason the photographs had been brought up from the dark room? Obviously it was unlikely that he would be blackmailing Hubert, but if by any chance the stolen photographs involved His Royal Highness—or one of his mistresses—the scandal that would ensue if such were to reach Her Majesty's eyes or were made available to the general public would be highly embarrassing, to say the least.

Such were my thoughts as Mr Windsor, his

curiosity about Vince's visitor satisfied, disappeared to continue his afternoon rest. However, I was delighted to be alone with Vince, to have a little time together, as we had a mere hour before the local train left for Morpeth where Wolf had promised to meet me with the carriage.

Vince did not know about Wolf Rider and was only mildly interested when I told him of our earlier meeting in Edinburgh and the strange coincidence that had brought us together again at Staines. I left it at that. Explanations would take too much time, time that was so precious and so fleeting in all our brief meetings.

'You're looking very well. So good of you to come all this way, Rose,' he added, hugging me again. 'Olivia sends her love and says I am to persuade you to come to London for a holiday and meet the children.'

All three of them, strangers to me, and growing fast as children do, I thought sadly. Promising to take up Olivia's offer, I wondered why he was with Mr Windsor but I knew better than to ask. As a junior physician to the Royal Household, the Queen seemed to rely on him to accompany, with vast quantities of remedial medicines, any members of her vast family should they be suffering from the mildest of indispositions.

Doubtless aware of my curiosity, Vince volunteered that Mr Windsor had been plagued recently by bouts of indigestion and other disorders of the stomach. A fact that did not surprise me, considering his vast girth and reputed appetite for food, wine and spirits.

'So I am here to have the powders at the ready after meals, and to make sure that he takes them regularly. Not a bad life, really,' he added with a grin, 'considering the life I would have had as a family doctor back home in Edinburgh. All thanks to Stepfather's good influence.'

'And to your own abilities, Vince,' I added sternly.

Vince shook his head. 'Inspector Faro just happened to have Her Majesty's ear on a case at the right time,' he insisted. 'What of you, Rose? Hear anything from Jack?'

I told him no, and I suspected he was sorry that Jack Macmerry and I had parted, but still had hopes that we might yet marry after all.

'And your dog—Thane? Is he happy to be back with his rightful owners again?'

I made this as easy as possible. 'He seems to have forgotten them, thinks he belongs to me now.'

Vince nodded, not terribly interested. 'And how is Hubert?'

I said, 'He is very well. Sent his best wishes, and hoped you would be able to look in at Staines.'

Vince gave me a rueful smile. 'Alas, we are heading in the wrong direction. But there might be a last minute change of plans—one can never tell with Mr Windsor—there have been hints of a lightning visit to the Northumberlands at Alnwick. But it would be brief indeed, and I certainly wouldn't be able to escape my duties. Tell me,' he added anxiously, 'how is the little girl—Kate?'

'The little girl, as you described her to me, Vince, is seventeen years old, a lovely young lady, who looks surprisingly healthy, in fact.'

This did not have the dramatic response I expected. Vince merely shook his head sadly. 'Poor Hubert. One can understand considering his tragic history—losing his wife and so forth. He is just being over-protective and still thinks of her as a little daughter. Besides, that glowing look, a fine complexion, is often a symptom of consumption.'

This was indeed a new slant on Hubert and Kate. He carried on, patting his rather tight waistcoat ruefully, 'When we reach middle-age, we tend to regard the young as children by comparison. Anyway, it is reassuring to hear your verdict on her present condition.'

I couldn't let it go at that, but I hadn't the heart to tell him that he had been misinformed by Hubert regarding the true reason for taking Thane to Staines. Should I tell him about the blackmailer?

At that moment I felt an urgent necessity to confide my fears, and Vince was closest to me. I knew from his situation with the Royals that he was also the soul of discretion, and no secret confided in him would ever be whispered to anyone.

But Vince no doubt had responsibilities enough and I did not want to add to them worries about my welfare. So I decided to tell him about the stolen photographs and Hubert's blackmailer, sparing him the details of Collins' attempt to poison me and Cedric's death.

He listened carefully, fingertips folded together, saying nothing, for all the world a physician in his consulting rooms. At the end he said, 'There might be an even stronger reason for their recovery. When our friend back there', he nodded towards the door through which Mr Windsor had disappeared, 'talked about Hubert's ladies, he obviously had seen some photographs and now I wonder— did he perhaps experiment with the camera himself on his visits to Staines?'

It was an interesting theory, which fitted my own suspicions regarding the photographs' presence in Hubert's study. I wanted to know more about those visits, but Vince held up his hand. 'I say no more than that, Rose. I have said quite enough.' And changing the subject, he continued, 'How do you get along with Hubert?'

'Very well. As a matter of fact, he has asked me to marry him.'

'What?!'

'Yes. He says he is in love with me—'

Vince seized my hands. 'That is not hard to understand, dear Rose.' He shook his head, suddenly speechless, then asked, 'And you have really just met?'

'Just a few days ago.'

He laughed delightedly. 'By Jove, such a conquest—that's wonderful!'

'No, it isn't, Vince.'

He stared at me, wide-eyed. 'You mean—you mean you have turned him down?'

'Exactly that. Even if I imagined I could ever be in love with him, I would certainly need more time for such a decision.'

Vince gripped my arm. 'Dearest Rose, I beg of you, think of the advantages before you say no. Hubert's a great fellow, a splendid ancient family. You couldn't do better, a great future, the prospect of a knighthood, a lovely home—'

I listened patiently. No mention of my career, or the vital matter of my feelings for Hubert. Alas, my stepbrother, in common with most men, regarded marriage as a woman's proper, and indeed, only valid role in life.

Vince was still eulogising as he put me on the train, and I promised him that I would do nothing rash, that I would think over carefully all those advantages he had painstakingly put before me.

It had been a remarkable day, one to remember. However, on the way back to Staines, Mr Windsor's remarks concerning

Hubert's 'ladies' were my main preoccupation.

Was the tearaway Bertie, Prince of Wales, also included in Hubert's images?

*　　　*　　　*

Wolf was waiting at Morpeth Station. I told him about my day and he didn't seem particularly impressed at my meeting the heir to the throne. His day's activities had been curtailed when Mrs Robson, cleaning a high cupboard, fell off a step ladder. She was in great pain, certain that her arm was broken, so Wolf had driven her to the doctor in Alnwick.

'A fractured right wrist, was his diagnosis. Unfortunately she's right handed, so the whole household is going to be disrupted. Hubert was very cross.'

'Cross—he hadn't hurt his arm!'

Wolf smiled, shook his head. 'Hubert is not very high on sympathy for others when it inconveniences him personally,' he said candidly.

We reached Staines village at five o'clock and I said I would walk back up to the house to collect Thane and then take him for a walk.

'Thane has been with me today. Kate didn't want him for some reason.'

There was no sign of Thane at the bothy. Tom's work on the roof was finished and he had also disappeared.

Wolf said, 'I expect he's gone with Tom. He

231

likes company. I never restrict his movements, you know. If he wants to wander about, that's in his nature.' And seeing my anxious expression, he added, 'Don't you worry, he'll be back.'

And so I climbed the hill and since I had a lot to think about, reviewing the day's events, I was in no hurry to return to the house, nor had I any wish to encounter Hubert at that moment.

I reached the rustic seat with its splendid overview of the village and, to my relief, confirming Wolf's reassurance, there was Thane, far below in the kirkyard, dancing around Tom, who was busily digging. *A grave for Cedric*, I thought. *How sad*.

Idly I watched the pair of them. Thane at Tom's side, getting between him and his digging. Tom trying to shoo him off, Thane barking and Tom obviously getting angry.

Such odd behaviour from the usually biddable Thane. It was obviously exercise he was needing, so I decided to remove him from getting in Tom's way by taking him for his walk.

Hurrying downhill, it took only a couple of minutes to reach the burial ground. Among its sad, lichened tombstones, a glimpse of Thane standing motionless by a mound of upturned earth.

'Thane!' I called, but he ignored me. Not so Tom, who came rushing over to the gate.

'That dog, missus, that dog of yours,' he panted breathlessly. 'He's just dug up a corpse.'

CHAPTER TWENTY-THREE

Tom looked pale and shaken. He gulped; 'I was trying to dig and he just wouldn't let me. Now he won't come away. He's back there, on guard like. I'll have to go to Alnwick, fetch the police.'

Grabbing his bicycle, parked against the railings, he shouted, 'See what you can do with him, missus, if you're not scared of skeletons. I'll tell Mr Rider.' And off he went.

Dead bodies were one thing and skeletons of the long dead quite another. I felt sick. Sick with apprehension as the full enormity of the situation struck me. Who could he have unearthed?

'Thane,' I called.

He looked briefly in my direction and then riveted his attention once more on the grave, standing stiffly, unmoving, like gun dogs I had seen 'pointing' at the shoot.

The grave wasn't very deep. Only his legs were hidden, and when I reached him and called again, he wagged his tail and jumped out to greet me, eager to share his discovery.

I had no desire to look any closer. Putting

my arms around his neck, I whispered, 'Who have you found?' as if he could provide the answer.

Wolf appeared, running swiftly towards us, jumping the fence, taking the short cut from the direction of the bothy.

Thane immediately ran to his side.

'What is it, Rose?'

'Thane has dug up a corpse.'

'I met Tom.' And pushing Thane aside he looked into the grave. 'A corpse—without a coffin.'

I shuddered. 'That sounds like murder, Wolf.' I felt nauseated, although the smell was not of death but only of freshly turned earth. Steeling myself for the worst, I glanced nervously over Wolf's shoulder. A skull, teeth showing.

Wolf, lacking my sensitivity, bent down and a moment later he picked up the skull. I didn't want to look closely as he shook off the loose soil and held it up.

Thane also lacked my sensitivity. Delighted, he watched, circling Wolf eagerly, I thought in dismay, for all the world like a dog being offered a juicy bone. And that it certainly was not.

'You've gone quite pale, Rose. Are you all right?' Then Wolf laughed and I felt angry. No need to make a joke of this horrible business.

'No need to be scared. This isn't a human skull. Don't you see?' He put it down and, as

234

Thane sniffed at it, tail wagging excitedly, Wolf took one of Tom's tools and removed the rest of the soil.

'Look, Rose. This is an animal's skull. In fact, to be more precise, it's a dog.' He held it out for my examination. 'When we dig out the rest, I think you'll find we have the bones of a very large dog. A deerhound, like Thane here, perhaps.'

And we both turned and looked at Thane, who was sitting down listening, head on one side, regarding us with a proprietary look of triumph.

'Tom said he wouldn't let him get on with the grave, kept getting in the way,' Wolf said. 'How did he know there was a dog buried here—in the kirkyard?'

And without one doubt, I knew the answer.

'Roswal.' I whispered. 'It's Roswal.'

Wolf looked up towards the house and whistled. 'Hubert's missing deerhound. Of course.'

'How long do you think he's been here?'

Wolf shrugged. 'Hard to say. A year or two, anyway.'

As he examined the skull, I asked, 'How did he die, I wonder?'

'Wonder no more, Rose. The answer is here.' And turning the skull towards me, he pointed. 'See, a bullet hole. Someone shot him.'

My mind was racing ahead. How was I to

tell Hubert and Kate that someone had killed their beloved Roswal and buried him, in the hope that he would never be found, in the disused kirkyard?

'I'll deal with this, Rose.' Wolf had shrewdly guessed my thoughts. 'You go back to the house. Take Thane with you. I'll wait for Tom to come back with the policeman, who won't be pleased to know the corpse has turned out to be a dead dog.'

Thane was happy to accompany me. He had the air of a job well done, an almost human swagger as he trotted ahead, while I was left to consider the enormity of his discovery and to find the right words to tell Hubert that someone had shot Roswal, the beloved deerhound he believed he had lost on Arthur's Seat three years ago.

* * *

It was not yet supper time. The door of Hubert's study was open. Sandeman was sitting alongside him at his desk; their heads were together, their voices low. They looked conspiratorial.

Hearing my footsteps, Hubert looked up, smiled, and called, 'Come in, Rose. Mr Sandeman is just leaving.'

The old man slid past me with an oily smile as Hubert pointed to the pile of papers. 'A lot of legal matters we are sorting out.'

Then, laying down his pen, he smiled. 'Welcome back, my dear. Had a good day? How was my old friend Vince—have you managed to persuade him to come and see us?'

I just stood there shaking my head.

'What is wrong, Rose? You must be tired, of course. Do sit down.'

I did so and he said patiently, 'Not time for supper yet. It may be delayed. You'll have heard from Rider about Mrs Robson's accident. Most unfortunate,' he sighed.

No sympathy, of course, I thought, as he added, 'I have to finish these, if you'll excuse me.'

Taking a deep breath, I said, 'Hubert, sorry to interrupt, but there is something I have to tell you—now, this moment—before we meet later.'

He threw down his pen, eyes gleaming. A look of triumph. 'You've decided!'

'Decided what?'

'To accept my proposal, of course.' He was about to spring to his feet and embrace me when I shouted: 'No, Hubert. This is about Roswal.'

As Thane was with me, he eyed him sternly and sighed. 'What has he been up to this time?'

'He dug up another deerhound—in the kirkyard.' And I stammered out the story.

Hubert listened silently. At the end I

paused, out of breath, and he threw down the pen he had picked up again.

'Yes, Rose. It is Roswal. I know. I shot him.'

I stared at him open-mouthed, horrified! 'You did—what?'

'I shot Roswal,' he said patiently. Then with a shrug. 'He was injured, sick—'

I yelled at him. 'Wait a minute—you killed Roswal. Then you tricked me—and Thane, pretending that you had lost him on Arthur's Seat and all the time you knew it was—a damned lie! That he was dead, here at Staines, buried in the kirkyard—'

'Where I knew he would be undisturbed,' Hubert interrupted calmly. 'Unlikely to be found, or so I believed,' he added regretfully. 'This is very unfortunate, Rose.'

'Unfortunate!' I screamed. 'Is that all you can say about it? You tricked me, Hubert Staines, lied to me. I'll never forgive you and what is more, I am leaving right now and taking Thane with me.'

Hubert held up his hand. 'Wait a moment, Rose. If you go now in a fury you will never know my reasons—and you will always wonder.'

That was true. 'They had better be good,' I said.

'Then please sit down and calm down. Right? Kate was very ill three years ago, not expected to survive. Roswal had an accident— he got onto the railway line and his back legs

238

were broken. I carried him home in the carriage. I knew he would die and I couldn't let anyone else do the job for me, so I shot him and buried him at night in the kirkyard, the day before I left for Holyrood.

'Kate had no idea about any of this and I didn't know how to tell her when I came back, so I invented this story about him having run away. She was so ill, believe me, I thought she was dying, and during the past months I believe we have Rider's treatment to thank that she is still alive.'

He paused, sighed deeply. 'One day, believing her days were numbered, I asked if there was anything, anything she wanted that I could do for her. She said all she had ever wanted after her mother and sister died was Roswal.

'Then I met Vince again. We had got along splendidly at Balmoral and when I visited him in London, I saw the painting of your deerhound, Thane. He had told me all about you being a private investigator. I was at my wit's end, being blackmailed about the photographs. And there you were, Vince's stepsister, who by a miracle also had a deerhound. It seemed such a marvellous coincidence that I got this mad idea.'

He paused. 'You know the rest. Roswal was my excuse for bringing you here—'

'Luring me here on false pretences, you mean,' I interrupted angrily.

239

He shrugged. 'Whatever you say. But can you blame me for taking advantage of such an amazing series of circumstances? However else was I to get someone here that I could trust to find my blackmailer without raising any suspicions?'

Then, with that smile I had thought so endearing, he leant over, took my hand, and said softly, 'How was I to know that I would fall in love with you? I vowed that, one day, when we were married, when I was sure of your love, I would tell you the truth of my little deception.'

Wrenching my hand away, I said furiously: 'A little deception, is that what you call it?'

He ignored my interruption. 'Please, dearest Rose, tell me you forgive me. I cannot let you go now; you mean the whole world to me. My whole future, the future of all you see around you here at Staines, depends on you becoming my wife.'

I stood up, lengthened the distance between us and said coldly: 'Hubert, you were being blackmailed. I believe I have solved that. Your blackmailer was Cedric. He is dead. Hopefully that is the end of the matter. If you receive any further threats, then you will have to find another private investigator. I am finished with you. That is final. And I am now free to go. Was that not our bargain?'

'You are turning me down?' His voice was cold, as if my response was incredible.

'That is right. I am turning you down. I am afraid, in view of all you have revealed regarding Roswal, I could never trust you again. Surely you realise that. You have destroyed any belief I had in your word. This monstrous deception, Hubert! Nothing but lies all along the line. You cannot imagine the agonies I suffered—that you put me through— believing that Thane was your Roswal and that I was about to lose him for ever, returning him to you here at Staines.'

'He is only a dog, Rose.' He sounded amused, contemptuous even, and that was the last straw.

'I came because you told Vince a lie. You told him that Kate was dying and allowed him to use that lie to persuade me. And what do I find? Another downright lie. Even Wolf says that although her lungs are delicate, it is possible that with care she should have a long and healthy life.'

'Rider doesn't know what he is talking about.'

'And nor do you, Hubert. As for me, I have had enough of Staines. I am leaving and taking Thane with me, and you can keep the fee for my professional services as an investigator.'

'I insist—'

'No. I do not wish to accept that either. You can consider it payment for your hospitality, my board and lodging here. The matter is ended. I wish to be free of any further obligation to you.'

As I stood up, ready to make a dignified and indignant exit, he seized my arm. 'That you will never be, Rose. I will never let you go. You belong to me.'

I laughed. 'Please don't be absurd, Hubert. I don't belong to anyone and certainly not to you.'

'So you think. But I will never release you.'

I laughed again, sprang away from him and said, 'Just try to stop me, that's all, and you'll soon see whether I belong to you or not.'

As I headed for the door, I heard a sound of scuffling and, flinging it open, saw Collins racing upstairs. She had probably heard every word and I thought that at least my decision to leave should make her feel happy. Her rival gone, Hubert could be hers now.

How wrong could I be? I was soon to find out the truth of the old adage, that two wrongs can never make a right.

*   *   *

It would be too late by the time I had packed and bicycled to Alnwick to catch a connecting train to Edinburgh. Besides, I could not go without seeing Wolf Rider again and telling him about Hubert's deception.

The more I thought of the devious way I had been tricked, the more indignant and angry I became. Too upset to face Hubert and

242

Sandeman across the supper table, for the first time I was not even hungry. Thane had been waiting in the hall while I was in Hubert's study, and I decided to keep him in my room that night.

I felt safer in his presence.

As we went upstairs I caught a glimpse of Mrs Robson in the kitchen looking very woebegone, her arm in a sling. Normally I would have rushed to her assistance, but as far as I was concerned now, Collins would have to help with meals, with fetching and carrying, as well as caring for Kate.

I did not really care what happened to them. Staines and Hubert and my brief sojourn here were already part of the past, for tomorrow at first light, I would leave before anyone in the house was awake. I would get my bicycle and go to say goodbye to Wolf Rider, who would have moved back into his bothy but, I suspected, would not be alarmed by an early morning visitor. Then I would head for the railway station and a train home to Edinburgh.

I felt quite jubilant at the prospect of being in my own home in Solomon's Tower and, despite some inevitable hunger pangs, I fell asleep only to be awakened by a fierce argument and a noisy banging of doors. It was still dark but the commotion suggested that perhaps Collins had not been so reassured after all by overhearing my rejection of Hubert's proposal.

At last there was silence and when I opened my eyes again it was to a happier sound, the dawn chorus. I packed hastily all I could take in my saddle-bag; the heavier items went into my travelling trunk. I struggled downstairs and deposited it in a corner of the gunroom. I would ask Wolf to take it in the cart to Alnwick Station and put it on an Edinburgh train for collection later.

With Thane at my side, and an unnecessary warning to silence, I opened the front door, where a spider had woven a gossamer web across the entrance overnight. It was like breaking out of a silken prison.

For a moment I hesitated. There was something else I must do before I left Staines for ever. That hundred guineas. I would never forgive Hubert for tricking me, however valid his excuses, and to take his money would be utterly repugnant.

So I took out the roll of notes, intending to leave them in his desk drawer with a note for him to find, but as I reached the study door, sounds from the kitchen warned me that I was too late.

The sound turned into an almighty crash, followed by a cry.

I seized Thane. I should have realised that, even injured, Mrs Robson would respond to the routine of a lifetime and get up at six in the morning. There was nothing else for it; I must go to her assistance. She might be hurt.

She wasn't but, one-armed and awkward, she had dropped the pan of porridge, which was now spreading rapidly all over the floor. As she knelt down, tearfully trying to mop up, she saw me.

'Let me do that,' I said as I helped her to her feet.

'I don't know what I'm going to do, Mrs McQuinn,' she moaned. 'I'm absolutely useless with my left hand and I've no strength in my left arm either. I broke it when I was a bairn and it's been weak ever since.'

She stood aside, but protested that I shouldn't be doing menial things like cleaning the floor. She never normally allowed animals, especially ones as large as Thane, into the sacred precincts of her kitchen, but this morning she was too upset to care. His presence ignored, he sped matters along by obligingly lapping up some of the spillings.

'Sir would be horrified if he saw you, Mrs McQuinn. He'd give me a proper telling-off. But God's truth, I don't know how I'm going to manage.' She touched the sling on her arm. 'Doctor says it'll be a week or two and that I'll have to rest it.'

She laughed harshly. 'Rest it, if you please. Not much rest in this house. Place will fall apart. Who's to do the washing, the ironing, not to mention the cooking, I might ask,' she moaned.

'Collins will give you a hand, I'm sure,' I

said by way of encouragement, but with little hope. My concern was immediately confirmed as Mrs Robson said, 'Well, I'm not sure. That Collins! She's far too high-and-mighty, and she's worse than useless in the kitchen. Besides, she's got more than enough to do—so she says—taking care of Miss Kate.'

'Someone from the village then?' I suggested weakly.

'Sir would never allow that. Not since that last girl—ages ago—he would never have anyone but me in the house. I'd be right scared. I have to watch my p's and q's—he'd send me packing, you know,' she added in frightened tones. 'And where would I get another job at my age?'

Poor Mrs Robson, all these years living under Hubert's reign of terror. And I remembered his ruthless treatment of Lily when she had worked here as a servant girl.

I offered to remake the porridge and thought it would be easy enough. I'd made many a pan in Solomon's Tower for Jack and me, but this had to be made precisely according to Sir's wishes, him being very particular about the amount of salt and so forth. Slicing the bread for his toast came under the same strict supervision.

As I carried the tray into the dining room, there was almost another nasty accident—the contents of the tray were heavy and they slithered dangerously on the smooth surface, but fortunately did not fall.

On my way back to the kitchen across the hall, I seized the opportunity of removing my saddle-bag from the front door and pushing it out of sight to be retrieved later.

I sighed wearily. So much for my planned escape from Staines. That was over—for today at least.

CHAPTER TWENTY-FOUR

As Mrs Robson rang the breakfast bell, Hubert and Sandeman appeared on the stairs and Thane retreated to his place in the hall.

He did not escape Hubert's notice. 'Shouldn't he be in the stables as usual, at this hour?'

'Don't expect to see our dogs before breakfast,' Sandeman put in cheerfully, but with slight admonishment, implying ownership which I bitterly resented.

I had hoped never to see Hubert again and did not mind distressing him in the least. He deserved it, but his good kind housekeeper was another matter. I could not rush off and desert that frightened, long-suffering woman to be at everyone's beck and call until she had suitable help.

I resolved to talk to Collins.

At the table, the two men were already

waiting and Hubert's look of smug satisfaction in my direction indicated that he believed he was forgiven. He asked if I had slept well, and obviously had not the least idea how near I had been to leaving that morning.

Wolf had returned to his bothy, Collins had not yet put in an appearance and Sandeman looked as if he had slept in his clothes. Unkempt, wild hair, eyes half-closed, he displayed all the symptoms of a man who was suffering from severe over-indulgence in fiery spirits.

Mrs Robson hovered, teapot balanced precariously between her left hand and the sling. I went to her assistance and apologising to Sir, she said that but for my help, no breakfast would have been ready on time that morning.

'You sit down now, Mrs McQuinn, the gentlemen can serve themselves.'

As Hubert bestowed an approving glance in my direction, I took a seat as far away from them as possible.

The door opened and Kate, still in her nightrobe, rushed in shivering. 'Where is she? Where is Collins?'

Hubert stared at her and she repeated. 'She isn't in her room. Her bed hasn't been slept in. And I need her.'

Mrs Robson, summoned by the disturbance, said no, she hadn't seen Collins since last night. Hubert shook his head. He hadn't seen her either. Which I knew to be a lie, as the sound of doors banging and their raised voices had awakened me.

'When did you last see her?' Hubert asked.

'She gave me my hot milk, said goodnight. Her usual time, about nine o'clock.'

'Perhaps she went out—down to the village,' Sandeman suggested with a beaming smile. 'Young woman like that. Probably has friends. Yes, I should think she has lots of friends—'

Hubert's crushing look silenced him. 'She didn't say anything to you, Kate, about going out?'

'No, she didn't, and she never goes out at night without telling me.'

I stood up and pushed my plate aside. 'I'll take Thane. See if she's gone for a walk in the grounds.'

Kate turned to me angrily. 'Not before breakfast. She hates walking at the best of times, and as for getting up early in the morning—!'

'That's very odd, then,' Sandeman put in. 'Isn't it?'

I thought it was odd, too, but decided that most probably, like myself, she had had enough of Hubert and, by a strange coincidence, our departures from Staines had coincided. A brave decision indeed for Collins, who must have succeeded in leaving before daybreak—not an easy task for a reluctant riser.

But it still didn't make sense. Kate followed me into the hall and I said reassuringly, 'I'm sure she can't have gone far. I'll bring her back.'

Kate gave me a withering look. 'She would have told me if she was going to leave.'

'Does she often go out at night?' I asked.

'Of course she doesn't,' was the indignant response.

'I just wondered, that's all, when you said she didn't go out without telling you.'

She bit her lip, shrugged uncomfortably. Definitely a guilty look.

Was she also aware of Collins' troubles with Hubert? Was she even a confidante? It seemed impossible that, unless she was a very heavy sleeper, she had not heard their angry voices last night. Especially as she slept in the room next to Collins.

She recovered and said firmly, 'Collins would never desert me, not after all these years together.'

'All right, I'll go and look for her. Perhaps she's only gone to the village for something—a surprise?'

Kate laughed scornfully. 'The local shop doesn't open until nine. Besides, who would she want to surprise? It isn't my birthday or Hubert's. There's nothing to celebrate.' At the foot of the stairs she said, 'I'll get dressed and come with you.'

She was shivering and I said, 'No. It's cold

and you might catch a chill. Besides I'll go faster on my bicycle.'

She stood at the banister, clinging to it, watching me leave. I felt very sorry for her as well as the missing Collins. Whatever the latter's emotional turmoil with Hubert, it was true what Kate said. She was utterly devoted to Collins, her only companion and friend since she had lost both mother and sister.

I could not shake off a very uneasy feeling and decided to consult Wolf Rider. But first of all, I checked the stables. The carriage was there, but then I hadn't expected her to take it, or either of the pony carts.

An idea came to me and, leaving Thane there with a promise to return for him later, I decided to question Kate again. Sitting at her window, she looked calmer. 'Did you find her?'

The answer seemed quite obvious, and I asked, 'Have you checked her room?'

I wanted to ask if anything was missing, in carefully chosen words, to discover if she had packed her possessions and gone of her own free will, or if she been removed by force.

'Of course I haven't checked her room,' was Kate's scornful reply.

'Shall we do that now?' I said.

She regarded me wide-eyed, about to protest. 'Oh, if you wish.'

I followed her, and the room was remarkably tidy. Kate looked round nervously and, opening the wardrobe with its few clothes on hangers, and slamming shut drawers, she said, 'This is quite useless. I never come in here and I have no idea what she has or what she would take with her. She has lots of clothes.' Going to the dressing-table, she continued, 'But her jewellery is still here.' And, pointing to necklaces and earrings, 'She loves jewels. Most of them were presents from Hubert.'

That she had left without them took on a sinister significance.

I asked, 'Has she any friends that she might have decided to visit?'

Kate looked out of the window as if expecting to see her outside. 'She has a friend who works up at the castle—I don't know her name, Collins just refers to her as "my friend",' she replied vaguely.

'The castle's a big place, Kate. A lot of people work there, have you any idea—'

'No,' was the firm reply. 'Just that she went there sometimes.'

That was not much help. I was puzzled by her disappearance but as yet not unduly alarmed, and relieved that Kate had calmed down. But after our search I had an odd feeling that she knew more than she was telling.

Had Collins fled to the castle to try to get work there? One thing was clear: whatever her destination, she would certainly never return to Staines or to Hubert.

She had suffered enough at his hands, although in truth it was as little his fault that she was obsessed by him as it was my fault that he was obsessed with me.

It is a sad fault of fate and the cause of much unnecessary heartbreak that we do not always have a choice about with whom we fall in love. I was lucky with Danny McQuinn that, eventually, I wore down his protests, that he was too old for me and not the marrying type. We then had ten years of a happy life together.

*   *   *

Wolf was up and about, already working in the little garden at the bothy.

'No, I haven't seen Collins. Come inside.'

So I decided to tell him the whole story, the sequel to Thane unearthing the bones of Roswal. And how shocked I was when Hubert admitted that he had shot him.

'As for his explanations, Wolf, he said he used Roswal to trick me and bring Thane here.'

Wolf shook his head. 'It seems to me that there are a few too many coincidences.' He paused. 'So you've decided not to marry him.'

'A decision was never involved. I never even considered it.'

He smiled. 'Very wise.' And frowning, he added, 'Now what about Collins? You are sure it was them you heard quarrelling last night?'

'It woke me up.'

Wolf considered this. 'From what Kate insists about Collins' behaviour and the fact that you were up before the house was stirring and did not see her, it seems an odd time to visit this friend Kate told you about.'

'And it would be a fair walk up to the castle.'

Wolf looked doubtful. 'There are plenty of carts on the main road at the crack of dawn going to Alnwick and to the castle. She could have got a lift and gone for a passenger train.'

He thought for a moment. 'A pity Kate wasn't more familiar with the contents of her room. What about the jewellery she left behind?'

'The answer to that is easy. If she was leaving Hubert, as I suspect, and had taken anything valuable he had given her, he could, if he was feeling vindictive, have raised a hue and cry and had her hunted down as a thief.'

Wolf shook his head. 'What an odd law!' And consulting the timetable on his wall, alongside that of Holy Island's tides, he said, 'We should check the railway station just to be sure. The first train to stop at Alnwick either way isn't until nine o'clock. That gives us half an hour. We can ride there. Fortunately Tom left his bicycle yesterday—had a puncture, which I repaired for him.'

'I didn't know you knew about such things.'

He grinned. 'Necessity is the great master,

254

Rose. Come along, Thane. You can run alongside. We might need you.'

We reached Alnwick Station in good time, Wolf with only the merest wobble, soon overcome. Among the passengers on opposite platforms, pacing up and down, awaiting the train south for Newcastle or north for Edinburgh, there was no sign of Collins, nor in the two waiting rooms.

When the Edinburgh train steamed in on time, I thought wistfully that Thane and I should have been boarding it, heading for home, but for Mrs Robson's accident.

The platform emptied and Wolf gestured from the opposite platform. I knew Collins would not be there either. As we bicycled back to Staines, I wished I could forget the sounds of that quarrel outside my door last night and throw off the increasing feeling that something had befallen her.

I saw Hubert at the front door, his carriage waiting. The forlorn hope that she might have returned in my absence was soon banished.

'Found her?' he asked. I said no, though surely that fact was obvious.

'Oh, I expect she'll turn up,' he said casually. 'I have business matters to attend to in Alnwick with Reverend Sandeman, so we'll keep a look out for her on the road.'

He did not seem suspicious and took the matter of her sudden disappearance amazingly lightly.

'Is this the first time she has disappeared?'

He gave me a hard look. 'I'm not quite sure what you mean by "disappeared". You make it sound very serious.'

'Perhaps it is serious.'

He laughed at that. 'Oh, come now. Collins is rather highly strung, you know.'

'Do you, by any chance, know the name of the friend she visits at the castle?'

'News to me. Wasn't aware she had any friends in high places.'

He laughed, amused at the idea. Angrily I thought that by rights he should at least have been morally more concerned considering their intimate relationship. But all I could detect was perhaps a sense of relief.

'I will look in at the village on my way back; try to get someone to help Mrs Robson.' He shook his head. 'Alas, I cannot guarantee that this will be successful. She is so particular, anyone I engage will cause endless trouble and we are all in for a very trying time.'

As usual he was thinking only of himself as he added, 'When Collins returns, I am certain she will be agreeable to helping Mrs Robson out for the short while until her arm is better.' He sighed and added sternly, 'Don't worry about Collins. She lives on her nerves.'

I wouldn't accept that excuse. 'She is in love with you, Hubert.'

'And I've told her that it is hopeless,' was the angry response.

'She told me, begged me not to marry you.'

'None of her business!'

'That's not true, Hubert. It is most definitely her business—as you are well aware.'

He sighed deeply. 'Well, I trust you disregarded her unwholesome advice.'

'Seeing that she has been living with you for some time—' He winced but could not deny it. 'She probably knows you much better than I do,' I answered sweetly.

'Dammit, Rose, this is getting us nowhere. All I am asking—I know you have told me you have made up your mind about marrying me— but I'd be very obliged if you could possibly see your way to remaining here until I get some help for Mrs Robson—or until Collins returns, whichever comes first.'

Pausing, letting it sink in, he said slowly, 'It must be obvious to you that Kate cannot manage on her own. She is much too frail. She needs someone to bathe her, to make sure she takes her medicines, to take her out sometimes in her bathchair. All I am asking of you, Rose, is a few days, that's all.'

Sandeman was in the carriage, leaning out, listening intently, and while I would have cheerfully refused Hubert anything he asked without a qualm of conscience, I could never refuse to help Mrs Robson.

As for Kate, I questioned Hubert's diagnosis regarding her medical condition, fast coming to the conclusion that Kate had been

257

talked into depending entirely on Hubert, for some reason of his own, since her mother died.

I had a feeling that there were hidden depths to Miss Kate that, once revealed, might surprise us all.

In all honesty, I did not relish the thought of being assistant-housekeeper and nurse-cum-lady's maid, but a day or two would not really make any difference, and if Hubert thought that by staying I might change my mind about marrying him, then he was in for a bitter disappointment.

With Collins' non-appearance and my own certainty that wherever she had gone she was not coming back, the next couple of days were rather dreadful, but I was kept too busy to make plans or to be sorry for myself, with Mrs Robson groaning downstairs and Kate moaning upstairs.

Helping in the kitchen, peeling vegetables, preparing meals, setting tables, rushing upstairs with trays and to attend to Kate's toilette was bad enough, but washing, ironing and sewing buttons on shirts for Hubert set my teeth on edge.

He insisted on a clean shirt and linen each day, and then there was the washing for the whole house, with the exception of Mr Sandeman, who had apparently been sewn into his clothes some time ago and was reluctant to be parted from them.

I soon discovered that, unless Kate was a

258

very good young actress, she truly was a frail creature, but I felt it was perhaps by habit, since everyone had insisted that she was so from her earliest days. Her eyesight was poor, and she soon complained that her eyes were too tired to read or sew. Mrs Robson informed me that she refused to wear the spectacles Hubert had thought suitable, which meant that she had to have someone to read to her.

It was clear that Kate had no desire to have Thane with her all day, and as my time was so fully occupied I suggested he should remain with Wolf, which no doubt pleased them both.

Kate now called him Thane. She told me that although Hubert had no suspicions of this, she had known from almost their very first meeting that he was not her Roswal.

'He was just—different. Animals are like that. They can look the same, but they are all individuals. And Thane has quite a different personality. I didn't want to upset Hubert. He was so desperately keen that this was Roswal returned to me. Felt I would be so heartbroken if I knew the truth.'

She shrugged and said sadly, 'I guessed that Roswal had probably died, and that he couldn't bear to tell me.'

I looked at her, but said nothing. She obviously did not know that Hubert had shot her beloved pet. It was certainly not my place to tell her. I hoped she would never find out the truth, and this was the closest we ever

259

came to having a real conversation.

Every hour through the next few days, we waited for Collins to reappear. Kate was so sure that she would walk in and Mrs Robson, also certain, was full of reassurances.

'Something upset her, that's what.'

I knew perfectly well what had upset her, but I felt there was something more than simply being upset involved, and each time I escaped for an hour, while I walked for some fresh air in the grounds, I knew I was also searching for her.

I looked at the pond every day, wondering if she had, like Kate's sister Amy, taken her life because of an unhappy love affair.

Yet what I had seen, heard and knew of her didn't quite fit that pattern. I felt Collins would have been more likely to have got rid of her faithless lover, or the woman who had taken her place in his affections. As she had tried, unsuccessfully, with me.

CHAPTER TWENTY-FIVE

Walks with Thane inevitably led towards Wolf Rider, who listened patiently to my trials and tribulations. Then, to my surprise, it was my turn to be the listener.

'So you will be leaving very soon, Rose, and this is also the end of my time here. I have known for some while now that it was drawing to a close.'

'I thought you were going to Chillingham for a bull calf for Hubert.'

He shook his head. 'He will doubtless find someone else to do that for him. I have had enough of Staines.' He sighed and looked towards the west. 'I need to be free again. To be back with my own people.'

'You really want to go back?'

Again that shrug. 'I have completed the tasks that have kept me here, and discovering my grandmother's identity led me to Staines.' He paused, smiled. 'And to meeting with you again.'

'I have heard that you have a right to remain at Staines—an even greater right by inheritance than Hubert himself.'

He grinned at that. 'You must have been talking to our amateur genealogist in the library. Am I right?'

I laughed and he went on. 'He has prepared a very convincing though slightly bewildering family tree about twins marrying twins. But I do not think I will be taking that very seriously. I really cannot see myself in the role of a typical English gentleman. Even if I ever inherited, which is extremely doubtful since Hubert and I are much the same age.'

'Are you really?' I had never thought of Wolf as a contemporary of Hubert. He looked younger, ageless somehow.

He said, 'I have been around for a long time.'

Perhaps even as long as Thane, I thought, looking at the deerhound, who appeared to be listening intently to every word.

* * *

Returning to the house, I was surprised to find Grace Sloan installed in the kitchen and busily rolling pastry, a task exclusively Mrs Robson's domain.

She greeted me cheerfully and I asked, 'What are you doing here?'

'What does it look like?' She grinned. 'Giving poor Maggie a hand. She was going to have a nervous breakdown as well as a fractured wrist if she didn't get someone to help. And Hubert couldn't recruit anyone from the village—not that that surprised me, he has never been forgiven for his treatment of young Lily and offers of employment are regarded with caution.'

'And so you offered.'

She nodded. 'Not altogether altruistic. Maggie is a friend and I like cooking anyway. And I'm being paid quite generously as Sir, as she calls him, is quite desperate. Every little helps and I'll do anything but wash and iron that man's shirts and linen. I have to draw the line somewhere.'

'How long can you stay?'

She shrugged. 'As long as it takes.'

My mind raced ahead, glimpsed freedom, Edinburgh and home. With Grace here, I was no longer needed. Or was I? I saw an impediment to my plans arising and asked, 'What about Kate?'

'What about her?' was the indifferent response. 'She'll have to learn to cope, that's all.' And, confirming my own thoughts on the subject, she added, 'Nothing wrong with her, except being spoilt rotten by Sir.'

Laying down the rolling pin, she looked at me and said earnestly, 'If I was you, I'd seize the chance to disappear sharpish, like Collins. You might as well, you know. We'll manage somehow until she gets back.'

It seemed too good an opportunity to miss.

Wolf Rider was going. Thane and I would go as well, leaving Hubert with his new-found friend, Sandeman, although from what I had seen so far, 'friendship' was too strong a word. 'Irritable tolerance' seemed a more apt description, with Hubert shouting and Sandeman whining in return.

Not at all a pleasant couple to have around. I shuddered. How refreshing it would be to leave Staines behind.

*   *   *

As I was walking Thane later, I spotted the familiar figure of Sergeant Sloan, gloomily contemplating the pond as if something nasty might erupt from its depths and scatter the overgrown weeds.

He gave me good-day and I asked, 'What are you doing here?'

'Supposed to be calling on my sister-in-law.' Pausing, he stared again at the pond. 'Grace has told me about Collins' disappearance and I have a naturally suspicious mind that goes with the job. It's my daily bread to solve mysteries, a perpetual itch, you might call it. Not often a missing person's inquiry comes to Alnwick. I'm lucky if I get a lad's head caught in the school railings or an old lady's cat up a tree.'

We laughed and I realised why I was not upstairs packing and recovering my trunk from the gunroom—this was my profession too and a perpetual itch described it perfectly. That's what it would be for me too if I went back to Edinburgh without knowing what had happened to Collins.

So I decided to introduce Sergeant Derek Sloan to Rose McQuinn, Lady Investigator, Discretion Guaranteed.

His eyebrows vanished into his receding hairline and he whistled. 'Well, well. A very unusual job for a young lady, but I do hear there's one or two with Pinkerton's Detective Agency in America. If this is your life story, then let's sit down. My feet are killing me.'

So we retreated to the rustic seat overlooking Staines village and the kirkyard,

264

where fresh flowers marked Cedric's grave.

Sloan asked if he might smoke a pipe while I gave him a brief outline of my life in Edinburgh and the events that had led me to Staines, including Hubert's proposal, though I didn't reveal that he had been the victim of blackmail and my role in solving that particular case.

He listened carefully, stroking Thane's head, which was well received.

As I reached the end, he said, 'I could have guessed that you aren't the usual run of middle-class ladies I encounter. That bicycle, too, created quite a stir, I bet.'

He chuckled then regarded me gravely. 'So Mr Staines wants to marry you?' When I told him I had refused, he shook his head. 'Think well about it. Many a girl would jump at the chance of being lady of the manor, aristocratic old family, handsome squire who is also a distinguished photographer with Royal connections, so Grace tells me.'

'You make it sound very tempting, Sergeant, but one reason I refused was that I wasn't brought up to that station in life.'

'Did your refusal have anything to do with being a policeman's daughter?'

'Not at all. I was and am very proud of Inspector Faro.'

He grinned. 'And so you should be. Personal detective to Her Majesty. We've even heard of him in Alnwick.'

I smiled. 'Well, let's just say that, like all little girls, I went though a phase of wanting to be a princess, but that was before I developed a social conscience and I've long outgrown such nonsensical notions. And living beneath the roof at Staines has certainly changed my ideas about the way high society lives.'

I watched as a spiral of rather nice aromatic smoke drifted between us. 'What about that Red Indian chap?' he asked. Did his casual tone indicate that he was detecting a romance?

'I met Chief Wolf Rider years ago when I first came to Edinburgh. He was with a Wild West circus and has proved to be a good friend. It was quite by a happy accident that we met here again.'

'Hmm.' Sloan sounded doubtful and asked, 'Is he, well, trustworthy?' betraying the prejudice of patriotic Englishmen who supported the Great Imperial Empire and its Empress against those people whose skins were not white and so were classed as redskin savages.

I decided not to tackle him on his shallow viewpoint, especially as I had a sense of caution about what I should tell this particularly perceptive policeman, who now changed the subject by asking, 'What do you know about Collins? I gather from hints via Grace that, to put it delicately, she is more than just Miss Kate's nurse. Also that the past history of Staines is very murky indeed.'

'What kind of murk?'

He shrugged. 'Well, insanity. Some of them would have been committed these days. And the present generation might well be included.'

Did he mean Hubert? I wondered, as he added, 'I know about Kate's sister's suicide and his wife's fatal accident. And Grace's husband, too. Not a safe place to live, is Staines.'

Turning his head, he regarded me very earnestly. 'As for you, young lady, if you were my daughter I'd have you on the next train home to Edinburgh.'

I laughed. 'But you're not and I'm not. So there it is. I promise I'll go when I'm ready.'

He rubbed his chin thoughtfully. 'What do you think has happened to Miss Collins? Three days missing.'

I paused a moment before asking. 'Are you thinking the same as me? Is she still alive?' It came out as a whisper. When he lifted his head and stared back to where we had met and said nothing, I asked, 'Is that why you find the pond so interesting?'

He looked worried. 'All the indications of her leaving in haste in the early hours, without any luggage, according to what Miss Kate told Mrs Robson, might be regarded with suspicion.'

'Collins wasn't given to early rising and Kate also said she didn't like walking—it would have been a long walk to the railway station, although Wolf Rider assured me that there would have been plenty of carts on the main road.' I added that we had checked the trains from Alnwick that morning.

'Had Kate any ideas of where she might have gone?' he asked.

'Apparently she has a friend who works up at the Castle, but Kate didn't know any more than that—if she was a servant, or what her name was.'

'It would be an almost impossible task to trace this friend on such scanty information. The castle must employ a hundred servants, male and female,' was the gloomy response.

Relighting his pipe, he considered it for a moment. 'Time will tell. It's too early yet for us to officially list Martha Collins as a missing person.'

A first name at last, I thought, as he went on. 'However, if she is dead, then it was either an accident—in which case her body will turn up—or murder,' he said gravely. 'In which case her body will by now have been carefully concealed by her killer.'

He pointed towards the distant colliery, where the ruined pitshafts stretched an ugly profile against the sky. 'Disused pits with all their tunnels, deep, dark and long, are ideal hiding places.'

If someone had killed Collins, the list of suspects was very short indeed, and at the very top I would put the name of her one time lover

Hubert Staines.

I wondered if Sloan was thinking the same, as he repeated sternly, 'I think you should go home to Edinburgh and leave this investigation to the police. If investigation it turns out to be and Miss Collins does not walk in the door and give us all very red faces.'

*   *   *

I had a letter waiting for me. From Pappa. He and Imogen were coming to Scotland, visiting friends of Imogen's in the Highlands on their way to Orkney to see my sister Emily. They hoped to see me, a last chance before their imminent return to France.

I looked at the date and panicked—they planned to arrive in two days' time. I was exceedingly fortunate that the letter had reached me in time. I might have missed their visit entirely if it had not been by the merest chance, I learnt later, that they saw Vince and Olivia in London the day after my Newcastle visit.

Much as I wanted to solve the mystery of who poisoned Cedric and the disappearance of Collins, the greater yearning was to take Thane, go back to Edinburgh, and for both of us to be free of Staines forever.

And now, most of all, I longed to see Pappa.

It seemed a long time indeed since we met in Solomon's Tower, and suddenly every consideration, except being with him for a couple of hours, was unimportant and abruptly vanished.

I had never ceased to regret that days with Pappa had been few and far between since I took a teaching post in Glasgow before going to Arizona to marry Danny McQuinn, and Pappa had devoted his retirement to travelling with his writer friend and companion Imogen Crowe—a patriotic Irish woman I respected and admired, an ardent feminist I secretly longed to have as my stepmother. Sadly, occasions to meet had been rare and very precious since my return to Scotland.

*   *   *

'You very nearly didn't get that letter,' said Grace as she was leaving, her daily tasks completed. 'Sandeman had it in his hand, but I'd looked through the post on the hall table. Nosey, that's me, and I'd noticed one for you marked "Urgent".'

'I had quite an argument with our reverend friend. "You are quite mistaken, Mrs Sloan," says he. "These letters are all for Mr Staines." "No, they aren't," says I. "Look through them again. You've picked up one for Mrs McQuinn by mistake." And I watched him. "You are quite right. I didn't notice. Not wearing my spectacles." Brazen old devil. Spectacles indeed. I don't trust that old fellow as far as I

270

can see him, and that's without my spectacles. I don't know how Sir can bear to have him around indefinitely.'

*   *   *

I looked forward to breaking the news to Hubert that I was leaving immediately. He would have to accept and take seriously the fact that I had not the slightest wish or the remotest intention of marrying him.

Was it possible that at our first meeting I had seen him as the present-day incarnation of my Borders warrior hero Harry Hotspur? Now his arrogance seemed absurd. Statements that he would never let me go belonged in some medieval chronicle and certainly did not fit in with my notions of a modern society in which, one day, when we got the vote, women would no longer be chattels of men.

How he intended to keep me here in Staines against my will I could neither imagine nor take seriously, so I decided to tell him outright that I intended to go. The alternative was to creep away like a thief in the night, leaving so many questions unanswered . . .

I could not see my departure being achieved and walking out peacefully without an angry exchange of words, a situation I knew I could no longer avoid. My chance came after supper that evening, with only Hubert, Sandeman and Kate.

We shared a silent meal in which Sandeman applied himself diligently to the wine and I observed that Kate's appetite was hearty indeed, in spite of her invalid state.

No reference to Collins was made by her, or any further alarm expressed at her continued absence, an omission that I found strange. The meal was punctuated by indifferent efforts at conversation from Hubert and, as we finally rose from the table, I said to him, 'May I have a word with you please?'

'Of course, my dear. We will be in the study,' he said, taking up the newly opened wine bottle.

I presumed that 'we' included Sandeman, who gave me a beaming smile. In return I looked at him sternly. 'I wish to talk to you in private, Hubert.'

Something like a gleam of hope shone in those remarkable eyes, a look of such sentiment and affectionate regard it would have thrilled the absent Collins had it ever been directed at her.

Motioning to Sandeman, who looked quite distressed at being excluded, Hubert ushered me into the study and closed the door, while I evaded any imminent physical contact by politely refusing to sit down and keeping a substantial armchair between us.

272

He looked at me, glowing: 'You have decided then.'

I took a deep breath. 'I have decided—'

He did not let me finish. 'This is wonderful—my dearest Rose. I always knew you would change your mind—'

I could not let him continue. 'Hubert, please listen to me. I am leaving Staines—now—immediately. That is what I have decided.'

As his face changed from triumph to defeat, for a moment I was almost sorry for him, sorry to inflict such visible pain on anyone. But he recovered, sprang to his feet, shouted at me, 'You cannot do that! I forbid you to leave. We are to be married!'

'We are not—not ever. Are you mad? I keep on telling you but you just won't listen.'

'You have not changed your mind then.' He sounded shocked, aghast. 'But you cannot leave. You belong here.' Bewildered, he looked around as if the furniture might have some means of persuasion.

I was fast losing patience. 'Hubert, please don't be absurd. Look, this is an impossible situation. I don't love you, I never will, and at this moment my presence is urgently needed at my own home.'

'Why?' he demanded. 'Why is that?'

I looked at him. That wasn't his business, I thought angrily, but said as calmly as possible, 'My father and his friend are coming to Edinburgh. I had a letter this morning—as you

273

know already from Mr Sandeman,' I added heavily.

His face coloured. 'Oh, that letter Mrs Sloan made all the fuss about.'

'Rightly so. It was addressed to me and marked "Urgent".'

He avoided my eyes and I said firmly, 'I have to return immediately. My father is looking in on his way to Orkney.'

He sighed deeply. 'Is that all? A family visit—you can see your father any time!'

It would have been impossible to explain, to make him understand, so I simply said, 'No, I cannot,' as patiently as my rising anger would allow. How dare he adopt this possessive attitude and tell me what I could or could not do?

We had known each other for only a few days and the whole situation was bizarre, outrageous. I was beginning to suspect that Hubert was mad. I thought of a recent case in Edinburgh of a lawyer stalked by a woman obsessed with the notion that he was in love with her.

I wondered if Hubert was suffering from a similar mental disorder. And for the first time I was afraid but, putting on a brave face, I said, 'I am leaving tomorrow and that is all I have to say on the subject.'

'You don't care that I will be desolate without you.'

In all truth, I didn't care in the least, but I

274

said, 'Perhaps Collins will be back soon. She will be very happy that I have gone so she can have you all to herself again.'

I knew it was twisting the knife but I was utterly sick of this ridiculous conversation.

'Collins,' he said slowly as if the name was new to him. 'Ah yes, Collins. She leaves me, without the courtesy of a word. You women, you are all alike. Utterly ungrateful, all of you.'

If there was a clue here to the missing Collins, then I wanted to hear it. 'Doubtless we have our reasons.'

'Collins protested her love, her undying devotion, then one night, because of a slight disagreement . . .' He went on with a shrug of despair, 'No explanation—nothing!'

I closed the door on his protests. It would be a lie to say that I had enjoyed my stay, although there had been moments at the beginning when I had liked him, had even wondered if fate intended Staines as my destiny. But his persistence had destroyed that and, even after a few days, any warmer feelings I had towards him seemed long ago.

All I wanted was to escape, and not even the temptation of a catalogue of unsolved mysteries could have kept me from seeing my beloved Pappa again.

*   *   *

It was too late to leave that evening to ride

into Alnwick to catch an Edinburgh train. However, I would look in and see Wolf and consult his timetable. I found the bothy empty and Kokopele was missing from his perch.

Suddenly I felt quite lonely and I was relieved to find that Thane had been returned to the stables. I would keep him with me in preparation for an early start, although I did not expect to sleep very well that night.

Meanwhile I would see Kate.

She was sitting at her window as usual, engrossed in a new novel, and I had to ask her twice whether she needed any help to prepare for bed. Without lifting her eyes from the page, she shook her head. 'I can manage perfectly well, thank you.'

So I told her that this was goodbye, that I was leaving, and added. 'But no doubt Collins will be back soon,' offering a small consolation, though I didn't believe it for a moment. I was certain that Collins was dead.

Kate nodded absently. 'Yes, I expect she will. I don't know what is keeping her away.'

'You have heard from her then?'

She bit her lip, stared at me.

'Well, no. Not exactly. But I just feel it somehow,' she said hastily, and I was sure that was a lie.

'When you see her again, tell her I wish her well. She will know what I mean.'

Kate obviously knew what I meant. She smiled wanly at my request.

How did you send good wishes to a dead person, possibly a murdered one?

CHAPTER TWENTY-SIX

As I had predicted, sleep evaded me that night, my last in Staines, with so many unanswered questions all perplexing my mind.

When slumber came at last, it was shallow enough to be disturbed by sounds in the corridor. I thought I heard Kate whispering but decided it was all part of a dream. Too exhausted to rise and investigate, I dozed uneasily, only to fall heavily asleep then awake with a start from a vivid nightmare horrifying enough to make me sit bolt upright in bed, but with the details already receding to leave only the sickened feeling of terror remaining.

It was time to leave and Thane looked as eager as I felt at that moment. I knew he would be sorry to leave Wolf Rider, but he was still my dog, my friend, and his first loyalty was to me.

We crept downstairs. In the hall I hesitated for a moment.

There was something I must do before I left Staines.

That hundred guineas. I still had it with me, afraid that Hubert's discovery of it in his desk would lead to arguments. Now more than ever

I was certain that I had made the right decision, that to accept any money from him would be utterly distasteful. So, taking the roll of notes out of my valise, I slipped into his study.

I opened the curtains, then the desk drawer, looking for a suitable envelope, aware that I had little time. There were sounds from above stairs already.

The first thing that came to hand was a large brown envelope addressed to Hubert. With nothing more suitable available, this one would have to do and, as increasing sounds of movement overhead indicated urgency, I shook out the contents.

Several photographs fell onto the desk.

One look told me yet another truth—yet another lie.

The nude girls provocatively posed were nymphs in a glade. With a satyr. Bearded. Also naked, his expression full of lascivious delight as his hands fondled the breasts of one of the nymphs.

His face was one I recognised. I had seen it just days ago in Newcastle at the Station Hotel.

The satyr was none other than Mr Windsor, otherwise known to all the world as Bertie, Prince of Wales.

And what I held in my hand were undoubtedly the stolen photographs, those with corners snipped off, the blackmailer's confirmation of authenticity to convince Hubert that he meant business.

Small wonder that Hubert was so scared. If these images ever fell into unscrupulous hands and were made public, gone for ever would be Royal acclaim for the popular Royal photographer, and lost for ever any possibility of a knighthood.

I thrust them back into the envelope, and laid the roll of notes alongside, with the full knowledge that these photographs were the reason why someone had searched Cedric's lodging so thoroughly after he died.

And what shocked me most was the realisation that whoever had retrieved these incriminating images and placed them here in Hubert's desk was also Cedric's killer.

I had solved the mystery of Cedric's death and I now knew the identity of his killer. With such dangerous knowledge, I must leave Staines with all possible speed. To linger would also mean my own life was now in peril and this was a strange, new and terrifying experience. In the past, I had faced killers who hated me but never one who professed to love me.

However, had I not gone into the gun room to check my travelling trunk, the final act in the drama of what had happened to Collins would never have been revealed.

The trunk was tucked out of sight where I had left it days ago when my original intention of leaving Staines immediately was frustrated.

Thane was behaving oddly.

Fascinated not by the stuffed pet dogs and cats, or the birds who, glitter-eyed, regarded us from their branches over our heads, or by the giant bear on his pedestal, but by one of the three mummy cases. He ran back and forth, looked towards me, whining softly, trying to get my attention, to tell me something.

I went over. One of the cases was not quite closed and, with a fast-beating heart, as I threw all my efforts into raising the heavy lid, I knew what I would find inside. I dreaded to look—

Blood!

It gave me little joy to realise that I would have left Staines and never have made the dreadful discovery had it not been for Thane. There were dark stains on the wooden interior, and a white silk scarf I had seen Collins wearing. I lifted it carefully between finger and thumb. The blood was not fresh. It was dark, congealed.

Horror stricken at its significance and wondering what to do next, I was startled when the door suddenly opened to admit the two men I least wanted to encounter at that moment, or ever again.

Hubert and Sandeman.

Hubert looked at my luggage on the floor beside me, 'We are early birds this morning. So you think you are leaving us?' he added cheerfully, indifferent to the open mummy

280

case, the blood-stained scarf in my hand.

I held it out. 'Look!' And thrusting it at him: 'Look at this. This belongs to Collins.'

He made no move. 'Oh, does it?' He sounded quite indifferent to the enormity of my discovery and what it meant.

'Yes, it does. And you know how it got here, Hubert.' I pointed. 'In the mummy case.'

He smiled, shook his head. 'I don't know, as it happens,' and with his most winning smile, he added, 'but I know you are going to tell me.' He sounded patient, a man with all the time in the world.

'I certainly am,' I said angrily. 'You killed Collins and put her body in the case here three days ago. Doubtless you were in haste, but by now you have had ample opportunity to remove her, put her in a more permanent grave.'

He sighed wearily. 'Don't be ridiculous, Rose. Of course I haven't killed Collins or anyone else—'

'What about Cedric?' I interrupted.

'Cedric?' His head jerked upwards. 'Why on earth should I kill him?'

'Because he was your blackmailer and I have just been in your study to return a fee I did not want for that particular assignment. Looking for an envelope, I found one— containing the photographs you allege were stolen from you.'

He took a deep breath. 'Oh, those

281

photographs. Did I not tell you? Someone returned them to me. It was Mrs Robson, I think. She found them under Cedric's bed or somewhere when she was tidying his lodging. Saw an envelope with my address.'

He paused, sighed. 'A relief, I grant you. I was grateful to her. Most grateful.' And then, with a puzzled frown, he said, 'But why do you think I should want to murder Collins?'

'To keep her silent about the mushrooms. The Destroying Angel, Wolf called it,' I replied, exasperated, as the two men stood solidly together faintly smiling as if at some secret joke. What made their attitudes even more sinister was the fact that the huge bear was just behind Hubert, its fierce face and yellow teeth grinning over his shoulder.

I looked around for an escape, and it was then that I began to feel scared, thankful that I had Thane at my side. Anticipating an attack of some sort, I did not have long to wait. But I did not realise until too late the reason for my growing awareness of danger.

Hubert was smiling. 'I am glad we found you here, Rose. I had a feeling you might be about to leave us. Well, well, this is as good a time and place as any for the little ceremony we have in mind. Do you not agree, Sandeman?'

'I do indeed. Absolutely perfect!' Sandeman rubbed his hands together in almost boyish glee as Hubert turned again to me.

'We are here, dearest Rose, for a wedding. Our good friend Reverend Sandeman is to officiate.'

I stared at him. 'Who is he going to marry?'

Hubert laughed. 'Us, of course, you and me, dearest Rose . . .'

'That is impossible—'

'I assure you it is not. Our friend is an ordained minister and I have all the necessary documents. Indeed, we went into Alnwick the other day, you met us as we were leaving, to acquire a special licence. We even have witnesses waiting out there in the hall. Two of Sandeman's rather disreputable drinking cronies from the village, at a price, of course. Now we can proceed—'

I sprang back. 'No, we cannot. I am not going to marry you now or ever, and you cannot make me do so against my will.'

He smiled. 'Oh I think I can, my dear.' And from his pocket he withdrew a gun, which he levelled not at me, but at Thane.

'First, the dog. I will kill him. I think that will change your mind.'

'You're insane,' I said. 'What do you think we are living in—the Middle Ages? You can't be a feudal lord in the nineteenth century; your kind vanished long ago.'

He ignored the taunt and said solemnly, 'You will marry me, Rose—or Thane dies.'

We both looked at Thane. He was very still, so still he might have been one of the stuffed animals surrounding us.

'That's good,' said Hubert. 'Good dog.' And to me. 'If he makes one move, I will kill him.'

He smiled. 'Well, Rose, and what is your answer now? All I ask is that you are reasonable. Marry me because I love you, have loved you from the first moment I saw you. And the fruit of our consummated love will be a child—the son you will give me—who will one day inherit Staines. After that, if I have not managed to gain your love, then I will set you free—reluctantly, of course—to return to your old life in Edinburgh.'

Sandeman regarded him with a grin of triumph and for one horrible moment I thought I must be dreaming. This was the year 1897 and such melodramas belonged in the pages of penny novelettes or grand operas.

'I am waiting, Rose. I am a patient man, as you know, and am not asking a great deal in exchange for your life and the dog's—just as long as it takes us to produce a child, a year at most.'

'There is one small impediment. Even if I agree to marry you, in order to save Thane's life, you cannot force me to consummate the marriage—'

He looked at me, laughed, and turned to Sandeman, who grinned.

'Oh, I think two strong men against one rather small girl can do the necessary—do I have to paint the picture any further? You, my

284

dear, can easily be taken by force. And if you are too difficult, then a little starvation might work wonders. We have an abundance of empty rooms—and dark cellars—where you could be kept securely and indefinitely until you changed your mind.'

I could think of nothing to say. I was literally struck dumb by what was happening, the certainty that I was dealing with a madman who would try to get a child by rape if necessary. A madman and a murderer who would not hesitate to kill me in the end, if I failed to produce a child.

'Is that why you pushed Kate's mother out of the window—because she could not give you a child?'

'Yes, that is the truth. He did it. He wanted rid of her.'

The voice came from behind the men. The voice of Collins.

Collins with a gun pointed not at me, but at Hubert.

'Is this how you repay me for all those years, you devil? Is this all I get for giving you a helping hand, getting rid of—?'

'Collins!' Hubert yelled. 'Don't do this.'

'You can't stop me. You want witnesses for your wedding, those two outside, well, you shall have witnesses—for your deaths.' And turning to me, she said, 'If I can't have him, you won't have him either.'

As she levelled the gun at Hubert I cried

285

out: 'No, Collins! For God's sake.' And in a desperate plea for time, I asked, 'What happened? We all thought you were dead. Look!' I held up the scarf.

'Oh that. He threatened to kill me that night if I interfered with his plans to marry you! He hit me across the face, made my nose bleed. I ran downstairs. I was scared of him and I hid in the case yonder till it was light.'

We stood shocked into stillness. The two with guns wondering who was to make the first move. A tableau to any casual observer with as little life as the stuffed animals and birds, the sole congregation at this unseemly marriage.

Suddenly Thane shook himself, as a dog does leaving the water. A trivial action, yet with it the whole room began to move. As it shook, I thought of earlier reported tremors, of the house built against all warnings on an earth fault made worse by the coal seam.

Now the quivering turned into a rumbling. The rumbling became a roar as the stuffed animals, long dead, were suddenly quivering into life, teeth showing, legs moving, mouths open ready to devour.

Then the great bear lurched forward from its pedestal and caught the staggering Hubert, thrown off balance, in its huge arms, as both fell together in a deadly embrace.

Sandeman made a dive for the gun but Thane got there first, held him at bay as birds released from their high branches rained down

286

on us, scattering feathers. Tame cats, wildcats, came to life again, leapt from shelves and fell to mouldering dust as the walls and ceiling rattled around us.

A moment later and it was over. The room no longer moved, and silence reigned. As the choking dust from long-dead feathers and fur settled, we were ourselves again, the nightmare ended and reality restored.

We were not to be buried alive.

I helped Collins, covered in dust, to her feet. Sandeman had rushed out, and we went over to Hubert who was lying still, knocked unconscious by the huge bear, its claws buried deep in his bleeding chest.

Mrs Robson appeared through the dust, her choking turning into a scream when she saw the scene of carnage.

Collins, kneeling by Hubert, looked up at her. 'Sir has been hurt and the house is about to collapse. Will someone help me please—we must all get out. Don't just stand there, Mrs Robson. Kate—get Kate before the staircase collapses.'

Mrs Robson continued to stand, staring, unable to believe her eyes. 'There is nothing amiss with the rest of the house. Nothing at all—just this one room—I don't understand. And as for you,' she said angrily to Collins, 'where do you think you've been, scaring us all?' An appeal that sounded somehow rather inappropriate in the havoc surrounding her.

287

Two figures appeared at the door behind her. Wolf Rider with Sergeant Sloan, who demanded, 'What on earth has happened in here?'

'An earth tremor, that's what,' said Collins. 'What is it like outside—the rest of the house?'

'I've told you if you'd only listen,' protested Mrs Robson.

'We should get out now, before the ceiling collapses,' I said and Wolf took my arm, steadying me.

'What are you talking about, Rose?'

'Look around you—you can see—another earth tremor weakened the foundations.'

Collins remained on the floor beside Hubert, dabbing at his chest. 'Someone should take him to the hospital. He's been badly injured.'

The giant bear had been pushed over and now lay on its side, as if asleep, Hubert's blood on its claws.

Collins regarded us tearfully. 'We were warned this would happen, after the pit closed.'

A very bewildered Sergeant Sloan held up his hand. 'A moment, miss. A moment, if you please. We met two men tearing out of the house, yelling about an earthquake, but I can assure you that there is no sign of any earth tremor outside.'

Kate appeared at the door, sleepy-eyed. 'What is happening?' And before anyone could tell her she ran across to Hubert and screamed, 'Is he dead?'

Everyone shouted together, trying to explain. And Mrs Robson, who had rushed out while we were talking, now appeared again breathless and looking round in bewilderment as the dust settled and we began to see one another clearly again.

'It was only this one room—nowhere else in the house. I have checked. There isn't even a cracked ceiling.'

'You are sure?'

'I am sure,' she said firmly.

Three more figures appeared. Two uniformed policemen with Sandeman between them in handcuffs.

'What has he to do with all this?' Collins demanded.

Sloan said, 'He's the reason we're here, and just in time it would seem.'

'Nothing to do with Mr Staines then?' quavered Collins.

He shook his head. 'Only that he has been harbouring a criminal. Sandeman has a police record. He is wanted in Newcastle, Durham and York. A forger under many aliases. We have been trying to track him down for several years and he was here right under our noses.'

To me he said, 'Now that there is a little calm, can someone tell me what has been going on here?'

Collins said, 'I can tell you. Hubert, who is

engaged to me, was about to force this—this person—to marry him—' Pointing at me, she managed to make it sound like my fault. 'I came in the nick of time,' she added, omitting any mention of the gun she had also carried. 'He was going to kill her dog—'

I looked at Thane.

'What happened then?' asked Sloan.

'He shook himself, the way dogs do, and then—then the room started to move.'

We all looked at Thane as if expecting an explanation. He stared back at us and, trotting over, sat down obediently by my side.

Sloan shook his head wearily. What was implied seemed impossible, but there was the evidence all round us, a museum of stuffed animals and birds, as if they had been struck by a hurricane.

Other images floated across my mind—the white cattle herd halted before Thane, the way Hubert's dogs treated him as if invisible, and how he had saved Wolf and me from the white cow deprived of her calf.

Sloan had turned his attention to Hubert, who lay so still. He looked far from well and the covering of dust added to his deathly pallor.

Sloan briskly gave instructions and we watched as the police van carted him off on a stretcher, with Sandeman handcuffed in the back, protesting his innocence, and Collins protesting that she should be allowed to accompany Hubert to the hospital in Alnwick.

I longed to discuss it all with Wolf as we followed Mrs Robson into the kitchen, where we sat down, staring at one another, speechless, round the table while she poured out the tea. And no one objected to, or seemed to notice, Thane lying peacefully at my feet.

I was free, safe, Thane and I could be on the next train to Edinburgh and home. But before we left, there were one or two questions I still needed answers for.

I looked at Collins, so tearful, with Kate holding her hand. I desperately wanted to get these two alone, to find out just how exactly Collins had been helping Hubert and who she had been getting rid of.

My chance came when I went upstairs to take a last look round the room, making sure I had left no belongings behind in my hasty packing. Wolf was waiting downstairs with the pony cart to take me into Alnwick.

Collins was leaving Kate's room. She would have walked past me without acknowledgement but I held out my hand, saying, 'I'm leaving now. I hope Hubert will soon be back with you.' And in a rush, I added, 'I never wanted to marry him; I never wanted to cut you out. Please believe me.'

She looked away, said awkwardly, 'All right, I believe you.'

'We were all very concerned by your

disappearance.'

'I came back last night, Kate let me in.' So that was the whispering I heard. 'I went to stay with my friend Elsie up at the Castle. And to have an interview for a situation there.'

'As a governess?'

Her face clouded. 'Alas, no, a sort of upstairs personal maid. But I felt it was rather beneath me. I had hoped for at least Her Grace. I was disappointed. And, of course, I didn't want Hubert to know. After the way he'd treated me, I decided he deserved to suffer.'

I thought of how little she had succeeded and of his indifference as she went on, 'But I didn't want to distress Kate. I didn't just disappear, you know. I left a note for her inside the book she was reading. Didn't realise she'd started reading a new novel and wouldn't find it right away.'

There was a silence. Then because curiosity got the better of me and I had to know, I said: 'Incidentally I know about poisoned mushrooms—Wolf told me about them. How did Cedric come in contact with the Destroying Angel, the deadliest of the lot?'

She stared at me, her suddenly flushed countenance giving away her guilt. 'You might as well know the truth, though no one will ever believe you, and if Hubert recovers I will deny every word. Hubert wanted rid of Cedric because he knew that he was in love with Kate.

And he had other plans for her.'

'What other plans?'

'I'm not certain, he never spelt them out. Just that Cedric wasn't good enough for her—thought he was just after her money.'

Which was probably true, I thought.

'So we talked about things—and I thought the Destroying Angel would give him a bad fright.'

I knew that was a lie, but I let her go on. Her obsession with Hubert had taken her well out of reason's grasp.

'I think Cedric was a danger to Hubert, blackmailing him, from hints he dropped. And that was terrible, he deserved what he got, but I was sorry that Kate was so upset. First love, and all that sort of thing. But she's young, she'll get over it.'

Again I wondered if Collins had ever noticed the thin line between reason and madness that lurked in the Staines family due, no doubt, to so many generations of intermarriage.

'Do you think he is going to die?' she asked.

I said: 'I hope not—for your sake,' and as I left her, I had the feeling she had wanted to confess, to tell someone, even someone she had no reason to care for.

Downstairs Wolf was waiting with Thane. The story was almost told.

CHAPTER TWENTY-SEVEN

The Edinburgh train was late, delayed by signal failure at Newcastle.

Wolf waited with us and we took a seat on the almost deserted platform.

'So this is goodbye, Rose.'

'When do you leave?' I asked.

'Soon.'

'Back to Arizona?'

'Yes. Pick up the threads of the life I left long ago. There will be plenty to do on the Reservation—another kind of fighting—for justice for oppressed tribes. I will apply for a job with the Indian Bureau of Affairs.'

That was the way my Danny had chosen—the Indian Bureau and Pinkertons, doing the same kind of fighting Wolf had in mind.

My face must have betrayed my emotions. With that uncanny ability to read my thoughts, he took my hands.

'Come with me, Rose. I know I'm old enough to be your father,' he added apologetically.

I laughed at that. The contrast between Wolf and Pappa was ludicrous. Sad too, for this was the conventional 'out' for men who did not really want any emotional involvement.

'I mean it. It is a good, worthwhile life. And we can be married, your way, the Christian way, if that is what you want.'

I was flattered by this totally unexpected proposal and I would have enjoyed spending the rest of my days with this man, whose strange and very remarkable qualities I had instinctively recognised on our first meeting in Solomon's Tower.

But as for his version of a rewarding life, I wasn't sure that really appealed. I had my own rewarding life. I had done the pioneering part for ten years with Danny and I knew first-hand the hardships of living on Indian reservations. Our baby son had died on one, in a tepee. I thought so often, so longingly, of that tiny unmarked grave in the desert, and knew I never wanted to see another tepee ever again.

A return to Arizona would be too painful; too many memories lurked in its cathedral-like red rocks.

'We can have a proper house,' said Wolf, a mind-reader again. 'Say yes, Rose. There is no one I would rather be with.'

There was no one I would rather be with either, come to that; I would miss him when he had gone. I was flattered, yes, but not tempted. Hero-worship, at close quarters in everyday living, soon vanished.

I knew I could never resurrect the rapture of that first all-consuming love for Danny as, alas, I had discovered with Jack Macmerry. The breakdown in our relationship was all my fault. I could not forget the dream I had once

295

lived.

Thane was looking into my face. 'What of Thane?' I asked. 'I could never take him with me.'

Wolf smiled. 'He would go back to the wild, to his life before he found you.'

But I couldn't think of those years that might lie ahead without Thane. He was probably about eight years old, and this did not make him, by my calculations, immortal.

Suddenly, I thought of the old Edinburgh ladies I met in Jenners' tearoom. Some were my clients, well-to-do widows saying they could never have a holiday and clutching a fat old lapdog to a well-padded bosom:

'Dear little Boysie can't be left alone. He is too old now and he would die of neglect.' And, with another hug and kiss, they would say, 'No holiday would ever be worth that.'

I had thought it silly, but now I was one with them. I understood such feelings, and Thane was no fat, overfed, asthmatic old lapdog. He was my friend, my protector, and I owed him my life. However the world might regard such devotion, he was as precious to me as any human, and as long as he lived and needed me, I would remain in Edinburgh, on Arthur's Seat, where we both belonged.

I wondered if he, too, was sharing my thoughts, as while we talked, I patted his head and, as if he felt the reassurance, he looked up at me and wagged his tail, knowing that he was safe too.

A bell rang signalling the train's approach. We stood up. Wolf kissed me lightly and we held each other for a moment. Then he took Thane's head between his hands, looked into his eyes, and whispered something in his own Indian language.

A moment later, it was over. We were on the train, gliding out of the station, and Wolf had vanished, hidden from us by the smoke. As if we had never been in his life or he in ours.

I looked at Thane, who settled down beside me, muzzle on paws in the empty compartment. He sighed deeply, a sigh for the loss of Wolf Rider, his soul mate. But I came first. Thane was mine and I was his dear human.

*   *   *

Vince provided the ending of my disastrous visit to Staines. He had been hopeful that he was to hear that his stepsister was to marry Hubert, and was shocked to learn of Hubert's accident, reported to him as being caused by the accidental collapse in the gun room of a large stuffed bear which fell on top of him. Left paralysed by this weird accident, it was a sad end to his photographic career, but at least he had a devoted companion nurse.

I thought it ironic that Collins had won a

sour victory. Years later I learnt that, despite Hubert's rejection, he was hers for the rest of his life. For worse, not better, faithful to the end, she followed him to the grave after an unspecified illness soon after his death.

Their guilt in certain 'accidental deaths' went with them unproven. In particular, Hubert's, for his wife Mary. For Cedric's death they were both responsible.

A short time after my return I read in *The Scotsman*, with considerable surprise, that Kate, now orphaned, was living with the Dowager Countess of Southwell until her forthcoming marriage to the young Earl of Southwell, who, according to Vince, was a penniless aristocrat to whom Kate's fortune would be a welcome relief. But this was a love match. They had met, without him revealing his identity, during the Duke of Northumberland's September 1897 shooting party.

I was intrigued. Could this be the same handsome young man, the Duke's travelling companion, whom I had briefly glimpsed talking to Kate that day, when a shot rang out and Hubert alleged that someone had tried to kill him?

Perhaps the final irony was delivered by Mrs Robson. The faithful retainer, she remained with Sir and Martha Collins to the end. Afterwards, Staines became a boys' boarding school and Mrs Robson retired, to live next door to her friend Grace Sloan.

More out of curiosity about subsequent events in Staines than anything else, I admit, we had kept in touch and she enjoyed the excuse to come to Edinburgh and have tea at Jenners'.

Despite many hints, I never found out from her any sinister reason for Hubert's devotion to Kate or his intentions for her future, or if there was any truth in the village gossip, regarding 'goings-on' with under-age girls.

However, on one of Mrs Robson's visits I learnt, as I had long suspected, that she knew more about Cedric's birth than she had been prepared to admit while employed at Staines. Before she died, Cedric's mother had revealed that his real father was Hubert Staines.

I spared Mrs Robson the true facts of Cedric's death, but now I knew why, looking at that young man's face in death, he had reminded me of someone.

Hubert Staines.

So desperate for an heir that he was prepared to go to any lengths to get one, including a forced marriage, by a bitter stroke of irony, Hubert had conspired in the death of his only son, Cedric Smith.

And as I write the final words of this the strangest of all my cases, I have resumed my life as Lady Investigator, Discretion Guaranteed, and Thane is still with me, back again running free on Arthur's Seat.

Sometimes, during the night, when the wind carries the sound of trains from Waverley Station, I think of Wolf Rider and his parting with Thane, those words, once so familiar to me:

'Till we meet again, the Great Spirit be with you.'

Chivers Large Print Direct

If you have enjoyed this Large Print book and would like to build up your own collection of Large Print books and have them delivered direct to your door, please contact **Chivers Large Print Direct**.

Chivers Large Print Direct offers you a full service:

✧ **Created to support your local library**

✧ **Delivery direct to your door**

✧ **Easy-to-read type and attractively bound**

✧ **The very best authors**

✧ **Special low prices**

For further details either call Customer Services on 01225 443400 or write to us at

Chivers Large Print Direct
FREEPOST (BA 1686/1)
Bath
BA1 3QZ